DIRTY RAINBOWS

a Tale of a City

billy zaidi

billyz68@ntlworld.com
07590 430385

Author's note

Although this novel is loosely based on some amazing gigs that took place in Manchester in the 1980's, such as The Festival of the Tenth Summer, this is very much a work of fiction and is intended to be read as such.

Before you start reading, I apologize profusely for anyone who is distracted by any liberties I might have taken with the timeline of gigs that form the backdrop of the narrative. I have always been a lightweight when it comes to alcohol, so my memory is as unreliable as the politicians who were running the show back then. Where possible, I have checked the dates of specific gigs and amended the narrative accordingly to add a veneer of authenticity, but this is an inexact science.

Furthermore, I can't vouch for the longstanding cultural worth of all the bands referenced in the next 230 pages, but if the names of any of them are unfamiliar, you could do a lot worse than to check them out. Some of them deservedly found fame and fortune or have fallen into disrepute, but almost all of them I'm certain would welcome the attention. And if you find a new band to fall in love with, then I have done my job; if not, all I can say is that you had to be there. This is dedicated to Ian, because he was always there,

Enjoy!

BZ

One

It was most definitely the worst of times. We were running hard, the pavements slick with drizzle and overspill from rubbish bags piled high in front of boarded-up shopfronts hosting pickled tramps and a new breed of desperate homeless. We had been to see The Ramones at a run-down rock club, not our usual haunt but needs must when rock royalty is in town.

It had been a great night, hard music played loud at 200 miles per hour, perfect bubblegum punk. The problem started when we were forced to walk past Rotters on the way home, a notorious trouble-spot if you chose to wear leather jackets and boots rather than Italian leather slip-on shoes and smart slacks. Sometimes, the door opened as we walked past and you could catch a glimpse of cultural hell, where people with no imagination went to strut their stuff on an illuminated dancefloor under non-ironic glitterballs that scattered rays of light like false promises. The smart thing to do was not to look, like avoiding the gaze of a gorgon. If you timed it badly and walked past when the hard lads had given up hope of pulling or run out cash, it usually ended badly.

Like tonight. One of them took a dislike to Tom who barely managed to slip a sneaky punch and heated words were exchanged. Heavily outnumbered, there was nothing for it but to run, only occasionally turning back to see if they were gaining ground while taking care not to slip on dogshit. If we fell or found ourselves trapped, things could very quickly go from bad to worse, anywhere from a hard smack or two in the mouth to a proper kicking, or worse. These were big men who did hard labour. Real men, as Tom called them. Nasty bastards.

So, there we were, heading fast towards Portland Street. If we could make it anywhere near the bus station, the presence of other people might put them off, and we might even be able to find sanctuary on the night bus. Luckily, we were younger and still football fit, so the odds were in our favour. We had also drunk a lot less. I could hear them breathing hard, their threats mostly lost as they started to run out of steam and struggled to fill their lungs. I wondered why it always ended up like this. Beside me, I heard Darren slip on discarded food waste, but Tom expertly caught his arm without breaking stride and pulled him along. At night, Piccadilly Bus Station could hardly be described as the bright lights – and certainly not a place to feel particularly safe – but on this occasion it was a very welcome sight. To lose them, we took a right through Chinatown, zigzagging through narrow streets and hurdling benches to put more distance between us and them.

Behind us, we would hear them finally giving up the chase. There were a few curses and the sound of breaking glass not very close by. Emboldened, Darren turned round and goaded them over his shoulder, still running hard. As he described it later, a lamppost came at him from nowhere.

'Screw y—'

There was a sickening crunch. Tom still had a firm hand a hand on his shoulder and was spun around by the impact in time to see him hit the ground hard. I took a few more steps before I was able to stop. Tom was helping him up, dragging him with forward momentum in case we were still being pursued.

'Daz, you are such a twat!' he was shouting. 'Get on your feet, NOW!'

Dazed and confused, Darren allowed himself to be dragged along, one hand held hard across his forehead to stem the flow of blood. A bus was waiting at its designated bay, its engine filthily belching out diesel. The driver looked at us and held up a hand, but we threw what coins we had down into the slot and headed upstairs before he could raise a serious complaint.

'Shit, that was close.'

The bus drove away, the hydraulic swoosh of the doors confirming our safety. The route took it down Oxford Road so we made plans to jump out at the Royal Infirmary so he could get stitched up. The cut was deep. Luckily, Darren had a funny animated face so he could get away with little imperfections and still look okay. A bit lacking in brainpower, he had been built for a life of hard graft, so this felt like useful life-training for him, getting into scrapes and being patched up again good as new. Tom was a breed apart, his face perfectly symmetrical with hair that changed with the light, coppery in the dark but softer in the daylight. He had rare poise and a quiet self-assuredness that drew people to him because he always seemed one or two steps ahead and knew exactly where he was going. Darren always said Tom was shiny, and I knew exactly what he meant. The golden one.

'You need a good cover story,' Tom decided, wincing at the prospect of the repair work required to staunch the flow of blood. 'Running into a lamppost makes you sound like a total twat.'

Oxford Road was one of the main arteries out of the city centre into the outlying suburbs, though that made them sound nicer than they were, so the hospital was well situated.

We debated what would make a decent story to tell others once we had him patched up to spare him further embarrassment but, in the end decided a mismatched fight against idiots wearing leather ties was more than enough to justify what had happened.

'Why always me?' he moaned.

'Because you're the only one dumb enough to run headfirst into a lamp post.'

'True.' He grinned, then grimaced as his forehead wrinkled with self-mockery.

The whole thing was depressingly familiar. Almost every time we walked past certain pubs or nightclubs it would kick off. Gangs of drunks looking for kicks. I couldn't see what made them hate us so much, just because we chose to dress differently. Someone had ripped my ear ring out a month or two earlier. It still smarted.

'We make them feel like we think we're better than them,' said Tom. He sat in front of us, turned around. The night bus had little to no suspension, and he jerked around spasmodically as it rounded a corner near the Royal Exchange.

'We are better than them,' I snapped.

'We're just the same,' he said.

'They're wankers. We don't go round kicking people's heads in for no reason,' said Darren.

'Or wear leather ties,' I said. 'I agree with Darren.'

'Daz,' he corrected. He hated being called Darren. Over the years, he would take on many names, from Daz to Dazzleships when he went through an electropop phase. He even briefly became Bobby Dazzler in the short period where he was popular with girls, impressed with the tall tales he told about his scar, or Bobby for short. He was always the same person, though. Daft. Fun. A really good friend.

'You need to remember their lives are shit,' said Tom. 'They work hard for very little, and it makes them angry. Just by trying to look different, it's like we are just taking the piss out of them.'

I wasn't convinced. 'What do they expect when their idea of a good time is to listen to Dire Straits trying to impress some secretary on the dancefloor?'

As I heard my own voice, I knew I sounded like a cultural snob and I didn't care. Maybe Tom had a point, after all.

Darren jumped up and pinged the button to stop the bus as we approached the hospital.

'I'll stay with him,' said Tom. 'He can stay at mine tonight if there are no more buses. My mum can have a look at him in the morning. No point both of us staying up.' I didn't protest. Tom's mum was a nurse, so it made some kind of sense.

They waved up at me as the bus pulled away, Darren still pressing his hand against his head to staunch the flow of blood although he looked ridiculous, like a third-rate actor in a Hammer Horror film pretending to be shocked. Even in a potentially serious moment like this, he had the ability to turn drama into comedy. Typical.

The bus jerked me through Rusholme and further until my stop arrived. My heart rate had returned to normal but the angular shadows disturbed me more than usual as I made my way home. The orange glow of streetlights threw menacing shapes against brick walls that stretched and distorted them to monstrous proportions, and I mocked myself for such childish thoughts. I pulled the collar of my jacket up as if that somehow made me look more tough and I checked my reflection in car windows as I made way through the labyrinthine streets of terraced houses towards home. My eyes looked hollow in the reflected glass, but I knew it was a trick of the light.

At home, things were quiet, and I made myself a cup of tea with as much care as I could manage in the dark, not wanting to disturb anyone. I didn't care to think of what horrors lurked in the bottom of the mug I selected, but I gave it a quick sniff and decided it seemed safe enough. There was even half a bottle of milk in the fridge, although it barely kept things colder than if the bottle was left on the side with all the other debris of the evening. Again, I gave the bottle a tentative sniff, but the whole kitchen smelt so bad that I would hardly have been able to tell if it had congealed to mouldy sludge. Finding a biscuit was too much to hope for. I leaned against the wall and took slow steady sips of the tea as my mind raced through the close shave we had just about managed to survive. I noticed that a new picture had been taped to the wall by my head, a portrait of me one of my sisters had presumably painted at school. I loved that they always drew me with a smile on my face and my mood brightened. I did the best I could to put on a happy front for them and I was always relieved that they couldn't see what really lay behind the mask. The ritual of tea-making and the time it took to cool enough to drink it gave me the time and space to switch my brain off. I strained my eyes through the darkness to look around me, the chaos of abandoned kids' toys and colouring books and piles of old newspapers stacked floor to ceiling, turning the living space into a kind of crazy maze that led nowhere and made nocturnal movement around the house quite treacherous. I had no idea how we could live like this, as if any of us had any choice. I took my time with the tea, but the adrenaline finally started to wear off and I was suddenly knackered and conscious that I had an early start the next day. College.

*

In many ways, the city overwhelmed us, as vast and functional and dehumanising as the factories that for a short while had made Manchester the epicentre of the world. Now the wealth had moved elsewhere and what remained was depleted and redundant, like the people who had been left behind. Poverty had stripped the city of colour and turned matchstick men and women fat. It was quite something.

As was customary, the moon was obscured by looming warehouses and smog and the few stray people who hung about were either looking to score or settle a score. We sat with our backs the statue of Marx or Engels, I couldn't remember which without turning round and looking up. Tom would have known, of course. Before he died, his old man had taken him to all the important parts of the city, so he knew who he was and what he was made of. Politics was in his DNA. He could have talked about it for hours if I let him. Perhaps when I finally shook off childhood I would care about such things, but that felt some way away. My back obscured the letters *omnia sunt communia* etched into the plinth which Tom had patiently explained to me meant that, apparently, everything belonged to everyone. I had commented at the time that it was a nice idea and, not wanting to openly hurt my feelings, Tom silently sneered at the poverty of my expression. It didn't really feel that way as I looked around me. Litter and boarded-up shops signalled how hard life had become. Every other person I knew was unemployed.

We sat there in silence for a while, in no hurry to go home. The ambient whoosh of the city at night was receding to a low hum, and we felt no need to make conversation for the sake of it. The deep cold of the plinth penetrated our bones, but we didn't really feel it. At times like this, I didn't feel much of anything. We shared a blistering bag of chips, which I guessed the old man would have approved of. Sharing our limited resources and all that. My ears were numbed by frost but were buzzing from the gig at the Palace. Morrissey and Marr hadn't disappointed despite the absurd hype surrounding their band and the unlikely coming together of the kitchen-sink poet and the great guitarist.

'That was pretty good,' I said.

Tom nodded in agreement. 'Yeah, but I think they'll end up killing each other, one way or another. You can feel the tension.'

Though his intelligence naturally lent itself to pessimism, Tom had an extraordinary capacity to embrace and celebrate exciting new ideas. It was brutally cold, but adrenaline fuelled our excitement, and we were content to sit there and debate whether the live performance enhanced the music or whether the record had the edge. It didn't really matter either way. What was important was that people were making music that had something to say and helped others to orientate themselves in the world. Something that you either loved or hated. Even if you didn't quite fit in, there was something that could be yours, words and sounds and a dazzling lightshow that lit up the cultural gloom even as it articulated a growing sense that the world we were inheriting had been stripped of anything of real value.

A girl walked over and sat next to us.

'Do you mind?' she asked, helping herself to a particularly fat chip. We had both seen her before at various gigs over the past few months, sometimes alone or with girl friends or various slightly older boys. She smiled in a way that seemed ironic, though I couldn't explain why. It was a knowing smile, I guess, though I was too young to understand what it was she knew that I didn't. Her teeth were small and clean and perfectly straight.

'Sure,' I said. 'Help yourself.'

'You both look nice,' she said. 'Been anywhere good?' Again, the way she pronounced the word nice suggested something more than I completely understood. Her hair was darker than the night sky, but her skin glistened even in that desperate light, her cheekbones threatening to slice right through like razors.

'The Smiths,' I said. 'At the Palace.' I wasn't sure why that extra little detail mattered.

'Oh. Any good?'

'Very.' I tried to sound convincing.

She had fine, delicate features but there was nothing child-like about her. She was friendly, but there was something a little feral about her, almost preternatural. She could easily have been a vampire, if you believed in that kind of thing. I would have guessed that she was a year or two older than us; a student, maybe, though her accent was local. It never occurred to me that anyone would choose to study in their hometown. She helped herself to another chip and sucked the salt off her fingers in a way that made my head spin.

'Good for you two,' she said. 'Not really my thing, though. I can't stand Morrissey. All that shyness and self-doubt and whatever else he thinks passes for a personality. There's just something about him that's off, like he's got something to hide he knows people won't like. He's so conceited and desperate for people to like him.' She shuddered, or maybe it was just a shiver. I wasn't sure I agreed with her, but I knew what she meant. Besides, people were entitled to their opinions.

'It's a nostalgia thing,' Tom explained.

She looked up at him and he held her gaze in a way that I couldn't. 'Aren't you boys a little young for nostalgia?'

He shrugged. 'Everything started there. We saw them at Rafters in '83. It was the first gig we ever went to, the first time I met someone with decent taste in music.' She smiled knowingly but said nothing, taking time to select the perfect chip. In the silence. he looked her over. 'We've seen you around,' Tom declared. 'You've got good taste.'

'Why, thank you,' she smiled. Dimples appeared in her face where her cheekbones ended. 'I've seen you around, too,' she said. 'That's why I thought I'd come over and say hi. You boys like a little bit of everything, don't you?' It wasn't a question.

Tom smiled enigmatically. 'Eclectic is electric,' he said.

She laughed and turned to me for help. 'Does he always talk like this?'

'Oh, you'll get used to him. I think we're a bit drunk.' I held out my hand and she took it. 'Nice to make your acquaintance,' I said, for no particular reason. Her hand was warm and small and fit perfectly inside mine.

'Hi,' she said. 'How very formal of you. I'm Miranda.'

'Yeah, hi,' said Tom, though he kept his hands to himself. 'He's Alex. I'm Tom.' As usual, he was wearing fingerless gloves, which I thought pointless.

I was still of an age where I was wary of girls as much I was enthralled by them. Against alabaster skin, her dark hair glowed red under the glare of streetlights. She reminded me of a painting that Tom had dragged me to see depicting a heroic youth ensnared by beautifully sinister nymphs. To let her know that I was not stupid, I told her so. She seemed bright, and it suddenly felt important for some reason to let her know that we were a cut above the usual drunken idiots you encountered on a night out.

She quizzically raised an eyebrow. 'Are you calling me a nympho?' she teased.

'He's talking about a painting at the Art Gallery,' said Tom, shivering suddenly with the cold. 'I think Alex is trying to pay you a compliment.'

She nodded, as if to let us know that she knew a thing or two herself. '*Hylas and the Nymphs.* I love that one. Good choice.' Totally relaxed, she sat down with her back against the statue. 'The thing people don't realise is that he's gay, the boy in the painting.'

'So, they're wasting their time?' I asked.

She looked at me sideways and laughed. 'Of course not, silly. They're not trying to fuck him. They're going to eat him all up.' She laughed again. I loved the way she swore, her voice echoing through the deserted streets. 'You could learn a lot from that painting.' I didn't doubt it.

'I don't see it that way at all,' Tom countered. 'It's all about sex.'

'Of course that's how you see it,' she teased. 'You're a boy. All you are capable of seeing is nubile flesh and pretty faces.' She pushed her shoulder against mine. 'Totally blind to the danger.'

Tom bristled at her use of the word boy. He wasn't used to others getting the upper hand, so much smarter than me and the other people he hung around with.

'There's more to the painting than that,' Tom retorted. 'The boy's lover is Hercules, who trained him as a warrior.' He pointedly articulated the word boy. 'He may look like a boy but he could look after himself.'

'Clearly not,' she hit back, licking her lips. 'You know how the story ends, right? He's hopelessly out of his depth, no pun intended. He goes missing and poor Hercules goes crazy with grief for his lost boyfriend.' I laughed. She was funny.

'How very modern,' Tom said.

We were on the edge of a notorious gay hang-out, back when being gay was still stigmatised and it was safer to stick to the shadows.

'How very Classical,' she corrected him. 'Can you imagine a gay hero nowadays?' she asked pointedly. Of course we couldn't.

'They were very open-minded back then,' she went on. 'Hercules had even killed the boy's father but fell hard for him and took him under his wing.'

'That's one way of putting it.'

I shifted uncomfortably, partly with the cold. Any talk of fathers and sons was prickly territory for Tom.

'Bloody hell,' I said. 'This is getting deep.' I checked my watch. I was enjoying myself and was in no great hurry to leave, but it was almost time for the next night bus. It was a long walk home and a taxi was out of the question. Alex saw me and nodded. He jumped to his feet and stood over us, backlit by the spectral moon.

'It's been a pleasure,' he said, 'but we need to be going.'

She walked with us as far as Piccadilly bus station, although she explained that someone was going to pick her up. We gallantly offered to wait with her, but she declined.

'I'm a big girl,' she said, 'in case you haven't noticed. You two are in far more danger than I am round here.' Echoes of the painting. The 42 was already waiting at the stand, looking warm and uninviting.

'It was nice talking to you,' she said. 'No doubt I'll see you around.' Her smile illuminated the night.

Without saying a word, we both watched her walk away, the rhythmic sway of her slim hips, until Tom turned to me and raised an eyebrow and we both breathed out together, laughing under the few stars bright enough to penetrate the gloom.

Two

Two nights later we were drinking in The Briton's Protection on Great Bridgewater Street. It was mostly inhabited by cursing old men hiding from the vicissitudes of life behind a pint of bitter, but increasingly there were younger people here, too. The dickheads who haunted many city centre pubs tended to steer clear of this ancient establishment in favour of modern venues which were brightly lit and full of dull people with nothing to say. As we walked in, Tom nodded knowingly at a couple of drinkers around whom the tortoiseshell tiles seem to have grown organically over the years. People always knew who he was, or he acted like they did. His dad had been big in the trade union movement, and everyone knew who Jack Barton was. There was a table for two at the rear of the narrow pub beside the mural depicting the Peterloo Massacre. Some of the drinkers looked like they might have remembered it.

Tom was keen to share with me a couple of articles he had written for potential inclusion in a fanzine we were working on. It had become important to both of us to be more than mere passive spectators in the burgeoning music scene that was developing around us. At that point, neither of us had demonstrated much talent for music beyond over-enthusiastic appreciation of those we hero-worshipped for pushing back the boundaries of popular culture. It felt like a vibrant time to be alive, although you wouldn't have known it looking around as we nursed our beers, too impoverished to rush and too callow to have properly developed an appreciation for what we were drinking. I was unusually quiet as he handed me the articles he had written.

'You're thinking about her, aren't you?' he asked.

I looked up over the first sheet. 'That obvious?' He nodded. 'She is something else,' I conceded, a little perturbed by the ease with which he read my mind.

'That she is.' He waited for me to read on but he could soon see that he had fatally distracted me. 'Forget about her, though' he cautioned. 'She's lovely, but she's way out of our league.'

'Too old?'

'Too everything.' He sat back in his chair. 'She's a great girl, but she knows she can do better.'

'Then why bother talking to us?'

He shrugged. 'I dunno. She was just bored, I guess, humouring us.'

I nodded. 'I guess so. She makes me wish I was a couple of years older, though.'

He laughed. 'Alex, it wouldn't make any difference.'

I put the article down carefully, avoiding spilt beer. 'Do you think she's a student?'

'I don't think so.' He considered the possibility. 'Maybe. She's a bright girl, that's for sure. But she's definitely one of us.'

'Maybe she just wanted to stay in Manchester,' I said. An old man next to me coughed, his shoulders heaving with the effort as he hawked up a great clog of phlegm that he wiped on a yellowed hanky. A breedless dog cowered at his feet. 'Why would anyone want to leave?' I wasn't being ironic.

I read the first article. It was about the aftermath of punk and its legacy. He loved punk and everything it stood for but was alarmed by the way a movement which had literally started on the streets had become commercialised by stores nationwide, the message diluted with every mass-produced T shirt worn by a public-school prick wanting to shock daddy. As always, we bounced ideas back and forward, and I was taken aback by the suggestion that we had missed our moment, born a few years late for the great cultural moment of the century. As he talked, I became distracted by the depiction of a worker's head crushed under the hooves of a cavalryman in the Peterloo mural behind him. The anguished faces of the others caught up in the massacre could still be seen reflected in the downtrodden faces everywhere you looked around the pub. He turned and followed my gaze.

'It's incredible, isn't it?' Whereas my interest had always been solely to do with the music, slowly Tom was opening my eyes to the importance of other forms of creative expression like art in articulating the many trials that life threw at us. Literature, too. Written as a nightmarish vision of the future, Orwell's 1984 was becoming more terrifyingly relevant by the day as the appointed year had come and gone. The north was suffering, on its knees. As she grew in confidence, Thatcher's rhetoric grew more confrontational by the week as she seemed intent to wage war on the common man.

'Do you know what this place was originally?' asked Tom, looking around him.

I nodded towards the mural. 'I assume to commemorate the massacre.' I already knew that would be incorrect or he wouldn't have asked.

'That's what it became,' Tom explained, 'but it was actually a safe haven for drinkers to escape being press-ganged into fighting Napoleon. The Briton's Protection, see? They were running out of people to fight the French so they would grab drunks off the streets, put a gun in their hands and off they went.' He pantomimed someone getting shot in the head.

He was an encyclopaedia of local knowledge, thanks to his old man. He had listened well, and now the knowledge was his, and mine. 'You know, at the turn of the century street gangs used fight each other in the streets dressed as Napoleonic armies. Huge fights. Literally hundreds of people. It didn't much matter which side they were on, English or French, just as long as they could knock six shades of shit out of each other.' He laughed. 'And if gangs turned up from other cities like

Liverpool or Birmingham, they would just join forces and batter them instead.'

'Happy days,' I said.

The second article was more political, about Thatcher and the mining unions. I wasn't convinced that people wanted to read this sort of thing, though it was well written for sure, not just passionate but well-researched and persuasive. 'Do you think we should just stick to music?' I wondered out loud.

'It's all part of the same thing,' he argued. 'I want to write about football, too. All of it. It's all connected, part of the same problem. People in power treating the rest of us like scum.' Like gangs at the turn of the century, the city was divided into red and blue, each convinced of their superiority and blinded to the bigger picture that they were rooted to roughly the same spot. We were decidedly blue, though it was an arbitrary choice. They were in decline and had a self-destructive tendency towards maverick individualism, so it seemed like a logical choice.

I wasn't sure, and I said so. 'I think we need to decide what we want to get out of it. The more we try to include, the harder it will be to sell.'

'What we want to get out of it? I just have all this stuff inside me that I want to get out. It doesn't really matter who reads it.'

Still, I wasn't sure. 'Really? Then what's the point? If no one wants to read it, why bother?'

He was adamant. 'If it's good enough, people will read it.' He spoke with a decisive tone that signalled the end of that topic of conversation so we changed the subject back to Miranda.

'I could tell right away you liked her,' he said. It was a loaded statement, emphasis on the like. I wondered if he fancied her, too, which would be odd as we had very divergent tastes but she was extraordinary, nothing at all like the other girls we knew.

'Like you don't.' He didn't disagree. He couldn't.

Then one of the old men came over with two pints and put them on our table. 'You're Jack Barton's lad, aren't you? He was one of the good ones alright.' He looked like he didn't have two pennies to rub together. We thanked him and invited him to sit down and join us, but he staggered on. 'Thanks, lads,' he said. 'I'd best be off.'

I was aware that Tom's old man was a bit of a celebrity although we were a bit embarrassed to take a handout in this fashion. I knew he missed him and didn't tend to talk about him a lot, but his presence was there in a lot of what Tom talked about, the way he thought and how he saw the world, always older than his years, wise beyond his experiences.

'Maybe you're right,' he conceded. 'Maybe music is a good starting point.' That was typical of him, always willing to consider other points of view.

We talked about what gigs we had coming up in the next few weeks and how we were going to fund them given our meagre income. That was part of the rationale behind setting up a fanzine, to try to get our foot in the door of the main music venues without paying for it. It was worth a shot. We had some articles written already but even thinking of a name was hard. Tom had suggested Paradigm Shift.

'What does that even mean?' I asked.

'It's about seeing things in new ways,' he explained. 'I want people to look at music differently, not just as something nice to listen to. It's so much more than that.'

'I get it,' I said. 'But I don't like it. It's too exclusive. People wouldn't get it.'

'Too pretentious?' He pulled a face.

'Just a bit. What about Teenage Rage?' I suggested. He pulled a different kind of face, like something smelt bad. 'Too juvenile?'

'Yup.' We knew it would smack us in the face when we stumbled on the perfect name. We kept on coming up with lame ideas while we carried on drinking on and afterwards, all the way to the bus station, but at least it stopped us talking about Miranda, which was probably for the best. The last thing we needed was a rivalry, especially one I knew I wouldn't win. We talked and walked. Above our heads, a few scattered stars twinkled red and blue in the night sky, their brilliance distorted and disfigured by the halo of pollution that sat perpetually above the city. The toxins haunted our very DNA, turning our voice into that distinctive nasal twang that softened the dialect. 'You know what this is?' Tom gestured broadly at the vast expanse of hideous run-down buildings which scarred the landscape, squat and now functionless in their dilapidated state. I didn't respond at first, guessing it was more of a rhetorical question, a linguistic trick to signal another profound statement about the city with which we endured such a love-hate relationship, more of the former than the latter. Close by, the ambient whoosh of traffic on wet roads created the urban soundscape than mocked the child's trick of putting a seashell to your ears.

'It's a concrete Eden,' he said after a lengthy pause. We screwed our eyes at the brutality of the vista, the sharp angles that sectioned off the view into a sequence of grotesque sections of what might loosely be termed architecture, though there was not a single nod to form over function, no artistic flourish to ameliorate the impression it left on us. 'It's what we turned Paradise into.' He laughed at the bleakness of the observation. I started to get what he meant. 'Dark satanic mills.'

'Exactly.'

He continued to stare. 'The thing is, I love it here, but sometimes it's just so depressing that we're supposed to accept that this is good enough.'

As I looked him, he seemed simultaneously to be ancient and young, a part of the landscape that had crafted him and yet set apart by the vital energy of his refusal to bow to the wicked inevitability of capitalism. 'Do you ever think you think too much?' I asked him.

He looked at me like the question had a faulty logic and then laughed.

'I guess so,' he said. For a moment, it seemed as though he was going to offer another piece of adolescent wisdom, but then thought better of it. 'Sod it, let's get another drink.'

*

As ever, half-hearted rain was coming down made gritty with soot, turning the pavements slick but failing to wash the streets clean of filth. We were having lunch at a café near Affleck's Palace. Tom had been offered an office job two afternoons a week which meant he would have to skive college.

'It's worth it,' he argued. 'I need the cash and I'm hardly struggling with work.' He had a mischievous look as he drank. 'It gives me access to a copier. If we ever get the fanzine off the ground, I might be able to run off a load of copies when no-one's around.'

'That's genius,' I said. 'It's typical of you to find a way to seize the means of production.'

He smiled wildly. 'The company I'm working for are loaded,' he said. 'It's not like they are going to miss a few sheets of paper.'

We were sitting with Colin, a friend of ours from college who worked sometimes as a freelance photographer. He had that faraway look in his eyes of those who obsessed about something, a reluctance to make eye contact that made him even more endearing, as if he was letting us into his secret world. His pride and joy was a Praktika camera he had picked up in eastern Europe somewhere behind the Iron Curtain. It was ugly and functional in design, and he was always vague about how he had picked it up but it took great pictures, or rather he did. He had taken photos of food at the café were in and they gave him and his friends free food from time to time when things were going off.

'Doesn't that make you a sell-out?' he asked. 'Working for the man?'

Tom knew he was teasing. 'I'm the enemy within,' he said. 'Requisitioning supplies for the masses.' As it transpired, that wasn't all he helped himself to while he was there. He shagged the office manager across the photocopying machine within the first month, a posh girl called Emily. She even turned up at a couple of gigs where she knew Tom would be, but you could tell she hated the music. It was a shame as she always bought a round of drinks.

In the meantime, I had reconsidered Tom's ideas for the fanzine and realised that he was right, that what might just give us an edge was the ability to write about more than just the local music scene. If we made it bigger, and wrote about art and culture and politics and everything else that we considered important, it would elevate the music that shaped our lives to an equal status. Whatever other people thought, music wasn't just something disposable, a backing track to life like the tinny muzak they played in the Arndale Centre to lull shoppers to buy more crap they didn't need and couldn't afford.

'I'm glad you've finally come round to my way of thinking,' Tom grinned. 'I've had an idea.' He always wore a canvas army surplus bag across his shoulder. With a pen, he had drawn on the strap to make it look like a bandolier of bullets, like he was a revolutionary armed with a chunky magic marker out to change the world. He fumbled around inside and pulled out some sheets of paper on which he had designed a masthead for a magazine called The Manifesto which cleverly mimicked and mocked more established magazines and duly doffed its cloth cap to the godfathers of egalitarianism.

Colin nodded his approval. 'Yes,' he said. 'Very yes. I love it.' He didn't speak like other people. He quickly showed us some photos he had taken which he placed under Tom's design and they looked perfect. He was developing a style of photographing the industrial landscape, taking abstract angular shots of factories and mechanical equipment back-lit against the polluted mancunian sky. They looked grim and epic, brutal and beautiful.

'You're a poet with that thing,' I told Colin as he hugged his precious camera. 'These are amazing.' You could give a hundred people that camera, a thousand, and ask them to take photos of the same thing and none of them could come close. He was modest and smiled shyly, but inside I knew he was beaming.

'Can we use them?' asked Tom. Apparently, it was a done deal that The Manifesto had been approved as the working title. 'We can't pay you at first, but it will help get you noticed.' I didn't recognise it then, but that was a business model that would become his signature in the years that followed, quick to identify useful talent and embrace the work of others for little if any recompense. Like his great hero, Trotsky, he saw himself as a ruthless pragmatist; I saw him as a cheeky idealistic opportunist, like his Bolshevik heroes, but I loved him like a brother even then. We played around some more with the photos and text that Tom had created. It was a great moment. Everything was coming together, and you could tell that we were really onto something that might become important. Of course, we were still young and assumed that life would be a stream of such moments, when everything just seemed to naturally fall into place without any effort.

Right on cue, Miranda walked past the café on Oldham Street, saw us and walked over to see what we were getting so overexcited about. Naturally, I was really pleased to see her, especially at that auspicious moment, which perhaps explained why I increasingly found it difficult not to see her as a kind of omen of better things to come. Tom patted a seat. 'Sit,' he instructed. Colin already had his camera out.

'Do you mind?' he asked, snapping away, adjusting light meters and framing her face like a seasoned avant-garde cinematographer.

'Christ,' she exclaimed. 'Is he always like this?' She posed anyway, enjoying the attention despite her protests.

'Not really,' I said. 'He normally only gets excited by chimneys and wrought iron and brickworks.'

'Should I be flattered then?' she asked. I didn't have a good answer, so I shrugged. 'I suppose it's better than being called a nympho.'

I blushed hard. 'That's not what —'

She pressed a finger to my lips to silence me. 'I'm joking, silly,' she said. 'It was a nice thing to say.'

She made me flustered, eager to change the subject. I mentioned the film of *Jason and the Argonauts* had been on TV the previous evening. 'He was in it,' I said. 'Hylas. He was one of the sailors. Only he wasn't eaten by nymphs, he was crushed by a bronze giant.'

'Artistic license,' said Tom. 'That's not how it went down. It just made for a better scene in the film.'

Miranda raised an eyebrow. 'Better than a pool full of beautiful women?' She had a point. It was a great sequence, though, better in my mind than the celebrated battle with the skeletons. Hercules had prised open the giant's ankle with a spear, so his life force ebbed away. I said as much.

'Beautiful *topless* women?' said Miranda. Clearly defeated, Tom conceded the point. Miranda smiled at my discomfort, as if she knew I was thinking of her unclothed.

She looked at Tom's designs scattered across the table, scrutinising them carefully as if she knew what she was doing. 'These are good,' she said. 'Really good. Is this your doing?'

She looked at Tom differently, really looked at him. 'Maybe I've misjudged you.'

'You should read what he writes,' I said. 'That's his thing.'

'Is that right?' she said. 'Writing. Is that your thing?'

Unblinking, he retuned her gaze. 'Maybe. We'll see.'

Colin had stood up and posed her face, tilting her head this way and that and taking more photos. 'I'll send you these when I'm done,' he said, his face screwed up with concentration. Finally, he used up all his film. 'All done.'

'I think you've just become his muse,' Tom said drily.

She ordered a beer. 'So how did you like The Ramones? I meant to ask you the other day.'

'I thought they were brilliant,' I said. 'My ears are still ringing.' I have no idea why that was ever an indication of a good gig, other than the fact that it made it hard to forget you were there.

'I don't normally see you boys in the rock clubs,' she remarked.

'You need to look harder,' said Tom. 'We go wherever the action is.' For some reason, she made him talk in an unusually macho fashion, as if he felt threatened by her in some way.

It was true. Normally, we tended to hang out at the indie clubs, but they were not always open, so we were happy to frequent the goth and rock nights as well. Our tastes were not that easy to pin down and we felt a sort of kinship with people with similar but different flavours of alternative culture. We all peacefully coexisted, united by a common rejection of the bland ubiquity of force-fed mainstream culture. Tom put it best one day as we walked in a drunken haze beside the River Irwell. The Styx could not have looked more wretched. Tom wondered out loud what would happen to people compelled to drink from that monstrous source of water. He had likened it to mainstream culture, which was like a river full of industrial waste and turds. Everything just caught in the flow, being pulled in the same direction towards God knows where. We thought

25

we had seen a dead baby swirling in the dirty water, but it might have been a doll. Either way, he was drunk and upset. 'Alternative cultures flow wherever they like,' he said. 'Unpolluted. Undiluted.'

We talked about the places we went and what we had planned for the next few weeks. The big one for me was The Chameleons at The Ritz.

'That's quite a leap from The Ramones,' said Miranda.

'Not really. They're both just trying to find a way to do something that feels real.' It sounded a bit hollow as I said it, childish, but it was how I felt. I wanted to try to express myself more clearly but I couldn't find the words, so I changed the subject. 'What have you been doing? You look nice.' She was wearing a fitted navy blue dress with heels, far more conventional than the way she had dressed the other night.

'Nice?' She was taken aback. 'Thanks, I guess. Not quite the effect I was hoping for, though.' She checked her reflection in a mirror behind the bar. 'I just had an audition.'

'What was the role?'

'Just a pretty face.'

Colin clapped. 'Ha. Then I'm sure you got the part.'

'You're sweet,' she said, patting his head. 'I'm not sure I was quite what they were looking for. The director wanted me to be innocent.'

'You're an actress,' said Tom. He was clinically dissecting his beer mat.

'Only in the same way that you're a writer.' She meant it playfully, but his comment had clearly touched a nerve and she took a long swig of her drink.

'Couldn't you just act innocent?' I asked.

'Theoretically,' she said. 'That is what acting is supposed to be. But I think it's hard to appear innocent if you're not. It's not just about dressing nicely. They can always see right through you.'

We had to think hard about that.

'Put it this way,' she explained. 'You boys can wear leather jackets and boots, but you'll still look like what you are.'

'And what's that? *Nice* boys?' There was disdain in Tom's voice.

She stood up, laughing. 'Well, you're nothing like the other boys who always seem to take an interest in me, that's for sure.' She paused. There were a million stories in what she wasn't saying. 'Put it this way, it wasn't meant as an insult,' she teased. 'Far from it. You look really great, just as you are.' She finished her drink and banged the glass on the table to signify that she was going. 'Stay gold, boys,' she called as she started to walk off, 'and good luck with the fanzine. I'm sure it's going to be brilliant.'

Colin spoke first once she was out of sight.

'Where on earth did you find her?' he asked, his eyes wide with wonder, his pupils flicking back and forth between me and Tom. We looked at each other and exchanged glances as we considered the question.

'I'm not entirely sure we did,' said Tom after a while. The new single by The Bodines came on the radio and he paused for a moment to acknowledge the fact, then carried on. 'If anything,' he concluded, 'I think it's more like she found us.'

I nodded. 'It's like she hunted us down,' I agreed, though it was the first time the thought had occurred to me. I had no idea what it signified, if anything, although if she was the predator, then that made us the prey. The thought made me laugh, but it was a thin and nervous laugh as if I was a swimmer suddenly finding myself a little out of my depth.

Three

Saturdays in Manchester was all football, even in an age when the balance of power had temporarily switched to Merseyside. After a late Friday night at The Venue, we would drag ourselves out of bed and hit the streets, the cold slowly clearing our heads. In the mornings, we would play at Hough End, a vast flatland of football pitches where men of all ages did pitiless battle against one another. Whatever time of year, a cruel wind would skitter across the pitches while you did your best to avoid lunging tackles and dogshit supplied by the police dogs who were trained nearby. A few of us had made the transition from youth football to the men's league to do the running for those too old and hobbled by age and hardship to do much more than lumber around the pitch. It was still a decent standard and occasionally you would recognise a face from an old football card you had treasured or traded at school and wonder how on earth they had ended up playing here for small change. A few months earlier, a scout from one of the big clubs had turned up to watch us play.

'Go out there and dazzle them,' our coach had advised us, and we did, but not enough apparently. It was a useful lesson that you have to take your chances when they present themselves, and one that we took to heart when it came to music.

There was a carefully prearranged routine. I was on the road first because I was already up with the girls, even on the weekend, making breakfast and setting them up for the day with something to do. I would then go and call for Darren who more often than not was still asleep. I knew his family well and would let myself in the back door and drag him out of bed while he swore and cursed and splashed water on his face to wake himself up. Then we would jog over to Tom's as he lived closest to Hough End and then we would be on our way, full of banter and bravado about the night before and what we were going to do on the pitch.

We were always the last to turn up. While the manager abused us, Tom hurriedly took off his Death Cult T-shirt and pulled his purple football shirt over his head. He had a six-pack even back in the days before everyone worked out in air-conditioned gyms. I was just fit and skinny. Darren played, too, with more enthusiasm than skill, but he had to sit this one out because of the six stitches holding his face together.

We won more than we lost, especially when Tom was able to get on the ball and control things from the middle. Even on a football pitch, he had the ability to see the bigger picture, played at his own pace even when psychopaths from the seven corners of Greater Manchester were doing all they could to disable him. That day, he found himself up against some George Best clone with long hair and an oversized shirt, but little talent to complete the look. Tom was always Colin Bell, the maestro making the team a better collective than the sum of its parts. Mostly, the other team couldn't get near him to kick him off the ball, and when they did, he could look after himself. We had a decent black kid up front called Jason who always seemed to score a couple of goals, but half-way through he ended up squaring up to one of their full backs who had racially abused him. I heard the other guy spit at him so Jason headbutted him and was duly sent off, and it all kicked off. In the ensuing melee, Tom dragged Jason away to spare him getting into further trouble.

'You alright?'

He laughed bitterly. 'Same old bullshit. I should be used to it by now.'

Tom had his arms round Jason's shoulders. 'You did the right thing, standing up for yourself. It won't always be like this, you know.'

I don't know if he believed it, but he tended to mean what he said. I almost always came away with blood on my shirt, but I enjoyed it all the same, even if the stain never quite washed out. In the afternoon, we would head to Maine Road if City were at home, never questioning why we were happy to be a part of this vast crowd of people in a way that we would never have tolerated when it came to music. Perhaps it was because of their underdog status. They also had a promising young team of local boys much better than I would ever be, and it felt important to support them, although within a couple of years the idiots in charge of the club had cashed them in for a bunch of journeymen and mercenaries. City were very much the footballing underdogs of the city, the imbalanced indie counterpart of United's mainstream status as a global footballing superpower. Supporting the blues was more a question of blind loyalty and faith, with little expectation of any kind of joy beyond sporadic glimmers of short-term success, where past glories had faded and expectations were low. In other words, a team who epitomised everything that Manchester now stood for as a city, although it helped that we had players like Mark Lillis and Clive Wilson, local lads who played their hearts out every week and wore their shirts with genuine pride. No wonder all the best bands were blues. United had Simply Red and, frankly, they could keep them.

As we walked down Platt Lane, Tom dropped a bombshell, casually mentioning that he wouldn't be able to play anymore.

'I've got to work Saturdays, too,' he said. 'I couldn't afford to say no.'

'It won't be the same without you, though,' Darren complained. 'Nah, you're just as good as me,' he lied, ruffling Darren's carefully sculpted hair just to annoy him. He talked to us about priorities and putting away childish things, although there was nothing childish and getting kicked black and blue by a team of thugs every week. He also pointed out that at some point in the not-too-distant future, going away to university was a distinct possibility, so he would have had to give it up anyway. There was no dissuading him, though, and that was that. With an almost Stalinist attitude to necessity and sacrifice, access to a photocopier had suddenly become more important than just about anything else. That's just how it was.

*

Like a novice vampire, the night-time was mine to explore and do what I liked, which mostly involved watching bands, slowly developing a taste for beer and developing crushes on girls who were out of my league. The daylight hours, however, were a very different matter. My homelife was a car crash. It would be grossly inaccurate to say I was raised by a single mother despite the fact that I shared a house with the woman who had given birth to me, and two subsequent half-sisters, but I effectively looked after myself and did what I could to care for them. At best she was barely functional, meaning that Maxine, as I called her, largely neglected her maternal responsibilities at my expense, not that I needed or expected anything more of her than I received, but because the chore of raising my siblings largely fell on me. I hadn't called her mum for as long as I could remember; I guess I felt she hadn't earned the right. Around noon, she might raise herself from the dead, but the task of preparing breakfast and getting my younger sisters off to school largely fell on me. They were good kids and didn't know any better, so it was mostly fine. There wasn't a lot of love to go around, so I tried not to be resentful and do my best for them, but I would be surprised if I hadn't failed than in more ways than can be easily counted.

31

For obvious reasons, getting to college on time was a considerable challenge. The fact that I was there at all was, to me at least, some kind of success, but it landed me in almost constant conflict with my educators. I liked to think I was relatively bright, though my physical appearance seemed to suggest to others than I was mentally deficient, as if the way you wear your hair or the crease in your trousers is in some way indicative of the quality of thought going on inside. God only knows how, but I got by well enough, mostly because I was quick at picking up new skills.

Although I did well enough to justify staying on at school, I decided to cut my losses and make a fresh start at college, where I hooked up with Tom, who I knew well from football, and others with a similar passion for good music. Not having to wear a uniform eased my issues with authority in terms of my habitual lateness, although it was still an issue that plagued me from time to time. I did well enough on my chosen courses to get cut a bit of slack, earning a reputation for thoughtful and imaginative work, but with a maverick spirit so that I tended to write about what I thought was interesting rather than doing what I was told to do. It never really occurred to me that what we were being asked to do was to regurgitate someone else's opinions about a topic rather than thinking of something vaguely original or interesting to say. What the point of it all was I couldn't really say, except to ensure that one generation to the next held roughly the same views whilst making sure that young people were discouraged from holding meaningful opinions of their own. Literally how to maintain the Status Quo.

'You need to compromise,' they would tell me. 'Play the game.' Which would be fine if only someone had bothered to tell me the rules. Tom would later explain to me that education was just as much about politics as everything else, which to his mind meant that it was always loaded in favour of the elite at the expense of working people. It was a game at which he was expert.

Either way, I was doing fine, well enough in fact for people to start putting the idea of going to university into my head, although it was hard to see how that could possibly happen unless Maxine miraculously got her act together. Otherwise, even if I managed to build up to escape velocity and move away, my sisters would be consumed in the afterburn.

I had also discovered girls at college and learned that if I made a bit of an effort, I could get some attention, although my circumstances meant that it was not possible to get even vaguely serious, even if I had wanted to. It was hardly like I could take anyone home. The thought of it made me shudder.

We studied History together, me and Tom. He was so smart that he really sharpened me up intellectually just to keep up, in the same way that certain girls made me strive to be better. Most of the course was the study of one revolution or civil war after another: Russia, China, Spain, Cuba. The sense of people's lives being redirected towards something better, rejecting the corrupt and moribund values of the feudal system and its decrepit aftermath, was something we both found quite intoxicating. It was very old school, mostly taught as the narrative of great and terrible men of formidable character single-handedly shaping destiny, which is of course as much a fairy story as the idea that a benevolent deity created the world. It made no sense. We argued that charismatic chancers like Lenin or Castro were remarkable for their capacity to harness and exploit mass discontent in a time of weakness for one faltering regime or another, but that it was ultimately the people who brought about the seismic shifts in the redistribution of power. Out teachers patiently tried to talk us round to the orthodox view of published theory which was what the examiners wanted to hear. They gently dismissed us as naïve idealists, which is exactly what we were and what we wanted to

33

be. There was plenty of time later on to embrace that cynical view of humankind that is perhaps the destiny of us all. For the time being, we were ablaze with hope that things could only get better as long as you were prepared to fight. Even Thatcher, that political archfiend, had used the phrase social mobility to suggest that the days when you died in the class into which you were born might become a thing of the past.

But in the meantime, I had fallen for a girl from Sale called Zoe who Tom had dismissed as a C&A goth, meaning she was superficially one of us but the way she dressed was more an affectation rather than something she really believed in. Things were good between us but there was no way I was prepared to take her home where she would have to literally clamber over piles of jumble and bundles of newspapers just to make it to the stairs, where I shared a room with my half-sisters. She had dark hair but had taken to bleaching it and decorated herself with fantastic silver jewellery from the classified ads in the back pages of music magazines which she wore dangled over tight black dresses. I knew it was just an infatuation, but I was flattered that she saw something in me to which other girls were seemingly blind so I chose to forgive the fact that she clearly lied about the music she listened to. Tom would cruelly make up the names of bands and she would swear she had their latest record.

She was a talented artist and would meet me after college so I could carry her art portfolio and walk with her to her bus stop which was over a mile away in the wrong direction. Although she admitted she had gone to a private school, she had switched to the public college at the first opportunity, and I chose to interpret that as a good sign, too captivated by her prettiness to take much notice when Tom mocked me for dating a posh girl. She habitually wore a T-shirt depicting Thatcher bearing the legend 'WE ARE ALL PROSTITUTES' which was what had first attracted me to her, but she claimed not to be interested in politics and had bought the shirt because it was shocking, which amused her.

More importantly, she taught me how to be in a relationship. Without me saying anything to give me away, I think she sensed that we came from different worlds; in fact, that was probably part of the attraction for her. She read classic romantic literature like Wuthering Heights but reacted badly when I tried to read it and described it as silly schoolgirl snuff porn, a critique I had borrowed from Tom. I suspect she probably tried to see us as doomed lovers and pouted sulkily at any indication that I was making fun of her. Her art was incredible, although for one of her show pieces she drew a portrait of Tom from secret photographs she took, portraying him like a doomed poet, his face emerging from a darkened canvas like something Caravaggio might have painted. I never asked why she chose him over me as a subject. Never ask a question if you don't want to know the answer.

Recently, she had taken to begging me to come and meet her parents, one of whom lectured in something or other at the university, but I resisted in case she wanted me to reciprocate, which was never going to happen. Whenever she brought it up, I abruptly changed the subject to delay that inevitable moment that she realised we were from different worlds and she moved on. For the time being, I liked being with her and I didn't want it to end before it had naturally burned itself out. When her bus pulled up, she would kiss me ostentatiously and wave from the top deck like a schoolgirl. It felt good, for once.

Back at home, I forced my way through the piled maze of hoarded clutter to the kitchen where I started to prepare food from the scant provisions I could find in the fridge. God knows how we survived from one day to the next. My saving grace was Deb, the neighbour, who always brought the girls home from school. She had a boy roughly the same age and they got on well enough and she instinctively did what she could for us out of her abundant sense of common decency, the kind of community spirit in the face of hardship that Thatcherism sought to destroy. Without her support, I think the world would have collapsed in on us. Maxine would be up and about by then, but she couldn't really be trusted to cook. More than once, food had been forgotten on the hob and it was more luck than judgement that the house hadn't been burned down. The last time, Maxine shook her head and laughed at her own foolishness.

'It's like my brain just doesn't want to remember,' she said, tutting at herself.

Deb had given me a look that warned me that unless I stepped up, Social Services would become involved again, and there was only one way that was going to end.

'Beware the child-catcher!' Maxine often cooed to herself absently in a silly sing-song voice as if it was all a great big joke.

The really sad thing was that Bella and Sindy were good kids, their upbeat names mocking the squalor in which they were unknowingly dragged through childhood, although they were incredibly good natured. It was as if Maxine thought their jaunty names would somehow guarantee them a good life, though who knew what the hell went through that foggy mind of hers. When she spoke, her voice was slurred, always out of step with the hardships of real life faced by those around her.

Deb's husband, Gary, was a United fan but a decent enough bloke, one of ten kids. He had a theory that children grew into the space available to them, physically and emotionally. I'm sure it wasn't his theory originally, and that someone else had been able to express it more articulately, but it made sense. I watched my sisters grow up to be easy-going and likeable little girls because they didn't know any better, floating happily around the house on the periphery of Maxine's dwindling grasp of reality. Her dereliction of her maternal duties drove me to distraction, and only Deb's intuitive interventions stopped me from the darker emotions that burned away in me. Occasionally, if I raised my voice, she would hold out a bottle of her prescription pills to me and urge me to help myself.

'You should try these, son,' she would say, as if her advice had any value to me. 'They take the edge off. You need to chill out.' They took a lot more than the edge off, though, as far as I could see. She had become completely dislocated from reality, like a living ghost, haunting everyone she was supposed to protect.

'Fuck off, Maxine,' I would say if the girls were out of earshot. I hated it when she called me *son* and would slap the pills out of her shaking hand onto the floor so she would have to crawl in the filth she had accumulated to recover them like they were pearls from a broken necklace.

My saving grace was the fact that Gary's brother had done well for himself and had been looking for a tutor to help his kids pass the 11-plus exam to get into the local grammar school. He lived miles away but Gary and Deb had convinced him that I was some kind of child prodigy, so he paid me twenty quid every Sunday morning for two hours of personal tuition while the girls went to Sunday school. The deal I struck with Gary was that I had to be in a fit state to work, and that I didn't take the piss too much whenever City beat United in a local derby, which was not that likely the way things were going. That money was a godsend, but Deb made me promise that the money was mine to do with what I liked, and I was happy to comply. My days were manic, but at least the evenings were mine, and I learned to function well enough on little sleep, a gift that has always served me well.

*

Of course we weren't out every night. Even in a thriving cultural hub like Manchester there were quiet nights, but we always had more than enough to keep us busy, whether it was college work, girlfriends or club nights like Fridays at The Venue, unless an unmissable gig dragged us away. Lack of money was a constant problem, so often we would end up sitting on The Stoop talking about everything and nothing all night long. The Stoop was the crumbling stairwell to an old industrial building on Whitworth Street in the city centre, with about eight stone steps leading up to an ornate wooden doorway which some long-dead industrialist must have believed presented the right image of his success at turning natural resources into saleable goods. Fittingly, it now looked like the entrance to a modern horror film, the premises long empty and waiting to be repurposed at some future period when the area was economically rejuvinated and the premises could be transformed into something that could turn a profit, shops or residences or whatever. Crushed under Thatcher's heel, it was hard to imagine that ever happening. The city was literally falling apart like it was an abandoned industrial theme park.

There was an ever-changing mixture of like-minded people who might turn up on any one evening, usually centred around Tom and mostly male. For some reason, the prospect of sitting in cold drizzle choking on exhaust fumes and drinking unbranded lager or whatever was going cheap did not appeal to the few girls we knew. Situated on the fringes of the emerging gay zone, this meant we were occasionally targeted by self-titled queer-bashers as much as those offended by our subcultural identity, but for the most part there were enough of us to be left alone. Drugs were never an issue. We knew a few people that smoked pot, but never there. Perhaps it was too public for anyone to be so daft as to openly smoke a joint. A lad called Sean was often there clutching a ghetto blaster that was always running out of the jumbo-sized batteries it gobbled. He made amazing cassettes compiling the latest John Peel sessions of the bands we loved, and he created exquisite hand-drawn covers for them which he drew with black and silver pens and named the tapes after whichever girl he was in love with that week. He was not discerning judging by the few who had turned up occasionally to hang out with us, but he wasn't much to look at, either. The tapes were not chronological but often themed by intricate sub-genres of alternative music, and he would select tapes with care based on the people there on any given night. Despite his creative talents, he has shy and often struggled to initiate conversation, but seemed happy setting the mood and drumming along on the hard stone with his pens to whatever tune was playing. He occasionally referred to the fact he was taking drum lessons as an excuse for turning up late, but he never once mentioned anything about being in a band.

Mostly, the talk revolved around past or future gigs, sometimes girls but especially music. We self-identified through our favourite bands in lieu of anything more real to base our conversations on. Then as now, the lives of teenagers are not that fascinating except to the people living them, and often not even then. No-one shared problems beyond lack of girlfriends or money, but we all had each other's backs as far as it went.

Tom had turned up and Sean popped in a cassette starting with Billy Bragg from a case decorated with an image of Lenin holding the ubiquitous Sony Walkman and wearing bulky headphones. I noticed the tape was labelled Mary, but I had no idea who she might be. Inevitably, the talk turned to music and politics and whether the two were compatible. Naturally, Tom argued that of course they were.

'All music is political,' he said. No one felt able to oppose him, but he corrected himself. 'All good music is political.'

'What does that even mean?' snorted another lad who habitually hung out with us, Simon. Tom had got off with his girlfriend at a Fall gig a few weeks earlier and their tentative friendship had become antagonistic. They were quite similar in that they liked the sound of their own voice, so it was probably inevitable that they wouldn't really get on. 'There's no such thing as good or bad music,' he said. 'It's just a question of taste. Just because you happen to like something doesn't mean it's better than something someone else likes. Taste is subjective.'

Tom gave him a funny look and I actually wondered for a moment if he was going to bring up the subject of Simon's ex clearly preferring him.

'You know that's a very simplistic argument,' said Tom thoughtfully. He held up the Billy Bragg cassette to prove a point. 'Sean's doodles are great, but no-one's ever going to hang them in art gallery. I know that's not necessarily the true definition of art but being good at something is not the same as being great at something. Real art has the power to transform people.' He let that one sink in for a moment while he searched for an example. 'Put it this way: *Love Will Tear Us Apart* is a great piece of music. In fifty years' time, people will still be listening to it. *The Pipes of Peace*, however, is a piece of shite. It's not music and it's certainly not political. It's something else. A commercial product that imitates music with a bland message designed to appeal to the most people to boost sales. Fodder for the masses. Nothing more.'

He chose his example with care. Paul McCartney was Simon's hero and his current record was terrible by any standards. Horrified, Simon took the bait. 'You can't slag off McCartney,' he said. 'You just can't. I know it's a terrible record but McCartney, he's a genius.' His voice was incredulous. His dad was an old mod from Warrington or somewhere else in the hinterlands who ran a vintage vinyl shop in Back Piccadilly, meaning Simon had been brought up listening to bands who had theoretically paved the way for the music we all listened to and had a deeply engrained awe for the old guard. We had come to it the other way round, working back from now to then. To Simon, the bands we listened to were pale shadows of bands he would have killed to see play live; for us, music had evolved from what had gone before, borrowing the best bits of previous generations of talent to create something altogether more culturally significant. I didn't know the term post-modern then, but that's what it was.

'McCartney' said Tom, holding up his thumbs mockingly. 'I absolutely can slag him off.' His voice was as off-hand as Simon's was strained with disbelief. 'He wrote some good tunes a few decades ago, but even then there were better bands.'

'Better than The Beatles?' When he said it, you could hear the slight Liverpudlian twang in his voice. 'Like who?'

'The Monkees,' I suggested, only half-joking. They were always a guilty pleasure of mine.

'The Stones,' said Tom. 'The Kinks. The Velvet Underground for sure. Loads of bands were just as good, if not better. Just because it's been decided by popular writers that they were the best, it's not an indisputable fact. It's just an opinion, and I choose to disagree with it.'

'And you're wrong.'

'*The Pipes of fucking Peace.*' Tom spoke slowly for emphasis and rolled his eyes mockingly. 'Seriously? A genius? You've got to be kidding me.'

Almost inevitably, Simon snapped. 'Just cos he's a scouser. What does it matter where someone is from? Surely what matters is what they've got to say.' The emotion cracked his final syllable; you could hear the frustration in his voice. Even I wasn't sure if Tom was serious or just picking a fight for the sake of it, but tonight he was a dog with a bone.

'It doesn't help his cause that he's a scouser, but that's not it. It's not like I hate everything about Liverpool. Politically, it's spot on.' We all nodded in agreement with that. 'My issue is with the term genius, which is criminally abused. Yes, he wrote some good pop songs. Good for him. He made a shitload of money, too. Good for him. But he's not a genius.'

41

'There's nothing wrong with being successful,' said Simon. 'People deserve to make a decent living out of what they're good at. We shouldn't turn against everyone who sells a few records and makes a few quid.'

It was an old debate. Did a band cease to be credible because they became popular? Was it an unforgivable sin to sell out to the major labels? Back then, it felt like it was unacceptable ideologically to turn your back on the independent scene. Music was so important and personal to us that the artists we loved belonged to us somehow, they were connected to us in an indefinable way so that commercial success diluted their appeal in a way that felt incredibly important back before we had any bills of our own to pay. We had hit an awkward nexus in alternative music where it was starting to become more popular and smaller independent record labels and their bands were being picked up by the majors like they were collecting trinkets, for the fun of it, just because they could.

Simon was never one to give up. 'So, you're saying that Morrissey will never release a piece of commercial shit in the future.'

'God, let's hope not. But he's not a genius either, just some guy who writes good songs. The point is no one should be forgiven for *Pipes of Peace*, or *Ebony and Ivory* for that matter. He's becoming a cultural war criminal.'

'You're full of shit,' said Simon, clearly exasperated. 'You'll say anything to sound smart. You're so anti-establishment.'

'Not true,' said Tom. 'I fully intend to part of the establishment in the future. I want to be right in the middle of it, changing it from the inside out, making it better. I might be a non-conformist, that I will grant you. I won't agree that something is so, just because people tell me it's true. I want to be free to make my own mind up. Are The Beatles the best band ever? No. Does it matter? Probably not.'

A fight like this was rare. Normally, the people on The Stoop were an amiable bunch. Small disagreements happened all the time, but they were usually good-natured.

Darren tried to redirect the conversation. 'What about love songs?' he said amiably.

'What about them?'

'Well, you said all songs were political – all good songs – but what about love songs?'

Tom shrugged. 'Love is political, too,' he said. He flashed Simon a smile to rekindle his misery about his cheating girlfriend.

'Everything is politics.'

Simon stood up to go. 'It is to you. You're not always right, you know.' Petulantly, he took his can of lager from Darren's hand and walked away into the night.

'Low blow,' said Darren, and he tipped the non-existent can to his lips to illustrate his disapproval.

After that, we chatted away for hours until most people had gone home, so only me and Tom were left.

'You were pretty hard on him,' I chided gently.

'Who? Simon?' He thought for a little while and cleared himself of any wrongdoing. 'He's just a pseudo-Scouser with bad hair,' he said. 'It's not my fault his girlfriend prefers me. I never chased her, remember?' He was right. His attitude to girls was very non-committal. I never saw him let anyone get too close and always skilfully disentangled himself before things became serious. He believed he had a gift for doing it in a way that prevented anyone from getting hurt, but it had become noticeable that increasingly there were places he would avoid in order to dodge a scene, just in case. I doubt anyone else would have noticed. He wasn't heartless, but he was undeniably egocentric in the way he valued his freedom more than he seemed to care for anyone else's feelings. Maybe that's how you get ahead in life.

'You're probably right,' he said. 'Simon's okay, as far as it goes. But you can't really trust anyone who never gets zits, can you.'

It was a strange criticism, but as I thought about it, I realised that it was strangely accurate, although why that made him untrustworthy I couldn't say. I assumed Tom was just being whimsical. As ever, he had his bag with him and he took out a folder or portfolio of some kind, containing several pages of what I quickly realised was the prototype of The Manifesto. Considering he was using old-school scissors and glue, it was incredibly slick. Even without reading the completed articles, the aesthetic was everything he had described over many fresh evenings on The Stoop or slowly nursing beers in one preferred public house or another. Somehow, he had succeeded in creating a cohesive visual style using a combination of Darren's angular photographs overexposed to create post-industrial frames on which to hang his words. The style was cold, minimalistic but occasionally embellished with artwork I recognised as Sean's, which added a more human flourish. Without me knowing, he had even convinced Zoe to design elaborate designs to act as drop capitals to start off each piece with a decorative feature which somehow tied in the old and new, lending the text a more authoritative feel. He certainly didn't lack for ambition. Taken as a whole, it was outrageously over-blown for what was effectively a music fanzine, but equally it was hard not to be impressed. And I told him so.

He blushed, and I was inwardly delighted that he valued my praise so highly. 'It's not just me,' he said. 'This is your work, too.'

He was being generous, although we had talked back and forth about it for months, and I had contributed some content of my own.

'The photos look amazing,' I said.

'That's all Colin. He's got the magic eye.'

We had no idea what we sounded like, sitting there, admiring ourselves, wishing our creative selves into existence like starving poets in garrets in European cities we would probably never visit.

We became aware that an old lady was making her way towards us, pushing an old shopping trolley piled high with wretched possessions that only Maxine could have prized. What she wanted with us we couldn't imagine. Perched high up on the crumbling stairwell, we certainly weren't blocking her way. She was randomly angry in the incoherent manner of the mentally ill, meaning she could potentially be dangerous. It took us a little while to tune into her ramblings, but she clearly held us responsible for some half-remembered transgressions against her.

'It's all your fault,' she was saying. 'Damn you all to hell and back again.'

We pleaded our innocence.

'That's just what they always say,' she ranted. 'You're all the offspring of Beelzebub. The generation of filth. The dick-swing children.'

I tried to suppress a laugh, but I couldn't do it.

'Yes, you laugh as much as you like,' she hissed, 'but you won't be laughing like that when all the goblins and demons are having their wicked way with your little arses.'

'I guess not,' I agreed, trying to compose myself. She was a wretched creature and God only knew what terrible things she had lived through to become reduced to this pitiful state. Though he had a reputation for being unsympathetic, Tom was amazing with people like this, those who had made the streets their homes. Instinctively, they aroused his compassion. He stood up and walked over to her, keeping his distance. She visibly flinched as if in expectation of some form of abuse.

'What can I do to help?'

She glared at him with her terrible cloudy eye. 'Resist temptation,' she said. The hint of strict religious doctrine clung to her filthy clothes. 'Repent your evil ways.'

'We're just sitting here,' he said, 'minding our own business. Are you hungry?'

Still she glared. 'I'm cold,' she said, after a pause. He fumbled in his pockets and found some loose change, his bus fare home. He held out his hand.

She was very wary and took the money in slow motion as if it was a trick and was careful to avoid human contact as she took the coins as it to avoid contamination. 'You can't just buy me off,' she hissed. 'I won't fuck you, you dirty boy.'

'That's fine,' he smiled. 'You don't have to. It's yours.'

She stared him down, waiting for him to make a move. He held up his hands and retreated a slow step at a time. As she stumbled on her way, he waved and sat down.

'Jesus.' He breathed out heavily.

I had other things on my mind. 'That's three great names for a band right there,' I said. It was something we often talked about.

'What's that?'

'The Offspring of Beelzebub.'

'Nah,' he said. 'Too rock.'

'Generation of Filth?' I suggested.

He shook his head dismissively, pulling a face.

'The dick-swing children?'

He sat upright. 'Now that one I like.'

'Not very radio friendly,' I offered.

He packed his things away and we headed off. The evening had come to an end, as we debated the likelihood that The Dick-Swing Children would agree to appear on *Top of the Pops* if invited. Probably not. On the way, we found a pristine pound note on the floor, sparing us a long walk home through the filthy drizzle. Sometimes, it was hard not to believe in fate.

Four

Darren never liked drinking in the Gay Traitor, not because he was homophobic as such but because he constantly clung to the belief that the perfect girl was waiting for him out there and he was convinced that he would never pull a girl in there. He was always a dreamer like that, and as much as he knew he was an ugly bastard, he was a lot of fun to be with and that could sometimes be enough. Whatever people will tell you, The Hacienda was never better than in its early days when it was three quarters empty, a huge cavernous folly that bled the city's cultural pioneers of any money they might have made from their unlikely global dance hits. It was epic, iconic and absurd, so overblown in its fanciful conception that it made your head spin. Tom could have named every semi-famous person in there, people who would probably have been embarrassed at the idea that anyone would recognise them.

The Jesus and Mary Chain were in town and we were all buzzing with expectation. In many ways, the Mary Chain symbolised everything good that was happening with music. Although they borrowed heavily from the past, they also sounded exactly how the future was going to be, snatched moments of beauty in an uncertain howling storm. All those tired cliches – overlong sets full of second-rate songs, the tedious pantomime of stomping for an encore – they were having none of that, just a twenty-five minute onslaught of feedback and smacked-up cranked-up noise masquerading as music. After several over-hyped riots at recent gigs, they had been banned from playing most venues and only Manchester and Nottingham had the balls to put them on. Rock City was allegedly run by Hell's Angels, so it was a brave person who would kick off in there; The Hacienda just didn't give a shit. It was uncommonly busy, and for once it was so full that the conversation didn't bounce off the walls. It was a great line-up, too. The Pastels came and went with so little presence that months later we would argue whether they had actually played at all. Meat Whiplash properly kicked things off, a ferocious twenty-minute assault of howling guitars and feedback, and the crowd started to warm up. Inevitably, Darren caught a flying elbow and opened the gash on his forehead his again, his grinning teeth flashing red as the blood started to flow down his face. He was loving every minute. Next up were Primal Scream, all jangling guitars in the days before they accidentally stumbled onto the little pills that would turn their world and everyone else's upside down. This was Bobby Gillespie learning the hard way how to control a crowd that didn't care a damn about his music, but it was great to finally see him up there on stage, that iconic hair bobbing across his face through swirling clouds of dry ice that caught in your throat. Somehow, Simon pushed through the crowd with a handful of beers he had picked up from somewhere. He had a habit of helping himself behind the bar, and we were too hyped to care where they had come from to say no. He had his moments, and his timing was immaculate.

The Mary Chain took the stage almost apologetically, accompanied by a swirl of furious screeching feedback that knocked you sideways. Bobby G smashed out a beat and they were off. A load of old punks had turned up to see what the fuss was about, a bunch of scruffy Glaswegians making a sound that emulated punk in its cocky rejection of what currently passed for music, a swirl of edgy black-clad figures assaulting us with sonic frequencies that were every bit as confrontational as the well-aimed boluses of phlegm that the crowd gobbed right back at them. This was give and take, no quarter given. Songs melted into each other, no break for tuning or any other affectations of musicianship or mutual respect. No 'Hello Manchester.' It was snarling band and crowd facing off, and it was great. It didn't matter that some of the songs seemed half-formed, what was important was the experience of it, living in the howls of noise and Jim Reid straining to make his voice over whatever the hell it was his brother was doing to his poor guitar, furiously stamping on pedals and smashing the neck with his fist to push the sound into extremes of what might be loosely termed music. The brilliance of it was the beautiful melody fighting to makes itself felt though the chaos, like glimpses of glorious sunshine pushing through storm clouds, vivid beams of light from the heavens that suddenly made everything seem better. And then they were gone, and no amount of clapping and booing was going to bring them back. We had had our pound flesh and that was all. No encore. No cliches. Just pure beautiful noise and then a profound silence. Stunned, we stumbled out onto Whitworth Street. The night was still young and suddenly it seemed pregnant with possibilities. We realised that you didn't have to be virtuosos in order to make something worthwhile, all you needed was attitude and self-belief and a sense of what you wanted to say.

'Fucking hell,' said Darren. His forehead was a real mess and he couldn't have cared less. 'I feel like I've been beaten up.' We showed him his reflection in a shop window and he grinned like a lunatic. He stood and admired himself, posing. 'I look amazing,' he proclaimed, although passers-by were giving him a wide berth.

'You look like a fucking lunatic,' I corrected him, because that's what he was. I threw my arms around his shoulders only partly because I thought he might be concussed. We wandered off together discussing our most spectacular gig so far that year and whether or not gobbing was an acceptable way of showing your approval of your new favourite band, ultimately deciding that it should have died with mohicans and safety pins and sniffing glue.

We found ourselves back at the Stoop, just sitting there and keeping the cold at bay by imagining brighter futures for ourselves and stomping our feet occasionally against the unforgiving stone. Come daybreak, I would be back to reality, dealing with tired children rubbing their eyes and finding the energy to get them ready for school. I would do anything to keep the night alive. Name your favourite Mary Chain songs. Devise the perfect festival line-up. It really didn't matter, as long as we kept talking to stop our chattering teeth. When we looked down, we could see the stars reflected in oily pools as if to remind us that no matter hard it seemed, you could still believe in the beautiful impossible.

*

Later that week I found myself at Zoe's place. Her parents were out at a dinner party hosted by some bigwig at the BBC who would later become embroiled in a lurid sex scandal and we made the most of it, fooling around as much as we dared, jumping at every noise outside in case her parents had laid a trap for us and came back early. Her house had so much space it made me feel sad in a way I couldn't really articulate but I was determined not to let it show. As hard as I strained, I couldn't hear the neighbours screaming abuse at each other. It was another world. I couldn't tell if she was being herself or if she was showing off, but she poured us drinks like gin and tonic with ice from a dispenser on her fridge with slices of lemon and I found myself pretending that I had done it all before, trying to be nonchalant about a way of life that was as alien to me as if she suddenly started talking in a different language. We quickly got drunk and then she took me to her bed.

Afterwards, I took a shower for the first time in my life, letting a dozen scalding jets bounce off my juvenile body. It was incredible. I felt purified. Naked, I found my way back to Zoe's room where I had been so long she had fallen asleep. I poked half-heartedly through her things, not to invade her privacy but to try to develop a sense of who she was, this girl who had just given herself to me so openly. There was a photograph of me on her mirror which I could not remember her taking and realised from the clothes I was wearing that it pre-dated our relationship, which I found strangely endearing. There was a writing pad on a desk and a novelty pen with a semi-naked man whose pants disappeared when you turned it upside down. In the mirror, my body looked nothing like his, but I felt good about myself and allowed myself the luxury of a smile as I stared at my reflection. I considered waking her, but found myself writing instead. I owed Tom an article to complete the first issue of The Manifesto but had no idea what to write about. I had composed some reviews of gigs we had been to which he had much admired, but he had encouraged me to think outside the box and I didn't want to let him down. The words came to me easily, in a subconscious stream that flowed onto the page. I barely knew what I was writing but I instinctively knew it was good. Perhaps writing with a pen with a man's dick hanging halfway down his leg was what I had been missing all this time. Finished, I threw the pen down onto the desk and ripped the pages from the writing pad with an extravagant flourish of self-satisfaction which woke Zoe up.

'What are you doing?' she asked. The sheets on the bed were twisted around her as she spoke.

'Nothing,' I said. 'Just writing something.'

'A love letter for your favourite girl?' I assumed she was joking. She had a great laugh, as if she didn't have a care in the world. Her long blonde hair cascaded across her face and shoulders.

'You wish. It's just something for the fanzine me and Tom have been working on.'

'I know all about it,' she said. 'I'm a valued contributor, remember. Good of you to finally join the party.' Her lithe body tantalised me on the bed as she held out her hand. 'Let me see.'

I handed her the torn pages. I started to explain but she shushed me. 'No spoilers.'

I climbed back into bed with her and tried to distract her but she was determined and I soon gave up, keen to know what she thought. I had decided to write about horror films, DIY straight-to video horror films which had become known as video nasties. I had adopted the voice of a deranged deity ranting down a divine telephone to a chief of police about the tawdry details of films mostly based on the lowest common denominators of sex and violence. It was distinctly Old Testament stuff, full of fire and brimstone. I called it Punk Cinema and twisted the narrative to link the films in their inventive cheap blurring of genres to the music we loved. A new wave of auteurs was finding a way to make a name for themselves. Abel Ferrara. Sam Raimi. Wes Craven. With next to nothing to work with but their twisted ideas and mad energy, their snarling little films were being shared across the globe. She laughed out loud more than once, in all the right places. 'This is hilarious,' she said finally. 'Totally bloody brilliant.' She was a terrible swearer, pronouncing every last consonant but it didn't matter. I was relieved that she had understood the reference to God's Cop, the Chief Constable of Greater Manchester who famously published a list of films every week which were to be banned for outrages against public decency. Every Friday, the Manchester Evening News would publish a list of films to be immediately withdrawn from distribution, prompting the phenomenon of the behind-the-counter box in the local Superstar video rental store which you would ask to surreptitiously rifle through looking for uncut gems and hidden gold.

'I mean, you know I hate those misogynistic little films you make me sit through,' she said, 'but I think this is exactly what Tom was looking for.'

Maybe making her watch *The Hills have Eyes* had not been one of my finest ideas for a first date, although I didn't necessarily agree they hated women, as they evidently hated men just as much. Everyone had to suffer; that was the whole point. As I said, they were loud and angry and full of wild nihilistic energy appealing to our worst instincts. Totally punk. I found myself a little taken aback that she any idea what Tom was looking for. I knew he had asked her to design some fonts for him to work with but that was just him, calculating what someone could offer him. It wasn't jealousy I was feeling, but it was a niggling emotion that came somewhere close.

'I wasn't doing it for Tom's sake,' I said. 'It just came to me. I started writing and it all just came gushing out.'

She handed it back. 'What's the deal with Tom?' she asked. 'He's a real mystery man, isn't he?'

I thought for a moment before I spoke, still irked by her earlier hint at familiarity. I was as much annoyed with myself for being petty, but I gave myself time to gather my thoughts. We had spent so much time hanging out, talking about the things that seemed important to us, our hopes for the future, that he didn't feel that much of mystery to me, and I told her as such.

'He just sometimes seems so far away,' she said. 'In his own head.' She lay her head on my bare chest. 'I can't put my finger on it. He can be so full of enthusiasm and optimism, but he still seems sad or angry somehow. You're just so open and easy. He's not.'

Feeling her cool skin next to me, I shrugged. 'I guess so,' I said. 'We just talk and talk so I don't really see it, but I know some people find him tricky. I think what happened to his dad has screwed him up a bit, but he seems to be working it through.' She propped herself up on her elbows. 'What happened?'

'I don't really know. He rarely talks about it.' As I spoke, I realised that perhaps we talked and talked but not about the things we should have been addressing. The hurting inside. I didn't want to give too much away. For one thing, it wasn't my pain to share. Besides, there wasn't much to tell. 'His dad was a big shot in the local trade union movement. He led a big strike and it got nasty. I don't really know any details, but he didn't make it.'

'What do you mean?' Her eyes were wide.

'I dunno. He died. I think there was an accident, but there is talk that was a bit more to it. He's a bit of a martyr to a lot of people round here. It was a few years ago so I don't think Tom knows what really went down.' I brushed some stray hair away from her face. Her skin was flawless. 'They were really close, though. His mum's dead nice, but he was his father's son. That's why he knows so much about everything, because his dad never stopped talking to him. Local history. Politics. Class war. That sort of thing.' I tapped my head. 'It's all in there, swirling around.'

'Poor Tom.'

'Yeah, I guess so,' I said. I thought about it some more. 'But he doesn't want your pity. Or mine. Or anyone's for that matter.'

'So what does he want?'

'What do you think? To know what really happened. Revenge, I guess. Respect, for sure. It can't be easy being the son of Jack Barton. He's got a big shadow following him around, I know that much. When we go out, you can see people watching him, waiting to see the kind of man he becomes.'

'Really?'

'Well, I know it sounds crazy but that's what it seems like to me. He doesn't really talk about it.' And just like that we were back to square one. In that huge bed, I pulled her close to me again and she gave herself to me again.

But sadly, my life was not my own. An hour later, I was standing by a bus stop just as the heavens opened. As persuasive as she had been in trying to convince me to stay, there was just no way I could trust Maxine to behave like a reasonable or responsible human being. She never had as far as I was aware, so there was no reason to suddenly expect her to be anything other than what she was: an all-consuming black hole, mindlessly destructive.

Feeling an odd mix of euphoria and detachment, I watched the world pass by as rain rolled down the bus windows and everything was reduced to smeared neon and my own chaotic thoughts. I was relieved that Zoe hadn't asked me about my own family as she probed me for some insight into my best friend. I found it hard not to resent Tom a little for the timeless beauty of his relationship with his father, which would forever remain untainted by disappointment or disillusionment. The man had been someone people turned to in need and looked up to, a great role model and a template for how any decent person would want to emulate in manhood. What did I get? A ghost I would never get to meet but who still haunted me relentlessly with his absence, rendering me father, son and brother the moment he took to his heels and disappeared without a trace. It was impossible to know if his abandonment of my mother had been the catalyst for her breakdown or if he had foreseen a terrible future behind those dilated pupils of hers. Either way, I was the one who paid the price for his cowardice, and I hated him for it with a silent seething fury that burned hot inside me. I smiled bitterly at the words Zoe had just spoken so me, that I was so open and easy. On the surface, that was how I had consciously decided to present myself to the world, but I was aware that it was very much a superficial veneer, concealing the damage that lay beneath. When my half-sisters had come along, it was a simple binary choice. Either I could let their innocence become forever tainted by the dark stain of my mother's inadequacies, or I could compel myself through sheer force of will to fill the void that others had created.

I knew it wasn't Tom's fault and I didn't blame him as such, but it was difficult sometimes not to wish for someone in my life who might have similarly acted as such a totemic beacon to guide me through the dark days and long nights. I had felt the same way when friends got off with girls I could only dream of, pleased for their good fortune, but resentful of it at the same time. Bus journeys dragged me down like that, always pulling me away from the light. Seemingly endless, but sadly not.

By the time I got home, I was chilled to the bone. The house was freezing but all was quiet. Maxine was unconscious on the sofa and I was able to wrap her up in an old blanket and manipulate her into a safer sleeping position in something approximating the recovery position before going upstairs. The girls were out for the count, so I felt able to turn on the radio to see what obscure delights John Peel had to offer. It was the usual eclectic mix of the good, the bad and the downright awful. Rap music was slowly growing on me but world music mostly left me cold. The Fall were in session – of course they were – and I slowly fell asleep to the ecstatic rantings of the one true mancunian poet.

*

In the morning, Maxine was awake, which was something of a miracle, although it was often better if she just kept out of the way as I struggled to get the girls ready for school. She was not a morning person, though she was little better in the afternoons or evenings either.

She had been woken up by the postman and was brandishing a letter addressed to me. 'What this?' she asked.

'Well, it's mine, for starters, so what the fuck are you doing opening my mail?' I tried to watch my tongue in front of the girls in case they picked up bad habits, but she had crossed a line.

'Leeds Uni, eh.' she said. It was neither a question nor an exclamation, more of an accusation. Who did I think I was, getting ideas above my station. 'Thinking of getting out, eh?'

I flashed her a look to warn her not to start something in front of the girls. 'It's just an idea,' I said. 'Don't get excited. It's something college is making me look into.'

She slurped a cup of tea. I could see the teabag bobbing around obscenely in the chipped mug bearing the ironic slogan MUM OF THE YEAR. 'Typical man,' she said, determined to get a rise out of me. 'Clearing off first chance you get.'

'Yeah, why would anyone want to leave this fucking palace?'

She glared at me, framed on either side by piled bags of jumble and tottering towers of old magazines. She looked a real mess, her face red and blotchy, as if she had been roughed up by a boozy lover. She was in a mood for a fight.

'You need to turn that bloody music down at night,' she snapped. 'I didn't get a minute's rest.'

I thought of her, lying there obscenely, drooling over the arm of the sofa in a stupor. 'You were dead to the world last night,' I mocked.

'You wish.' Her puffy eyes were slits of malevolence. 'I hate that shitty music you play all the time.'

'Good,' I said. 'You're supposed to hate it.'

The girls seemed oblivious, dutifully putting their bowls beside the sink amid piles of washing up I would have to deal with later on once I got back from college. They looked perfectly innocent in their school uniforms, as clean and cared for as I could manage, and I was reminded once again of what I would be leaving behind if I selfishly decided to move away. I could feel the metaphorical chains clanking as I ushered the girls towards the front door.

Maxine sniffed. 'You smell like a ponce,' she said, accusingly. I didn't get it straight away, then remembered I had showered at Zoe's. What I smelt was clean.

'We'll talk later,' I said as I pulled the front door to, but I knew that we wouldn't. She would either be unconscious again or else propping up the bar at once of the local pubs who still let her in, bothering customers who didn't know any better. It was going to be one of those days.

I hurried the girls outside where Deb was already waiting to take them to school, as calm and patient as ever. She worked long hours and I had no idea where her energy came from.

'What's eating you?' she asked, taking one look at me.

I shrugged. 'The usual. Maxine is doing my head in.'

'I know, love.' She tousled my hair fondly. 'Don't be too hard on her.' It was a conversation we had run through so many times that we didn't even need to fill in the blanks anymore. I don't know how I would have ever got by without her. Her energy and optimism were unfailing.

'I got a letter from Leeds Uni,' I said. 'That's what started it. They invited me for an interview.'

She must have sensed my reticence. 'That's fantastic,' she said. She turned my face towards her so she could look me in the eyes. 'I know Leeds is a bit of a shithole, but it would be so great for you to get away. Do something for yourself.' As usual, I walked with them as far as the bus stop.

'I couldn't ask that of you,' I said.

'You wouldn't have to ask,' she said. 'I'd be happy to do it. For you. For her. Especially for them. I love those kids. You know that.' I suspect she had always wanted a girl, and they were indisputably good kids by any reckoning. She was a proper Christian and charity in the true sense of the word was encoded into her very essence. I let her take the girls to Sunday school every week, and not just for the break it gave me. I liked to think of myself as a godless commie, but I knew a thing or two about sacrifice and suffering and saw Jesus as something of a kindred spirit and a fellow revolutionary. Also, considering that I was their primary carer, I had little fear that the girls would become true believers. Given the shitty hand that life had dealt them, it was inconceivable to me that they could possibly believe in the existence of a benign being that watched over them. Even if they were converted, I couldn't see what harm it could do them if they grew up to be as warm-hearted and generous as Deb. Gary, too. I very much doubted that he believed in all the superstitious stuff, but he went along with it for an easy life. I watched them all toddle off into the distance as the bus pulled up and caught me in a tiny tsunami of oily puddle water.

At college, the conversation was still swirling around my skull when Tom informed me that he had been offered an interview at the London School of Economics, the spiritual home of the revolutionary spirit in academia, where great thinkers went to learn how to accomplish great things. I was delighted for him, but it also seemed so unreal. As unlikely as it felt that I could ever justify getting out, the idea that our lives might soon undergo such radical upheaval felt like an impossible dream. People from Manchester saw themselves as living in the centre of the known universe, self-sufficient and satisfied with their lot. You might temporarily move away but it seemed to exert its own gravitational force that sucked you back in. No-one stayed away for long.

I think Tom must have sensed my inner turmoil. 'You okay?' he asked with genuine concern.

'I'm good,' I replied with a warm smile. 'I'm pleased for you. Getting into the LSE would be amazing. You know you deserve it.'

He grimaced. 'London, though. Their bands are shite.'

'I'm sure you'll cope.' When we had first talked about what was coming next, we had scoured the music papers to see what different cities had to offer in terms of gigs and nightlife. It had become a short list. Sheffield. Nottingham. Leeds, maybe, if it upped its game. London. Bristol at a push. Birmingham. For me, I had to add the requirement that it had to be within easy reach of home so I could still be of use when Maxine's many inadequacies inevitably demanded my intervention.

That was as far as the conversation went. It was a topic we tended to avoid. Zoe was a year younger, but she bounced over and handed us a sheet of paper.

'For you,' she announced happily. It was a piece of artwork she had created for The Manifesto to illustrate the Punk Cinema piece I had written, which Tom hadn't even read yet. 'I woke up this morning and felt inspired,' she said, giving me a knowing smile. It was a picture of me and Tom as the anti-heroes of a horror gore-fest, both wielding chainsaws as the undead lumbered towards us. 'I even added voids for the text,' she explained. It was perfect. Tom looked a bit confused but loved the design.

'You'll see,' I said.

I had the article folded up in my back pocket and handed it to him. He had Economics first and I had double something else, but he turned up at the door halfway through holding up both thumbs approvingly like a manic McCartney. His eyes were sparkling with excitement. I made a lame excuse and left the room with no intention of returning. Tom actually hugged me when I caught up with him.

'I love it,' he exclaimed. 'I knew you had it in you. I literally laughed out loud.' That was it. The final piece. After months of hard work, the first issue was ready to go. There was no turning back. Compared to college work, it felt like I had actually produced something worthwhile, and I knew exactly how to celebrate.

Five

There was a horror double-bill at The Odeon that weekend and we made plans to go. The Membranes were playing The International, but we had seen them a couple of weeks before and decided against it. As good as they were, they were one of those bands you ended up seeing every month or so whether you planned to or not, though they never disappointed. Zoe opted out. She had already seen *The Evil Dead* and had no desire to sit next to a group of young men watching Debbie Harry in *Videodrome*.

'I think I would choke to death on the testosterone,' she said.

It was a fair point. We had a mate called Adrian who worked at the Odeon and he got us in for free. He was also our supplier of contraband films, usually lousy tenth generation copies of outlawed films that had been low on quality in the first place. He seemed to have an inexhaustible supply of Maxell videocassettes and had a load of recorders set up in his parents' garage where he ran off copy after copy of notorious films which he flogged us for a pound apiece from a green Gola bag slung across his shoulders. The films were almost unwatchable, grainy images flickering uncontrollably like a Tourette's twitch, but somehow it only added to the taboo joy of watching something that others had deemed unsuitable for public consumption. We had never seen a genuine snuff film apart from the Zapruder JFK footage, but this was about as close as you would want to get.

Sadly, Debbie Harry had dyed her hair darker for the role and I learnt that I really was a sucker for blondes. She wasn't up to much as an actress either, but Cronenberg was a true horror auteur, and the image of people inserting videotapes into their abdomens stuck with me for days afterwards. It felt like a warning that we were becoming overdependent on technology, but I couldn't imagine much worse than being disconnected from music and film. Alternative culture was such an essential part of my life that it almost felt like food and water; without it, I would wither and rot away.

We met Adrian afterwards and sat around sharing cans of Special Brew with soft-mints to thank him. Our thinking was that if you drank the strongest drink possible, you could still get pissed on next to nothing, although the taste was horrendous, hence the mints. He was a great guy, a real film fanatic and always well ahead of the game in knowing what the next unmissable film was going to be. Naturally, Tom told him about my article on Punk Cinema and then asked him to write film reviews for the next edition of The Manifesto, and I was happy to go along with it. I knew my stuff well enough when it came to video nasties, but Adrian was a grandmaster. We had no idea if we could write worth a damn, but he certainly talked the talk.

'You've been going on and on about this bloody magazine of yours for months,' he joked. 'You're always full of it but nothing ever happens.' He had curly hair and freckles, but a real love of life and the most infectious laugh.

'Believe it,' I told him proudly. 'We go to print next week.' I looked to Tom for some assurance and he nodded.

Adrian laughed. 'I'll believe it when I see it. If it's any good, I'll write something for you.'

As we gagged on our drinks, we discussed whether I was right and if the films we loved would be enhanced by using indie music as a backing as the soundtracks were usually pretty terrible, though this was not helped by Adrian's dodgy knock-offs. John Carpenter was the great exception, of course, proving that with one finger and a synth and a great idea you could create a brilliant backing to a film. Adrian shared a dream of his which was to persuade New Order and other bands to play along to cult films like used to happen in old cinemas before the advent of sound, but he knew it would never happen.

'It would be great, though,' we acknowledged. I loved these moments, totally relaxed, no responsibilities, just talking about the things we loved like music, comics or film. I was particularly taken with Adrian's T-shirt which showed a panel from a notorious old British comic a monstrous shark called Hook Jaw destroying a fishing boat, which a friend had screen-printed just for him. It was like an X rated version of *Jaws* which was good fun but at the same time a bit lame compared to what we were watching now.

'My mum totally bollocked me the other day for watching this stuff,' Tom confessed.

'Not a fan? I'm surprised. Your mum is cool.' She was a nurse so worked long anti-social hours, but she still managed to find the time to always be there for Tom, mother and father in one. It must have been hard for her, but she had incredible reserves of energy. Tom often joked that she must have helped herself to amphetamines from work, and maybe that was true. She was great with me, too, on the rare occasions we had met up. She was getting on a bit, but she had a great face too, broad, high cheekbones that Tom had been fortunate to inherit. I sometimes teased him that I had a crush on her, which wasn't true. For his part, he despised Maxine and made no attempt to hide it, despite his capacity to see the best in people.

'I think it was *I Spit On Your Grave* that did it for her. She walked in on me watching it and went nuts. I got a long lecture about what it's like for her at work having to deal with rape victims. Totally horrendous. I felt really bad.'

'She has a point, to be fair.'

'Of course,' said Tom. 'I tried to point out that the victim gets her revenge so it's not just rape fantasy bullshit.'

'And?'

Tom looked away. 'And she asked me to think about what kind of man chooses to sit through a realistic gang rape. She said they were films made by men for men and that I should know better.'

I shifted uncomfortably, a little shamed for being disappointed that Debbie Harry had dyed her hair for *Videodrome*. Perhaps his mum really did have a point about the way the media represented women. Instead, I blamed Mary Whitehouse for reducing all culture to a tally of fucks and dicks and pints of blood, as if context didn't matter. It irked me that some twisted proto-Puritan should be allowed by the media to act as the arbiter of good taste and public decency. An idea came to me to write another article for the next edition in which Whitehouse and her equally despicable husband watched *Ai No Corrida* and re-enacted their favourite sex scenes. I shared the idea and the others joined in with ideas of their own, laughing until tears rolled down our faces. The beer kept the cold at bay, and we talked long into the night until the last night bus came trundling round the corner onto Oxford Road. It felt great to be with like-minded people where you could bounce ideas around, even if next to nothing would ever come of it.

As Adrian said over and over again, 'You never know if you don't try, eh boys?'

*

Tom started his new job that week and we sent Zoe in on his second day to print a small initial run of The Manifesto so we could see how it looked. It ran to 24 pages and had an edgy distinctive look, combining the DIY ethos of other fanzines with a more formal aesthetic that could have been produced by Factory itself. With scissors and glue, I have no idea how he did it, but it almost looked professionally designed. We had just enough money to run off 20 copies. Tom's reasoning was that once we had paid for printing off a small run, it would look less suspicious if he was found to be printing off more. If necessary, Zoe could magically reappear and explain that she had phoned in a larger order.

He invoked his revolutionary spirit to justify his actions as being for the greater good. The company he worked for ripped people off with their pricing policy, so he felt no remorse. As we lacked the means of production, we had little choice but to resort to requisitioning paper and ink for the time being. I suspect he had grand plans for an old-fashioned printing press in a sweaty basement mass-producing pamphlets for the deserving masses, but an overpriced printers near King Street would do for now.

We met up after work on a bar in Oldham Street and he handed over a plastic bag containing the first print run. Although we knew every word by heart, we spent a silent half an hour flicking slowly through the pages admiring the fruits of our labour, savouring every detail. It was a hard feeling to describe as it was entirely new to us, that sense that we had been able to create something that felt important and worthwhile. In that moment, we knew we had done what we set out to do, which was to announce ourselves to the world.

We had found deep within us something that we needed to articulate and share with others, and we had found a way to accomplish exactly that. It didn't really matter if no one shared our enthusiasm and every copy went unsold, although for me that had undoubtedly been part of the point of it all, to feel like we were contributing in our own way to a wider movement of artists and musicians and creative people to rise above the mundane and create something unique and beautiful.

Zoe bought us drinks as we had spent every last penny we had and we toasted ourselves, and those others who had played their part.

We realised we had forgotten to add a price to the front cover and laughed at the oversight, although we both recognised that this had probably been subconsciously deliberate. How could you put a price on something so personal?

Zoe offered to draw the price on each front cover for us, which seemed a reasonable idea, but then we had to decide how much, and that became problematic. If we charged too little, we would barely cover our costs. If we charged too much, we might deter potential buyers who we had intended to be our target audience. It was a silly problem, trivial in the grand scheme of things, but it soon started to take the edge off our feelings of joy at having achieved what we had set out to do so many months previously.

It was Tom, of course, who noticed the significance of where we were, on the corner of Tariff Street that memorialised the free trade movement that had helped cement the city's global reputation as a place where important ideas were brought to life.

'I don't get it,' said Zoe. She was an artist and had no understanding of economic theory. I had very little, only what I had gleaned from Tom.

'It's hard to explain,' Tom said.

'Try,' she said. 'It's good to learn new things.'

'It doesn't really matter,' he said. 'It's just funny, trying to put a value on a subcultural magazine here of all places.' She looked blank. Pretty, but blank. 'There's a concept called comparative advantage,' he persisted. 'In order to make money, places should stick to what they do best.'

'And what does Manchester do better than anywhere else?' I offered helpfully.

She brightened. 'Music,' she said.

'Exactly. So, we should stick to what we do best, which is great music and art and culture, and let other places do what they are good at.'

'I like the sound of that,' she said.

'And that's just what we've done.' For once, I could be genuinely proud of something I had helped create. 'Made something we're good at.'

On the bus home, Tom laughed at himself for giving the worst definition of free trade ever, but there was some truth to what he said. 'If anyone at the LSE heard me talk like that, I would be thrown out for sure.' He was already talking as if it was a sure thing that he was in. But then he had a great idea, and he quickly forgave himself.

'What about this?' he said. 'How about if we just ask people to pay what they think it's worth?'

'No cover price?' I was a little taken aback. 'Okay. Interesting idea, I guess.'

'Remember what you said: what's the point of all this effort if no one reads the damn thing? This way, anyone can afford it. Either way, we won't be out of pocket. That's the beauty of getting it printed for nothing.'

When he was excited, he had a way of speaking fast so there was no way anyone could possibly challenge him, but I liked the idea and it solved a practical problem with the front cover. We had planned to mostly sell it at gigs anyway, and I decided it would be interesting to see how much people were willing to pay, if nothing else. We had split the first run between us, once we had set aside a few copies for people who had contributed, and the feel of them in my hands was incredible.

My stop was first, and before I got off we had started talking about what might go into the next edition. The euphoria of the first was still in our veins, but already in our heads we had started to move on. That's how it was.

*

We liked to walk the streets, as if were acquiring *The Knowledge* like a taxi driver. To us, it was a form of free entertainment. Sometimes, some of the others would come with us just for something to do, especially Colin with his perpetually clicking camera, looking for fresh inspiration. If we were familiar with one route, we would take the other. It didn't matter if we had no idea where we were. This was our city and we could never be lost, although it did occasionally lead us into danger.

We had found ourselves suddenly near Old Trafford, home of our arch-rivals, and realised that Darren was wearing a city scarf, which was tantamount to wearing an inverted crucifix in the Vatican. It hadn't gone unnoticed. They had made an incredible start to the season and assumed the title was theirs, but things had subsequently gone horribly wrong, and a mean resentment had settled in with the fans. The last derby had been a bloodbath, cross-town rivalry having given way to something far more sinister. This was serious.

We made our way down toward a tow path near the quay where the River Irwell had been engineered to form the start of the Manchester Ship Canal. This was long before new money gentrified the place into a cultural hub. Walls were daubed with artless graffiti, and the paths were littered with food waste, condoms and needles, the urban flotsam of the slums.

'Keep walking,' I said, trying to avoid eye contact. We were reminded of *The Warriors*, that breath-taking remix of Homer's Odyssey remixed by Walter Hill where a Brooklyn gang find themselves miles from safety in a pre-apocalyptic Manhattan pursued by various gangs hellbent on their destruction. The key to survival was to blend into the environment, become invisible, part of the post-industrial wastelands as if there was no issue with us being there. If we looked nervous, we would attract unwanted attention, and that would only end one way: badly. Darren couldn't even try to remove his scarf as to do so would be to attract attention. Eyes forward, alert to danger. Walking with purpose, but not running. Hands in pockets, looking casual but fists clenched.

The river had a devious current, swirling eddies of liquid that was polluted with two centuries of progress and 50 years of decline, dark and satanic and utterly unnatural. The Styx itself, the river to the underworld, could not have looked more terrible. We had an atavistic sense that we were being followed that was more than just the echoing footfall as we passed under long bridges supporting railroads that had once launched locomotives between us and Liverpool to the west. We didn't need to look to know that we were in danger. Darren snapped first, launching into a sprint and dragging me by the shoulder along with him. Tom soon took the lead, using his instincts to take us up concrete stairwells as the gap between us and them widened. As we crossed the water along a bridge that gave us an elevated view of the area, we allowed ourselves a quick breather that we didn't really need. We could see enough to assess the situation and realised that they were never going to catch us, those pie-eating denizens of Salford who were already starting to give up the chase. We counted silently to ten and then started on our way again, just to be sure, relieved that football had gifted us the stamina to evade danger on the rare occasions when we let our guard down.

Finally safe and breathing hard, we came to a stop against a wall, bearing the legend LIVERPOOL IS/ ARE SHIT. The whole area was an eyesore, derelict buildings and wastelands where even weeds struggled to take hold. This was the past and the future compressed into one. There were occasional signs of human life, grubby Dickensian children kicking bricks around and scrap dealerships run by squat hard-looking men who would not have been out of place in the horror films we avidly watched. It was as if the city was cannibalising its own past, sucking the marrow from its cadaverous industrial heritage.

'You daft twat,' said Darren, still catching his breath. 'You could have taken us anywhere but there.'

'Could have been worse,' said Tom, who had already recovered.

'You've got a point. They could have been scousers.'

We allowed ourselves a laugh. You could still just about see the river through rusted wire fencing. 'You know why they built this?' asked Tom. It was time for another social history lesson.

'The fence?'

'The Ship Canal. It was to piss off the scousers. They had the port and we didn't so we built this to have access to the sea, so we could trade without having to rely on them. It cost a fortune. It's the same size as the Panama Canal, more or less. An amazing feat of engineering.' We stared through the fence at a different world, like a portal to the past. No one of had been more than fifty miles of Manchester.

'Liverpool was the slave city,' he said. 'Nearly a quarter of Mancunians signed a petition to end the slave trade because we didn't agree with it so the Ship canal was in part a huge *fuck you* to Liverpool.'

'An expensive *fuck you*,' I suggested. 'But probably worth every penny.'

'Yeah, said Tom, 'Definitely worth every penny. But to be fair, we weren't a lot better. I mean, effectively we enslaved our own poor, working themselves to death in the factories. That's why Engels came here, and Marx.'

Darren started laughing. 'Only you could almost get us killed and end up turning it into a lecture about the working man and all that.'

'You're the one who chose to wear a city scarf,' I pointed out.

'Always.' He kissed the club crest theatrically to prove his undying fealty, oblivious to the reference to the ship canal on the emblem.

'And you are the living embodiment of the working man.' Tom reached over and playfully squeezed one of Darren's bulging biceps. 'You were created to do the hard graft.'

We meandered our way through Spinningfields and the intestines of the city, down Quay Street and past Cobden House, a Georgian townhouse which was the first university building paid for by a local merchant to improve academic opportunities for Manchester's young men. The city had always been a place for ornery nonconformists, people like us who were incapable of taking no as an answer. Ironically, it had been reincarnated as a county court where the authorities could do their best to enforce the law against people who were unwilling or unable to follow the rules. There was some kind of demonstration going on outside, so we stopped to take it in.

Tom nudged me in the ribs. Miranda was there, in full Edwardian costume, a tight-fitting bodice with fluted skirt in sombre black. Around her, other women were similarly attired, some holding placards. At first, we assumed this was some bizarre form of feminist protest in which women sought to reclaim the night after several high-profile attacks on young women had gone unpunished, but as she turned around, I could read that they were demanding equal rights for women.

She saw us and moved away from the group, looking somewhat embarrassed.

'What the fuck are you supposed to be?' I was teasing her, although in fact she looked great, even dressed out of time.

'*Who* the fuck,' she corrected me. I had no idea what she meant. 'It's an acting job,' she explained. 'There's a group of lecturers at the university raising funds for a Pankhurst Museum. You know, the Suffragettes.'

I nodded. 'Yeah, I said, 'I'm not totally stupid. Votes for women and all that.'

'Exactly. I'm supposed to be Christabel Pankhurst, enfant terrible of the movement.' Her pronunciation was intentionally awful, but I didn't laugh. 'I wanted to be Emmeline, but they said I was too young and pretty.'

'How dare they?' I joked. Usually free and wild, her hair had been scraped back and piled artfully on her head for historical authenticity and convenience.

Tom looked over at the other women on the demonstration, overly serious and seemingly oblivious to how absurd they looked. 'Coming from them, I'm not sure that's much of a compliment.'

'I know. I don't think they like me much.' Some of the women were glaring at her, talking to a group of dodgy looking young men. 'It's not really meant to be serious, just raising awareness of who the suffragettes were and trying to get people to dip into their pockets to raise a statue or get more funding for the Museum. It's another thing to put on my CV.'

We had studied the suffragists at college, and thoroughly approved, hardcore radicals intent on subverting the outdated status quo.

Tom couldn't help himself. 'Christabel was pretty cool,' he said admiringly. 'I liked her attitude, although she was only really interested in middle class women. I thought she missed the point a bit, to be honest.'

Miranda seemed unimpressed. 'The point?'

'Equality for all women, not just the nice ones.'

Miranda shrugged. 'Tell them,' she said, looking like the last thing she needed was another lecture. 'Although they will probably bite your patriarchal head off for daring to speak out against one of their heroines.'

He laughed. 'Yeah,' he said, looking over at their stern faces. 'I'm in enough trouble with my mum right now, so maybe not.'

She started to move back towards her group. 'See you at The Ritz tomorrow,' she called out.

The Cult were playing, and we absolutely had tickets. 'How did you know we were going?' I asked.

She tapped her head and gave me a knowing smile. 'Where else would you be?'

It was going to be some night.

Six

We were not alone. The city was crackling with creative energy. To the north, west, east and south of the centre, young people just like us were finding ways to express themselves artistically. From every direction, bands were forming and creating music that mattered, poets finding their voices and musicians discovering rhythms that had no logical place in a city that had previously only moved to the beat of industrial machinery, deafening, suffocating, endlessly repetitive. Somehow, the sounds had woven themselves into the DNA of villages and towns as they swelled into a formless metropolis of sorts, each area with its own distinctive identity that magically took form in the drums and bass and guitars that found themselves into the next generations that drank the water and breathed in that polluted particulated air and poured down in the dank drizzle that got into everything it touched.

There were always more great bands in the city than we could count on our fingers and toes at any one time, and countless more that were terrible, taking their shot at the fame game and missing the mark by a mile. It made for a vibrant underground culture where there was always a gig worth the effort of attending if you had the money, and endless support slots for those bands patient enough to learn their trade and nurture what latent talent they might possess. Inadvertently, the scene fed on itself. Bands had to get up to speed quickly and up their game or else find themselves quickly eclipsed by others more hungry or simply more brilliant. Earlier that month, james had supported The Smiths at the Palace, as different as they were alike, pushing themselves and each other to greater heights of excellence whilst struggling for enough money to buy a round of beers.

Our lives were not without stress, but it felt like a great time to be alive, although I am sure that every new generation feels the same way, no matter how absurd their clothes and terrible music might seem to others. New music venues were springing up as were independent clothes shops, largely based around Afflecks Palace, a sort of phantasmagorical shopping Xanadu which sprang up organically inside an abandoned department store. Stalls could be rented by the week, encouraging a grassroots entrepreneurial spirit that went hand in glove with the thriving music scene. The idea that we were contributing to this cultural melting pot was really invigorating. College work felt like a trivial inconvenience, although of course we were conscious that education was a far more certain pathway to self-improvement. It would have been easy to have developed a form of cultural myopia, where anything that wasn't locally produced could be overlooked, such was our enthusiasm for what was growing up around us. But there were great bands everywhere. The Cult were ostensibly based in Leeds, but they were still northern, and their gifted guitarist was both a Mancunian born and bred, and a City fan to boot. That was good enough for us. They straddled the indie and goth scenes, which probably accounted for the crowd they drew at The Ritz, a faded ballroom with a balcony and sprung dancefloor that had a life of its own. At the weekends it was a no-go for kids like us, but during the week it hosted some great bands. It was heaving. From everywhere came the jangle of glass bangles, the air thick with hairspray and expectancy and sweat and the mingled hormones of hundreds of horny youths waiting for Ian Astbury to take the stage to shake those hips as if he really was a mystic Navajo warrior and buffalo roamed through the dark streets of the northern cities and towns.

As we strained our necks to see what was happening, Miranda came up behind me and pinched my arse, then realised I was with Zoe and laughed at the glare she received in response.

'Fancy meeting you here,' she said.

'Glad to see you've changed out of that stupid costume,' I remarked. I was pleased to see that she wore her hair long and free, with a tight black dress that stopped halfway down her thighs.

'Whatever do you mean?' she said in mock dismay. 'I thought I looked very fetching.'

Before she could say anything else, the band took to the stage and Zoe grabbed my hand and pulled me into a furious mass of dancing bodies and we were lost in the brilliant chaos of the music. Every now and then I would see Tom thrashing around in the moshpit, grinning like mad as Billy Duffy's guitars crashed over us like wave after wave of sound and white noise so you couldn't catch your breath. Predictably, Darren caught an elbow and went under, but Tom reached out an arm and grabbed him and they hugged each other and laughed and roared with approval as each song came to an end. As *Spiritwalker* started up, the crowd went berserk and I lost Zoe, sucked into the melee where I found myself pressed up against Miranda who was half out of her mind. The heat of her body pressed into mine we threw our arms around each other and just let go. At moments like that, time simply ceased to exist. Then the music stopped and we were outside, pushed along by the crowd of bodies and the only thing we could hear was chatter and traffic and our own overexcited voices. Tom came over first, dragging a dazed Darren with him. He threw his arms around me and Miranda and hugged us hard.

'Sometimes...' he started to say. I couldn't hear any more, but I knew what he was going to say anyway. You could see the magic of the evening in his eyes, wide with wonder and the sheer thrill of it all.

We waited around for Zoe to emerge, the cold air kept at bay by the lingering warmth of our bodies and the adrenaline that lingered. Eventually I went back in and found her downstairs with her arms around some guy I didn't know by the cloakroom. She saw me and pulled away, following me silently as I walked back towards the exit and the cooler air.

'He's a friend,' she said, not even bothering to catch up or look me in the eye. I didn't react, not wanting to give her the satisfaction of getting upset. She trailed me outside where the others were still waiting. A car horn tooted twice, and Zoe obediently ran across the road to where her lift home was waiting for her, presumably one of her parents.

'I'll call you,' she shouted, though she knew I didn't have a phone at home. I walked back to join the others.

'How good was that?' I asked.

'Do you mean the gig or the little melodrama with your girlfriend?' Tom enunciated the word to express his mild disapproval at my relationship with Zoe. He needn't have worried.

'It's nothing,' I said.

'You two are so cute together,' said Miranda, as the car pulled away and Zoe waved awkwardly. 'Just adorable.'

I didn't take the bait. 'So,' I said. 'What next?' There was no way I was going to sleep any time soon, no matter what chaos the next day might bring.

'I'm out,' said Miranda. 'Sorry. I'm working again tomorrow with the lesbians. Another day, another demo, you know how it is for us hardworking ladies.'

'I thought they were suffragettes,' I said.

'They are,' she said. 'I think they're both. They're not mutually exclusive things, you know.'

We walked together towards the bus station, safety in numbers and still buzzing about the show. I was hungry but didn't have enough money to eat and get the bus home, and it was too cold to walk the four miles to Fallowfield, so I was relieved when Miranda insisting on stopping for some chips that we all shared. I didn't really join in with the conversation, trailing behind a step or two as Miranda was sandwiched by Tom and Darren on either side for warmth. I was frustrated, confused by the situation with Zoe while I could still feel the impression of Miranda's body against mine from earlier, watching the sway of her hips as her silver jewellery dazzled in the neon glare of the city at night. I had always thought that life would become less confusing as I got older, and I knew right then and there how very wrong I was.

Seven

It was a rare event, but we had a midweek cup game so Tom was available, and Darren's forehead had sufficiently healed for him to be able to play, too. It was a hard game which ended in failing light. I was still in a bad mood and put in some uncompromising tackles against a team of hard bastards from Stretford who used crude violence to compensate for their lack of skill and fitness. The ref was intimidated by them, and it seemed increasingly likely that someone was going to get hurt.

I had avoided Zoe all day at college but was frustrated with myself for being jealous about something that might have just been in my head. Tom was never with the same girl for long and was always totally unmoved if he saw an ex with someone else, but it appeared I wasn't wired the same way. I was in a dark place.

As always, the middle of the pitch belonged to Tom. While other players slogged through the mud, he had a lightness to the way he played so that he was able to glide over the pitch, head up, seeing the whole picture, evading lunging tackles designed to snap him in half and break his bones. They couldn't get near him by means foul and fair. A decent sized crowd had appeared, a few dozen maybe, not just dads and mates but the bored and curious, attracted by the beautiful game we played and the impending sense of violence that haunted every challenge. By half time, we had a slender lead and all of our limbs and teeth just about intact, but the outcome was far from decided. As we caught our breaths, our manager went to speak to the referee to file a complaint but was waved away.

Tom was addressing the lads, some of them ten years or more his senior. 'We're all in this together,' he said. 'If it kicks off, no one backs down.' Everyone nodded grimly.

It didn't take long. Jason scored again with a low drive soon after the restart and one of their defenders spat into his afro as he walked past. He didn't see it or feel it, but I did and sneakily booted the guilty party hard up the arse then walked away as if nothing had happened. Afterwards, I couldn't explain why I had chosen that form of justice, it was just the first thing that came into my head. Immediately, I got a hard slap across the back of my head and went down, and by the time I was back on my feet there were fights breaking out everywhere. Ever the primary focus of abuse, Jason was nearby waving the pointy end of the corner flag at one of their players.

'Call me a spear-chucker again!' he demanded, lunging with his bizarre choice of weapon.

By this time, some of the spectators and a few passers-by had run onto the pitch to join in. There was no way the game was going to restart. As big as they were, the Stretford boys were heavily outnumbered and quickly retreated and the ref attempted to resolve the situation by awarding us the win.

On the long walk home in the failing light, we were able to see the funny side of it. Darren mocked me for always going straight for the arse, and I retaliated by pointing out that once again he was going home with a blood-soaked shirt. He pulled up his hair that fell across his forehead to proudly demonstrate that this time the blood wasn't actually his.

'Aren't we getting a bit old for this bullshit?' I wondered out loud. It was exhilarating but the feeling lingered once again we had enjoyed a narrow escape.

'All I can say,' said Tom, 'is that on a Saturday morning all I can think of when I'm stuck in a shitty little office is getting out there on a pitch with you guys.' It was rare to see him express any kind of regret.

'Getting kicked up the arse and going home with blood and dogshit on your shirt?'

'That I don't miss,' said Tom, although at least he didn't have to wash his own kit. We followed Princess Parkway a little to the south then cut left through the badlands roughly in the direction of our respective houses.

'What got into you tonight?' asked Darren. 'It's not like you to get your retaliation in first.'

'Bad mood,' I said starkly.

'Oh, stop torturing yourself about it,' said Darren cheerily. 'You'll soon kiss and make up.' I turned off first and waved, watching them disappear into the darkness. I didn't know what I felt, I didn't know what I wanted, a slave to my hormones and self-doubt and the tough decisions that awaited.

When I got back, the house was unnaturally quiet. In my room, the girls slept on, oblivious to the world and blissfully carefree. They slept face to face, twinned in their own little world but open and sociable by day. I think it must have helped that the most important person in each of their existences was the other, so they were less reliant on others for comfort and entertainment, and less needy, too. They knew no different. If Maxine was having a good day, so much the better, but if not, they were quite content fending for themselves, with my support always on hand when required. Although they were fast asleep, I wore my headphones anyway, mostly so I didn't inadvertently disturb Maxine as she lay comatose downstairs on the sofa. I had missed the start of the *John Peel Show* but I quickly tuned into his mood. The Cure were in session, and I found myself enjoying them far more than I expected, experimental and playful and smart. There were some bands who were probably far more deserving of my attention than I ever gave them, but that was fine as it demonstrated once again that we were in something of a golden period culturally and there were many reasons to feel optimistic, despite the other distractions in my life. I fell asleep long before midnight and woke up hours later with the coiled wire of the headphones imprinted across my cheek.

When I dragged myself out of bed, Maxine was slumped on the sofa watching daytime TV as if watching other people's miseries and tragedies somehow made light of her own. The light of the screen illuminated her face with unnatural light that gave her the appearance of a corpse, an illusion emphasised by her medicated stillness. At least it made it easier to ignore her, and not take offence that the rest of the world passed her by so that her responsibilities were passed on to others, mostly myself. She was totally oblivious to me.

My facial imprint didn't go unnoticed at college, but like all embarrassing things, the sting of it soon wore off and I laughed along with everyone else. Zoe was conspicuous by her absence, which was fine by me, as Tom gave me a detailed account of how many copies of The Manifesto he had been able to surreptitiously run off at work. We were over a hundred and counting, although he went to great pains to tell me how soul-destroying the printing job was.

'It's a job,' I explained. 'The whole point is to destroy you then build you up again as the perfect employee.'

He did a terrible impression of a robot and we laughed.

There was a gig at the weekend that he was keen we went to, a relatively low-key event at a new venue where a local band were on. John Peel had played their single a few times and we liked what we had heard so we were keen to check them out. There was a support band Tom was particularly intent on seeing, so we planned to get there early, especially as the plan was to use this event to start selling the fanzine.

'Where's the girlfriend?" he asked casually. I shrugged as if I didn't care, which fooled no-one.

'What did I tell you,' he said. It wasn't a question, more a told-you-so observation and statement of his superior knowledge when it came to relationships. I had no idea how he could be so nonchalant about such things, when it was tearing me up inside. As I tried to sleep, every time I shut my eyes I could see her standing there with the other boy.

'What have you done to upset her?' asked Tom. 'She seems such a sweet thing. It's not like her.'

'I didn't do anything,' I said defensively. 'She's the one in the wrong.' I couldn't tell if he was being ironic and I was certain I was right, but his question still burned away at me all morning from one distracted lesson to the next.

I became the living embodiment of the Mary Chain song, walking sideways to avoid her, but she caught up with me anyway at the end of lunch. I tried to make an excuse and get away to my next class, but she stood in my way.

'Why are you being weird with me?' she asked, holding me with her gaze. Her eyes were the colour of a polished gem, bright and opaque.

'I'm not being weird,' I said. 'I'm trying to give you space.'

'And why would I want space? I thought things were good between us.'

'I thought so, too.' I looked down, trying to be composed. 'Who was the guy you were with?'

'Just some guy,' she said. 'I don't know what you think you saw. It was nothing. I could ask the same of you.'

'What the hell does that mean?' I was angry, but as much with myself as with her. I felt like I was being petulant but the rawness of the emotion I was feeling felt like real anger.

'That girl you were with is stunning,' she said. She looked up at me with those eyes and I could see the hurt. 'Who the fuck is she?'

'She's just a girl we met.'

'We?'

'Me and Tom. After The Smiths gig.' I could hear my voice trying too hard to sound reasonable and innocent. 'We keep bumping into her.'

Now her arms were folded in front of her. 'So, she's stalking you,' she said, as much to herself as to me. 'Or Tom.' She nodded as she said it as if that made a lot more sense, possibly to needle me even more.

'It's not like that,' I said. 'She's really interesting.'

Now her eyes burned with a raw intensity that ignited the green. 'Interesting,' she repeated coldly. 'Oh, I'll just bet she is. Does she have a name?'

'Yes,' I said, being petty. I made her wait. 'Miranda.'

'Miranda.' She rolled the word around her mouth as if tasting for poison.

'I don't know why you're being weird about it,' I said. 'She's just a mate.'

'A gorgeous mate.'

'Well, I can hardly help that, can I?'

'And how do you think that makes me feel?'

I had no idea how to answer that one. 'I don't know. Like you want to get off with some random guy just to piss me off?' We were standing close enough to kiss.

She pushed me in the chest, but not hard. 'Now who's being weird? It wasn't like that.'

My heart was beating hard. She waited to see what was coming next and I had no idea what I was thinking or what I was going to say.

'Okay,' I said.

'Okay?' She looked up at me intently. 'Does that mean we're good?'

'I think so, yeah.' I had to go. I couldn't afford to be late again or my freedom around the college would be limited. 'Listen, I'll see you later, okay?'

Tentatively, she took my hand and we kissed, and we both immediately knew that I was going to be late again, regardless of the consequences.

*

Tom had developed a pragmatic streak from nowhere which, in tandem with his boundless energy, was quite a force. He took it upon himself at work not only to run off as many contraband copies of The Manifesto as possible but also started contacting local music venues and record labels seeking to secure contracts for printing their posters and flyers. The benefits were many, not only in getting advance information about forthcoming gigs but also in making important contacts with the people who made things happen around the city.

As always, there as method in his madness.

His new employers were really impressed with his entrepreneurial spirit, especially with the boost in revenue, which in turn meant they were blinded to what else he was up to in the printing room and why he always left work with a bag of extra copies stuffed into his bag.

'You're becoming the perfect capitalist,' I teased him. 'The shareholders will be pleased.'

'True,' he admitted with a self-satisfied smile, 'I am quite the golden boy at the moment.' It would be a couple more weeks before he admitted that this included sexual favours with the office manager, a good-looking redhead with a penchant for tight blouses and leather skirts. 'However, I am also redistributing this newly accumulated wealth to the needy people of Manchester in the form of high quality culture. And the first round tonight is on me.'

Unusually, we got to the venue early, both armed with a bag stuffed with copies of The Manifesto. We sat at a table with a much-needed beer, self-conscious that this was a big moment for us. In the grand scheme of things, we knew our first attempt at selling a self-produced fanzine was pretty insignificant, but to us it felt huge. We were putting ourselves out there in the only way we knew how, trying to make our voices heard, trying to find something that hopefully was worthy of the effort we had put in. The area we were in was in a terrible state. Bags of rubbish were piled high and countless windows were boarded up, like a horror film where you had to wonder if they were boarded up to keep undesirables out or trap bad things inside. Thatcher had declared that there was no such thing as society and Tom wanted to see what I thought. I dismissed it as empty political rhetoric designed to distract people from what was really going on, selling the country out to the banks and tearing the hearts out of working communities. The country was already becoming totally lop-sided, with the financial institutions and banks based in the south whilst manufacturing bases all around the provinces and the north were being run into the ground. As bad as things were, they were only going to get worse.

'It's more than that,' said Tom. 'It's a really radical idea. What she's saying is that she no longer considers it the responsibility of the government to take care of the things that make society run smoothly. She's tearing up the social contract. Council houses. The NHS. Employment rights, social care. Everything is being thrown open to the wolves. The markets will run everything. We'll get screwed over, good and proper. Just look at it round here,' he said sadly. 'I love this city, but so much of it is a shithole. Post-war brutalist monstrosities built for function. What chance have we got?'

I knew it was a rhetorical question.

It was a common theme for us, how so much great culture and how many great ideas had been cultivated in such thin soil. Mostly it just made us angry and determined to make the best of things, although that in itself posed some difficult questions.

The beer eased our nerves but also loosened our tongues. We each knew the other's weak spots and tended to avoid them.

'So, what do we do about it?'

'Resist,' he said. 'Fight as hard as we can, with every weapon we have at our disposal. People like me going to the LSE, maybe I can get inside the system and try to change things.' Even to me it sounded idealistic.

'I know what you're thinking,' he said. I never doubted his determination, but my face must have given something away. 'You may be right, but I've managed to find a way in and I've got to give it a shot. That's why I didn't just want to write about music,' he said. 'It's what we do best, but there's more to life than that. It's just the thing that makes it all better.' There was a brief lull in the conversation.

'Have you thought any more about next year?' he asked. Tom was adamant that he was not going to turn down an opportunity as great as the London School of Economics if an offer materialised, although it meant we wouldn't be together for the first time either of us could recall. London wasn't even on my radar, and not just because it was so far from home. The thought of living there in the great metropolis never crossed my mind, for reasons that eluded me. I think he possibly felt guilty about leaving me behind, so encouraging me to make a decision that would enhance my own prospects eased his conscience somewhat.

'I try not to, if I'm being totally honest.' The thought depressed me. 'If I try to picture what my life could be like somewhere else, it just doesn't seem real. I can't really describe it. You know in bad fantasy films when someone has a vision of the future, and the image sort of shimmers, it's a bit like that.'

Tom smiled sympathetically although I suspect he didn't have a clue what I was on about. He had an idea about how he wanted things to go and somehow he was able to just make it happen. Getting into the LSE was the prime example, but far from the only one. If he saw a girl he liked, he would just walk up to them and they would hit it off. I loved that self-belief he possessed, like he was charmed. He made it look so simple, although in his case it was backed up by charisma and good looks and that easy way he had with people from all walks of life that probably he inherited from his father. He was fearless, or at least that was how he seemed to me. If he was afraid of anything, it was living up to the image that others had of him.

'Isn't it time to cut the umbilical cord?' he asked. It was a question as brutal as the building we were in.

'It's not like that,' I protested.

'I don't necessarily mean Maxine,' he explained, almost spitting the name. 'She's no kind of mother.'

'Then what?'

'I don't know.' He sighed with exasperation, not with me but at the situation I found myself in. 'The family responsibility? There's a great big world out there. A different kind of life. You have no idea the things you could achieve if you give yourself the opportunity.'

'You know it's not that simple. I can't just abandon them. My freedom would be their prison.'

He took a big swig of beer, emptied the glass. 'That's a bit melodramatic, isn't it?'

'You think I don't know that? But it's also true, and you know it.'

He didn't have a good response to that. This conversation always ended the same way: stalemate. Temporarily at a loss, he sauntered over to the bar.

'How's the love-life?' he asked, when he returned, a question perhaps designed to distract attention from himself.

I shrugged. 'I think things are okay. She's just being weird about Miranda. She's suspicious, like we're up to something.'

'You mean jealous. Look, I know you like her, but don't get sucked in. You've got too much going on to get distracted.'

I wasn't sure whether he was talking about college, universities, my responsibilities at home or the fanzine, and told him so.

'All of it,' he said. 'If it's fun, enjoy it. But the moment it becomes hard work, it's time to move on. She's a nice enough girl, but it's not like you're going to marry her. Get a bit of perspective, Alex.'

We finished our beers, and I went to get another round in. We were both a little nervous about what kind of reaction we were going to get when we started trying to sell The Manifesto. After all that work, we had a lot invested in it emotionally. If the reaction was lukewarm, it would be hard to take.

It was early but the first band were getting ready to come on. There were about ten people inside the venue, but even the greatest bands have to start somewhere. A spotty singer came onstage apologetically and announced they were called The Toast Rack, presumably named after that perfect piece of pop architecture on Wilmslow Road close to where I lived. Their name wasn't the worst thing about them. They played a half dozen songs, half-formed and of no fixed genre, a band in search of an identity. The guitarist was interesting though. He didn't belong, very technically competent and with an insouciance about the way he handled himself on stage that deserved better. He also looked strangely familiar.

After they had finished their set, I told Tom what I thought. He nodded.

'Totally agree. The guitarist, he's called Luke. He does music at college, and I think he's really got something about him. That's one of the reasons why I wanted to come tonight. He asked me to come along.'

'Why? The band is awful.'

'I think he's aware of that. But his next band will be much better because he'll have more of an idea about what he wants. It's the same thing with The Manifesto. We already know the second issue will be better.'

Sometimes his bluntness took me by surprise. 'I'm really proud of it,' I protested. 'You can't already be ready to move on.'

'I'm proud of what we've done, too' he acknowledged, 'but we both know there are things we could have done better. We've learned so much, but we have to keep moving forwards.'

I was irritated by his opinion, but Luke came over to say hi before I could say anything.

'Sorry about that,' he said. 'I know we're shite but thanks for coming.'

'You weren't shite,' said Tom kindly. He never lied but he was adept at ameliorating the truth. That was part of his charm. 'You got up there and did it. I really respect that. Lots of people never have the balls.'

Luke had come over with three bottles of beer and he generously passed them round. 'We got a rider,' he explained. 'A crate of beer. I feel I owe you for having to sit through that.'

'Thanks,' I said, laughing. He seemed like a decent guy. On impulse, I handed him a copy of The Manifesto. 'Fair trade.'

He gratefully accepted it and started to flick through it. I expected him to have a quick look at it out of good manners, but he quickly became engrossed. 'Have you done this?' he asked, not looking up. 'This is really impressive.' I burned inside. I could see Tom felt much the same way.

'Thanks,' said Tom. 'You're our first satisfied customer.'

'Well, I'm honoured. Seriously, this is good. Really good.' The place was starting to fill up. It probably held about a hundred people and it was half full. 'Thank God we managed to get off stage before this lot turned up.' He had an easy open manner and a self-deprecating sense of humour that made him easy to talk to. I excused myself and started to walk round trying to sell a few copies while they stood around chatting and waiting for the next band to come on. It was hard work. Not having a price on the cover was quickly becoming an issue.

'Just pay what you like,' I explained.

'Is this a trick?' The uncertainty seemed to make people suspicious. I tried to explain the concept that we wanted to make sure anyone could afford it.

'Are you saying I'm poor?' I noticed for the first time how big he was.

'Of course not,' I said. 'Poor isn't an insult, it's an economic circumstance.'

'Are you taking the piss?'

'Okay, just keep it.' I gave up and walked back to the table. This wasn't how it was supposed to go down, so I reached over and touched Tom's arm. 'Tag. Your turn.'

I watched him do his stuff, that natural easy charm of his, but he did little better. He came back with just enough cash for another round. 'Well. That was hard work,' he said. Perhaps it was too personal for us.

'Let me have a go,' said Luke. He helped himself to the rest of Tom's stash and walked off. We couldn't look.

'It's at times this I wish I smoked,' I joked. The plan had been to sell it at gigs, hoping to use it as an excuse to sneak inside for free but it immediately became apparent that neither of us were ever going to make a fortune as salesmen.

A few minutes later I felt a tap at my shoulder. Jake was standing over me, holding out his hand. 'Can I take these?' he asked. 'I can't keep up.' We hadn't even bothered to check but between us we had probably brought out about 60 copies. Half an hour later, they were gone. He handed us two pocketfuls of cash and sat down, looking very pleased with himself.

'I even got a girl's phone number,' he said, retrieving a scrap of paper from a bundle of pound notes. 'I play my heart out, and nothing. I start to sell these, and suddenly I've got myself a date. Thanks, guys.' Once again, it was turning into quite an evening, better than we had hoped.

'How come we never see you out?' I asked.

'I tend to stay in my room,' he said, 'trying out new things on the guitar. I'm a bit of a muso.' He grinned ruefully. 'A bit sad, I know.'

'Well, you definitely need to get out more,' said Tom. 'At least you're here.'

Right on cue, A Witness walked out. Singer, guitarist, bass player and a drum machine, what they lacked in technical skill they more than made up for in assured song-writing, making a virtue of their limited set-up and finding a distinctive voice, all choppy guitars and barked vocals. They were never going to make a dent in the pop charts, but what they did, they did very well. I was irritated that some people were still sitting around talking or reading The Manifesto, ignoring the band playing their hearts out on stage.

We hung around afterwards to tell them we had liked what we heard as they packed their gear away. Then Tom walked round picking up any discarded copies of the magazine to re-sell, a nice bit of cultural recycling, as he put it.

'Really?' I asked.

'Paper doesn't grow on trees, you know,' he chided me, parodying a phrase he evidently heard a lot at work, encouraging workers not to waste resources. 'Waste not, want not.'

It had been a modest but largely encouraging start to our venture. People had not only bought it, but read it and apparently enjoyed it, too. Maybe Tom had a point that we needed to move fast to seize our moment rather than letting the healthy jangle of coins in our pockets lead us into complacency. All the way home, the thought rolled around my head as I started to think about things to write about for the second issue. Already, as Tom had forecast, I was moving on.

Eight

Maybe Zoe had a point. Wherever we went, Miranda always seemed to be there. From our narrow perspective, it never occurred to either of us that Manchester was actually quite a small town when it came down to it. Whereas London was vast, with scattered communities of subcultural groups, in Manchester everyone more or less congregated in the same spaces. Inevitably, you would bounce off the same people over and over again. You might not notice it normally,

but if the other person was a beautifully presented and extrovert person then you most certainly would, although it seemed highly unlikely that she secretly harboured romantic feelings about any of us. More often than not, we would see her across crowded rooms in the company of a slightly older group of people we didn't know, and she would either come over to say hi, or not. It was not unusual for her to pull pleading faces for us to come and rescue her, or turn her fingers into guns to blow her brains out. Once, an older male acquaintance grabbed her by the arm as she came over to see us. Instinctively, I started to head over to sort things out and Tom held me back with a wag of the finger.

'She knows how to take care of herself,' he mouthed over deafening music, and I backed down, my Galahad complex held in check for the time being.

We had met up in Piccadilly Records, conveniently located immediately where the bus dropped us off in town and we would rifle through the racks as if we had money to spend. If it annoyed the staff, they never let it show, but after the night we had had selling The Manifesto, we were for once able to indulge ourselves. After that, Tom dragged me across 'the gardens' to Grass Roots, the specialist bookshop where pseudo radicals liked to hang out. I would flick distractedly flick through the collections of books of speeches by Fidel Castro or Trotsky as if I properly understood what they were talking about whilst Tom lost himself in obscure sections of Russian propaganda that made little sense to me at all. I felt like a fraud in there, although it had a great ambience. We both nurtured a naïve view of Russia that it was somehow a more virtuous and egalitarian society, although in reality I suspect both of us would have hated living under such an authoritarian regime where the expression of non-conformist ideas through decadent counter-cultural movements like music was hardly encouraged or nurtured by the state.

Miranda appeared over my shoulder. 'What are you reading?' she asked. She pulled the pamphlet from my hands and gave it the once over. She pulled a face, disappointed. 'I can't tell you how incredibly dull that looks.' She was clutching a copy of Medea, which I foolishly thought was a pretentious spelling of media until I saw it was a Greek tragedy. She had this effect on me, always scrambling my thoughts. She was wearing dungarees which should have been terrible, but looked great on her, pulled tight into her waist with a thick man's belt.

'That looks so much more exciting,' I replied with more than a hint of sarcasm.

'This?' She pulled a shocked face, holding the book up for me to see more clearly. 'This, my handsome little friend, is art. Actually, it's more than that. This is also my next job, or at least I hope it is. There are auditions tomorrow and I really want the part so I'm trying to get ahead of it. If I know what it's about, I can really get inside the character. See? I'm smarter than I look.' 'Well, I hope you get you want.'

She smiled at me knowingly. 'I always get what I want.'

'Like dressing up as a suffragette?'

'Exactly,' she said, 'the role of a lifetime. Who wouldn't want to be a hot sassy pioneer like Christabel?'

She was easy to talk to, open and fun. 'Did you at least escape the clutches of the lesbians?'

She pulled a face and I could see why she had been drawn to acting. We were standing next to the gay section, and someone had flashed me a dirty look. 'They're a bit up themselves, but they mean well,' said Miranda. 'I don't think I was in any danger.' She nudged me, gesturing towards the till. 'What's the enigmatic one up to now?'

I assumed he was spending more of his newfound wealth on books, but he was handing over several copies of The Manifesto. The silver-tongued maestro had managed to convince the coolest bookshop in town to stock it. We had passed the acid test for hip recognition.

Miranda held out her. 'Give me some money,' she commanded, and I did as I was told. I watched as she ostentatiously made her way over to the till, picked up a copy, negotiated a price and bought it. A sale in the first five minutes.

Outside, still clutching the copy of Medea to her chest, she thanked me for the money and told me she would reciprocate by providing us complimentary tickets for the show when she inevitably got the lead role.

'Did you even pay for that?' I asked her.

Again, she gave me a look that said more than a thousand words, disappointment and regret. 'I'll return it when I've finished with it,' she swore. 'I'm penniless today.' She turned out the pockets of her dungarees to prove the point, dropping her return bus ticket in the process. The wind caught it and we chased it across the concrete. On the corner of Piccadilly Gardens, on the cusp of the sweep up to the train station, she was far from the only one with no money. A bearded tramp scoured the pavement for discarded cigarettes. Grey shoppers shuffled by, clutching plastic bags containing post-dated vegetables. Others dragged miserable looking kids behind them. If this was Thatcher's vision of a better world, I would hate to see what was worse. Finally, we caught up with the bus ticket and she safely stowed it. Everything about her was melodrama.

'Thanks, boys,' she said. 'See you around.' And then she was gone.

Tom had a shift at the printers later that afternoon so we spent some time in Afflecks killing time flicking through racks of clothes we couldn't afford. All the same, it was diverting, and we even managed to convince a few stalls to stock a few copies of The Manifesto for us, on the understanding that any proceeds would be evenly split. The ad hoc nature of the arrangement appealed to us, and it felt great to be getting it out there on public display in stalls and shops that were important to us, as if we were already becoming a part of the scene not simply as passive consumers but as people participating in something that mattered. The nice girls at Identity, our favourite clothes stall, even offered to place an advert in the next issue, a sure sign that people liked what we were doing and wanted to become associated with it. Amongst other things, they did great T shirts using iconic Russian art-prints that chimed perfectly with our adolescent obsession with revolution so well felt that they were a good fit as a commercial partner, although we stopped short of using such a loaded phrase to describe the arrangement.

On the way across town, we had a horrible realisation that we didn't really have a clue what we were doing. We had failed to discuss the cost of placing an advert, let alone consider the ideological implications of going down a more commercial route at the first opportunity. The Manifesto was a labour of love, not a money-making scheme. Had we already exposed ourselves as ideological frauds? The thought horrified us.

In fact, it bothered Tom so much that he took greater risks printing off more issues as he worked into the evening, provoking accusations and an argument with the office manager that he resolved by resorting to charm which soon became physical and then sexual. 'Taking one for the team' was how he described it the next day.

'Giving one for the team is more like it,' said Adrian.

'I've thought about it a lot,' said Tom, 'and I've realised we haven't really got much of a choice. As long as we stick to places we approve of and that fit the ethos, I can't see what's wrong with it.'

'It's not like you to compromise your principles,' said Adrian.

'That's just the point. I don't think we are. By taking adverts from places like Identity, what we're actually doing is reinforcing what we stand for, small imaginative stalls taking on the big boys and doing okay out of it.' I wasn't certain he was convinced by his own argument, but I had nothing much to add. We hated it when bands we liked sold their music to use in adverts, even though the corporate cash probably transformed their lives in ways that their music careers never could. The word sell-out was used a lot. We didn't even like it when indie bands signed up to major labels, even if it meant the quality of their recordings improved a thousand per cent. That was the whole point. The low-fi nature of the music we loved was part of its appeal. Take away the rough edges and you could spot the imperfections and limitations. It occurred to me that this was an article for the next edition, though subconsciously it was probably a warning to ourselves not to let our modest success warp our values and taint the work we were doing.

We were sitting on a bench on Oxford Road outside the BBC studios near the cinema where Adrian worked. Stuart Hall walked past to hail a cab, a pretty young woman on his arm. I expressed my admiration for him, and Adrian gave me a look that suggested I was way off the mark.

'He's a right dirty bastard,' he warned me.

'He makes me laugh,' I said.

'Yeah,' said Adrian enigmatically, 'but I think he might be laughing at us, not with us.'

He had let us in to see *Top Gun* which I had found strangely enjoyable, in a cheesy Hollywood kind of way. As usual, we were passing round cans of barely drinkable beer to take the edge off.

'What did you think?' asked Adrian.

I let Tom go first. 'Jingoistic American bullshit full of preening peacocks.' I thought he was being a bit harsh and said so. 'No, I kind of liked it,' he said. 'In spite of myself, it was actually quite good fun.'

'I think it's the gayest film I've ever seen,' I said.

Adrian gave me a queer look. 'Really?' he said, artfully raising an eyebrow. 'You need to watch more films. And I think the word you're looking for is homoerotic.'

I passed him the can. 'I stand corrected. You know what I mean, though.'

He took a long gulp, then another. 'I do,' he said. It was another freezing night. The sky was unusually clear, and constellations blazed away up above. Coming from Manchester, you could have believed there were only about a hundred stars in the night sky. Nights like this were something of a revelation. Sandwiched in between me and Tom, his Gola bag nestled between his feet, he turned his face to look at me. His eyes were a little bloodshot. 'You do know I'm gay, right?'

I could feel his body next to mine. 'I didn't know,' I said, trying to keep my voice steady, mortified that I might have offended him.

'Seriously?' Tom was laughing. 'You didn't know? Really?' He held the can of Special Brew up as if to toast his gayness, and his courage to open us to us like this. 'Adrian, you are so totally gay, your pink aura must be visible from the moon.'

'Like the yellow brick road.'

Adrian laughed and I did, too. It was an obscure joke I didn't understand but I was relieved that things were okay between us.

'You're right, though,' said Adrian. 'It is a really gay film. And, for the record, I'm sure Tom Cruise is one of us.'

'One of you,' said Tom, 'Just to be clear. Although to be fair I fancied him more than Kelley McGillis.' We laughed again. I'm sure for Adrian that in his head coming out to us must have been a really big deal and yet within moments his big secret was out there, and it was all okay and nothing much had changed. I was starting to grow up a bit, learning that internalising things was harmful.

'Can we call you Gaydrian from now on?' asked Tom. He could be really silly when he was pissed.

'Erm, absolutely not.'

We chatted for a while longer then left him sitting there with the dirty dregs and a complimentary copy of The Manifesto, which had prompted him to present each of us with a VHS copy of Cannibal Holocaust by way of thanks. We walked towards home together through the curry mile into Fallowfield where we went our separate ways. He called me back.

'Did you really not know?' he asked. I shook my head and he laughed again as he walked off shaking his head and laughing until the darkness swallowed him whole and the only sounds were the usual ambient soundtrack of a city at night, stubbornly refusing to go to sleep.

Nine

As it transpired, Zoe's parents were lovely. In spite of my adolescent determination to see them somehow as part of a middle-class conspiracy to cling on to the better things in life at the expense of others, I found it hard to dislike them. They were warm, generous and socially conscious to the extent that even Tom would have struggled to provoke an argument with them on the subject of politics. I had witnessed him on a number of occasions turn normally mild-mannered people into spitting lunatics infuriated by his idealism and ability to take and defend extreme political views on subjects as varied as religion, abortion and the growing inequality of wealth that split communities, cities and countries into brutally separate entities. Like many modern parents, they were a little reluctant to accept that their daughter was turning into a young woman, so they insisted that they meet me which slowly evolved into an invitation to dinner. A refusal would have been tantamount to an end to our relationship and I was reluctant to let go, so I relented, much to Tom's amusement.

The mood was light-hearted, a world away from the tense passive aggressive interactions I had to endure with Maxine, and I quickly found myself relaxing. The thought struck me that maybe I was overly judgemental, condemning whole swathes of society based on faulty logic and pre-conceived notions of how I imagined people to be. Her father, George, was a lawyer and talked in broad terms about the kinds of cases he worked on, suggesting that it was a fine career for someone with a sharp mind like mine. I couldn't tell him that I associated the law with the many kinds of barriers that people like me faced, vague but very real threats from various people over the years that first me and then my sisters would be taken into care if certain conditions weren't met. Red letters from the utilities were an almost daily irritation, and only Deb's kindly interventions with emergency loans kept us out of the courts, or worse. All of this I kept to myself, of course.

He put on a Bruce Springsteen CD and caught me rolling my eyes. He laughed.

'Don't be so dismissive,' he insisted. 'You need to listen to this guy. There's a lot more to him than meets the eye, you know. He's the real deal.'

Highly dubious, I did as I was told, and found myself seeing something that I had somehow missed, authentic blue-collar storytelling that betrayed a real sympathy for the working man. I still struggled with the high production values, far too slick and overdone for my indie tastes, but I found myself being won over despite myself.

'If you're not careful, he'll put some Leonard Cohen on,' Zoe teased him. I was fine with that. Tom had already tuned me into his dark humour and the Mary Chain had previously cited him as an influence, something I struggled to hear, though it made me view him in a more sympathetic light.

George talked about his *pro bono* work with vulnerable families, and I quietly wondered if it was his way of letting me know that he knew what I was and that he was okay with it. He had a pleasant, honest face, a sharp beard and clear blue eyes that seemed able to penetrate your soul. As I listened, I became more convinced that the conversation was a subtext, a carefully coded message letting me know that he was aware of my social circumstances, and that it was fine by him as long as I caused his daughter no harm and treated her right.

He had a phrase he kept repeating as he talked about his work, although I don't think he realised he was doing it: How can that be right? He clearly had a well-defined sense of social injustice that was in many ways a reflection of my own, though we were coming at it from different sides of the mirror.

I think I said all the right things, keeping things as vague as possible, although I was all too aware that we communicate not so much by what we say as how we say it, subtle clues betrayed by body language and social etiquette of which I was largely ignorant. The mood stayed light, friendly, welcoming almost. I seemed to win their approval, which I found strangely reassuring. Her mum was lovely, a lecturer at the university, and in every way a blueprint for how I imagined Zoe would develop into womanhood, confident and self-possessed and well-presented. They were like a TV family, attractive, loving and mutually supportive in ways I could scarcely envisage. I knew I wasn't a lost cause but compared to this, I had to wonder what chance I had, dragging myself through college while doing my best to provide some kind of normality for my sisters.

Zoe sat next to me and squeezed my hand encouragingly. The question of next steps came up and I was skilfully manipulated to imagine a future for myself which involved university and potential future careers about which I had scarcely ever given myself the luxury of a moment's thought. It was hard for me to see from one week to the next in terms of how we were going to settle bills and put food on the table, whereas Zoe's family thought in terms of five-year plans, like Stalin, ironically, given that he would undoubtedly have sent them to the gulags.

They really took an interest in The Manifesto and seemed genuine when they asked if they could have a copy. Apparently, Zoe hadn't even told them of her artistic contributions, and they were delighted to hear how she was putting her skills to practical use, something which she could use for a portfolio for future use. For them, the future was something bright and attainable, not an elusive fantasy.

Inevitably, they asked me about my family. I tried to steer the conversation to my sisters and the closeness of our bond, but they gently probed about my parents. I should have been better prepared, or at least been quick-witted enough to gloss over the issues without having to fabricate a different kind of truth, but the best I could manage was that my mother was currently between jobs. At least it wasn't a lie. She had worked in an office briefly before I was born and had lived off the state ever since, but there was a possibility that she would be coerced back into some kind of employment if Thatcher had her way.

'And your father?'

'I don't really have a father,' I said, looking away. Zoe squeezed my hand protectively.

'I'm so sorry to hear that.' George even looked upset, possibly assuming that he had passed away.

'You can't miss something you've never known,' I said, possibly a little more defensively than I intended.

George nodded. 'I see,' he said. Instinctively, he seemed to understand the situation, an absent father in dereliction of his duty.

'That must be very hard for you.'

'We manage well enough,' I said. I had no desire to be pitied.

Quickly, the subject was changed and more wine was poured out into ornate glasses that made me fearful in case I dropped one as my hands were shaking slightly. The food was delicious although I doubt I could have named a single ingredient and I probably ate more than was socially proper but if my mouth was full I couldn't be put on the spot again by intrusive questions, although I know the intent had been kindly enough.

It was still a great evening, and I was a little embarrassed by how good it felt to be able to engage with such successful and well-educated people without making a fool of myself. They were entertaining and surprisingly open-minded. I was even offered the chance to spend the night, although I politely declined, explaining that I had to be home to look after the girls. Even that seemed to meet their approval rather than being a black mark against my name, facing up to my responsibilities and trying to do what was right.

When I started to set off for the bus, George shook my hand and expressed his desire that I come back soon. Her mum hugged me goodbye, and Zoe kissed me hard on the lips.

'You did great,' she said.

Then they called me back. 'I bet it's ages until the next bus comes along,' said George. 'How about I call a cab for you?'

Zoe must have felt me tense up. 'It's okay. He'll pay,' she said quietly.

I thanked him but told him the buses were really reliable and dropped me right outside my house, which wasn't really accurate, but I didn't want to feel in his debt.

'Okay,' he called.

His wife was by his side, waving. 'It's been lovely to meet you,' she said.

'Likewise,' I called back. 'Thanks for a lovely evening.' The words coming out of my mouth didn't feel quite right and I was worried about sounding fake, but it was how I felt.

The bus had a dodgy suspension and a driver who had never quite mastered the clutch and it rattled me all the way back to reality. I wondered if I was becoming the kind of person who could mix it up in different social circles. The city I glimpsed through the grime-encrusted windows seemed to exert a little less of a hold on me somehow. They seemed to genuinely like me, which wasn't something I had ever given much thought to, but it pleased me all the same.

It was a great John Peel Show that night, although I had missed half of it. The Wedding Present were in session and did an awesome cover of an old Orange Juice song that stuck in my head as I tried to switch my brain off and go to sleep without any realistic hope of success, there were so many things to work through before my night was done.

*

'So, how was the dinner party with the bourgeoisie?' asked Tom. He was mocking himself for his binary worldview as much as he was making fun of me.

'Strangely pleasant,' I told him.

'Pleasant,' he repeated. 'Ugh.'

'No, it was good. They were decent people.' I felt the need to be fair to them given how much effort they had made. 'Although they did make me listen to Bruce Springsteen.'

'I've said it before and I'll say it again,' Tom insisted, 'The Boss is one of us. My dad always told me he was one of the good guys. He donated loads of money to the miners last time he was over here touring, you know. I won't hear a bad word said against him.'

There was just no arguing with that.

'Just don't tell anyone.'

We were on our way to The Venue on Whitworth Street as it was a Friday night and Dave Haslam was DJing, which was always a treat. To save money, we were drinking beforehand on The Stoop, a short walk away, and quite a few of us had turned up. I was pleased to see Jake had turned up, too, having accepted our invitation. Unusually, Zoe was with us with a couple of girl friends, so the talk was a bit more refined than usual, and it turned out she knew Jake quite well from college. Colin was there, as well, with his camera in hand as ever, shooting away and stealing little slices of our souls with each snap of the shutter.

We got into The Venue just before ten so entry was free and the drinks half price, and we bought what we could afford and took handfuls of bottles over to a group of tables where we formed a base camp. It was mostly deserted in there, but Haslam was already finding his groove and Zoe pulled me over to the dancefloor where I self-consciously shuffled around until the alcohol started to take effect and I loosened up. It was all new territory for me, a girlfriend in tow, but it mostly felt okay. The music was a glorious mix of genres and always – always – something you'd never heard before that linked past and present and sounded bloody brilliant. Usually, Tom would be able to tell me what it was if I didn't know, but occasionally we would have to concede defeat and ask Haslam what it was, and he would give you his shy smile and tell you in a voice that didn't shame you for not knowing. Darren had joined us on the dancefloor to The March Violets and was trying to attract the attention of a girl who turned her back on him and stuck her tongue down the throat of another girl, who didn't seem to mind in the least. She pulled her onto the dancefloor where they made out without a care in the world and we danced on as if it was totally normal, which of course it was. The Loft came on and Tom got up and danced with us and we followed him up that hill and down that slope and laughed and drank until all the beer was suddenly gone.

We sat down in a big sweaty heap. Tom nudged me in the ribs and gestured towards the doorway where Jake was already heading home from the girl whose number he had got from the A Witness gig. He looked over his shoulder and we exchanged approving grins as he threw his arm around her and led her up and away.

It was starting to fill up, which was both good and bad. With more people, the atmosphere improved and you were less conscious of the grim décor. It was not so much minimalist chic as bereft of any kind of attractive feature, like a morgue that even goths would avoid. What this place looked like in the cold light of day was an awful thought. Like a crime scene, probably. More people also meant greater capacity for trouble.

It was the kind of place that idiots would sometimes turn up to looking for easy trouble, and so it proved. A scuffle broke out on the dancefloor, and Haslam was forced to leap gracefully over the DJ booth to split up the combatants. A bouncer came over and dragged one of them away, but unease hung over the place and we decided the moment had gone. *Hymn From A Village* came on as we walked away, up the stairs and into the unrefreshing night. It was relatively early, barely past midnight, but we were broke again. We surveyed the street up and down, assessing our next move, but none of us could come up with anything.

'So that's that, then, is it?' said Darren, always the last to call it a night. For once, he had not shed a single drop of blood. Zoe was clinging to me for warmth and support.

'Can I stay at yours tonight?' she asked.

It came out of nowhere and knocked me sideways, and I didn't react well.

'Absolutely not,' I said. I tried to make it sound jokey, but she was more than a little the worse for wear and instantly took it the wrong way. She didn't usually drink much and was unsteady on her feet so I had to take her weight. Apparently, she wouldn't give in without a fight.

'Why not? Are you ashamed of me?'

'Don't be so bloody daft.'

'Tell me why I can't stay at yours, then?' There was no good answer to that.

'Your parents will worry about where you are,' I said in desperation. It wasn't a lie and was definitely worth a try, except there was a red phone box a few feet away and she wasn't so drunk that she couldn't remember her number.

She wouldn't be deterred. 'I can just call them, stupid.' She pushed me in the chest, but in what she considered a flirtatious way. The word stupid stung me, though. Her friends were getting cold and came over to see what the issue was. 'I just want to stay at his,' she told them. 'I want to meet his sisters. They sound so cute.'

'Not tonight,' I said. 'It's no big deal, but I just can't.'

Her friends tried to pull her away, but she resisted. She looked up at me with that face of hers, her eyes huge, pleading. Tom came over, too. He gave me a look that was his way of letting me know that this was what it was to have a girlfriend.

'I think it's a great idea,' he said. I didn't know what his game was, maybe reverse psychology. 'We can all get the bus home together.' One of Zoe's friends put her arm round his waist, chancing her arm. She was a tall redhead. I couldn't really say he had a type, but he certainly didn't resist.

'Me, too,' she said.

I glared at him and he smiled back. Over his shoulder, I could see that most of the others had already walked off and Darren was making out with the girl from the dancefloor under a streetlight. I had been backed into a corner, and I didn't want to lose face.

Sod it, I thought. Let's do it.

I was quiet on the bus home, apprehensive. Reluctantly, I could see that this was a situation I couldn't contain indefinitely if my relationship with Zoe was to have any kind of future, and I liked her. Inadvertently, counter-intuitively, the dinner party with her parents had made her more of a real person with genuine feelings than even the most intimate moments we had spent together in bed. Tom knew all about my avoidance tactics; I had used them on him often enough in the early days of our burgeoning friendship and he had a brutal way of forcing me to confront my inner demons that I knew was probably necessary. In many ways, I was a coward although I would have preferred a gentler term.

She held my hand tightly as we bounced along Wilmslow Road past the Toast Rack and the university residences. Full disclosure was required if our relationship was to mean anything, or else I was just a fraud playing out a part to impress her and her parents. *The Catcher In The Rye* is undoubtedly one of the most overrated books ever written, but at that moment I identified closely with the idea of the phoney existence. I pinged the red button and dragged her down the stairs as Tom silently mouthed the words: good luck. His grin was infuriating.

Occasionally, I checked Zoe's face for signs that she was having second thoughts as I took her through a labyrinth of terraced houses, but she was resolute. I opened the front door carefully, trying not to disturb Maxine and immediately led Zoe upstairs so she couldn't see the inert figure prone on the sofa in her medicated wonderland. It was a blessing that it was so dark so she couldn't see the disarray and disorder that Maxine inflicted on us, but the morning would be a different matter. An only child, Zoe stared in wonder at the girls, curled up together in their single bed. I put a warning finger to my lips, but I needn't have bothered as she instinctively understood the importance of leaving them undisturbed. We partially undressed and manoeuvred ourselves giggling into my single bed which creaked riotously as we found a space in which to place our entwined limbs.

'Thank you,' she said in a whisper, kissing me hard on the mouth. She might have been a tourist in my misery for all I understood what was going on, but for the moment it felt thrilling to have her next to me, a tiny spark in the darkness.

*

The next thing we knew it was morning and Sindy was sitting on top of us.

'Who's this? Who's this?' she was saying, full of excitement.

Zoe stuck a hand out. 'Hi,' she said. 'I'm Zoe.'

'My name's Sindy. Like the doll.'

110

'Only much prettier,' said Zoe, sitting up. Bella was awake, too but she was not so forward and kept her distance, happy letting her sister be her public face. 'Hi, you,' said Zoe, sensing her presence in the room. She giggled. I could tell it was early by the lack of noise in the street. Luckily, our game had been postponed as I was in no shape to kick a ball or run, but City were at home so in a short while the streets would be full of fans trudging expectantly to Maine Road.

'Will you be alright here with these two?' I asked, standing up. I wandered downstairs to make some breakfast. Fortunately, Maxine was comatose. A bottle of vodka rolled across the floor as I tiptoed past the sofa. For a few hours, I was probably safe. There was no milk, so I popped next door to scrounge some off Deb, who as ever was awake and happy to oblige.

'You're in quite a state,' said Gary from the kitchen table. It was part jest, part warning not to be so dissolute the next morning when I had tutoring to be done while the rest cleared off to church. 'Big night, was it?' I grinned, despite myself.

Deb took a long look at me at laughed out loud. 'Get lucky last night, eh?' I blushed.

'I'm bloody glad someone did.'

'Shut it,' she said, though she knew Gary was joking. 'Christ, did you bring her home? You bloody did, didn't you.' She opened the fridge and pulled out rashers of bacon and eggs.

'You don't need to do that,' I protested.

'I bloody do,' she said. 'Poor girl's got a bit shock coming. Least we can do is give her some decent food.'

In its way, it was every bit as warm and loving as Zoe's house.

'This is going to cost you, mind,' said Gary. 'I need a hand with the car later. If you've got the energy, that is.'

They pushed me out of the door. 'You get back to the poor girl,' said Deb. 'I'll pop these round when they're done. Give you a chance to get some pants on, eh.'

She was as good as her word. By the time I had got the girls washed and dressed and down the stairs without disturbing their poor excuse for a mother, we had cleared some space at the kitchen table and Deb walked in through the back door with cooked breakfasts all round.

'Oh, but she's stunning,' said Deb, looking at Zoe to take her in. 'Lovely to meet you.' She looked at me sternly. 'You'd better look after this one,' she warned me as she made her escape. 'She's way out of your league, sunshine.'

'You swore,' said Sindy, pointing an accusing finger at me.

'Not really,' I protested. 'Eat your food. It took me ages to make.'

'Bloody cheek,' I said. I threw a crust of toast at her as she closed the back door.

'Deb did it,' said Bella.

I pulled a sad face. 'Not true. How could you say that?'

We kept our voices down but there was a lot of laughter. I could see that Zoe was enjoying it, but also trying her hardest not to look around at the dreadful chaos of the house.

'I know, I know,' I said defensively by way of apology. 'It's a bomb-site. Honestly, I clean it all the time,' I said, 'but it just ends up the same.'

'That's true, that is,' said Sindy. 'He does his best and that's what counts.' I had no idea who put those words into her mouth, but it certainly wasn't Maxine. Gary, probably, sticking up for me, just like my sister was now.

'It's fine, really,' said Zoe. 'The breakfast is great.'

'Thanks.'

'But Deb made it,' said Bella, getting cross.

'Oh, don't start all that again.' And I threw a crust at her, too.

'Ow.'

Before Maxine awoke and ruined things, I suggested we go to the park so the girls could get some exercise and something resembling fresh air, anything to escape. The house was small to begin with, but the piles of hoarded clutter made it almost impossible to move freely. Only Deb's endless supply of air freshener she got from work kept the stench at bay, and that was probably carcinogenic.

We stuck our heads in at Deb's to return the plates and see if her boy wanted to come along but he was doing something with his dad and said no.

The park was a park in name only, a few sorry see-saws and swings that required untangling before you could use them. It was fenced-in and I was always dismayed that dog-owners would open the gate to let their dogs use the area, adding to the hazards already present, great expanses of debris and broken glass. The girls knew no better. Occasionally, I would walk them over to Platt Fields where they were almost overwhelmed by the vast expanses of grass and open space, but increasingly I didn't have the time. Predictably, it had rained earlier on. For a moment, Sindy stopped and bent over, staring right into a puddle, waiting for the ripples to stop as if trying to see her reflection.

'Look', she said.

I strained to see something of note.

'What am I supposed to be looking at?'

'The dirty rainbow.'

Zoe laughed out loud. 'Yeah, I can see it. It's amazing.'

I leaned in. There was a sheen of oil on the ground and sure enough there was a sort of rainbow slickness just below the surface.

'Is that what you call them?' Zoe laughed.

'Yes, the dirty rainbows,' said Bella. 'They're trapped in the water and you have to splash to let them out.' The girls giggled as they sploshed each other by stamping in the puddles as we walked on. Zoe joined in, too, and I let them play, even though I would be the one cleaning and drying their shows for school tomorrow. I had the girls well trained so they were able to push themselves on the swings when we got to the play-park, competitively seeing who could go the highest while I got a break.

'I guess you're wondering why it's like that,' I said.

Zoe held my hand as we encouraged the girls. 'It's none of my business,' she said.

'But it's embarrassing,' I protested. 'You can see why I didn't want to bring you home.'

'Your sisters are lovely,' she said, sidestepping a repeat of last night's argument. 'How are they so sweet?'

'Living in this shithole? Damned if I know.'

'You're so good with them,' said Zoe, admiringly. 'They're really lucky to have you.' We watched them, oblivious, lost in their own petty competition to be better than the other, then giggling when one of them lost their nerve.

'It might be the other way round,' I said. 'They stop me getting too bitter. I have to keep myself under control or else...'

It was a sentence I could never finish. There was no or else, not without hurting the girls. We stayed a while longer and then Zoe called her parents to come and pick her up. It was her mum's birthday and she had agreed to go shopping with her. The closeness of their bond amazed me, although most of my friends had great relationships with their parents, too. Because of the football, I walked her somewhere easier to be picked up, but on the way I popped home to pick something up. Maxine had arisen, sort of, unsteady of her feet, stumbling around the kitchen like a mythological gorgon and I was relieved I had asked Zoe to wait outside with the girls. I handed her a copy of The Manifesto and asked her to give it to her mum. It was all I had to give.

When her mum came to pick her up, she made a big fuss of the girls and they gave Zoe a hug and a kiss that almost made her cry. I guess it's not so easy to be an only child. On the walk home, they both told me to always be nice to her, and I promised that I would. Sometimes they seemed ancient in the way they understood the world.

'Remember that God is always watching,' said Bella, and she pointed upwards as if the great bearded deity was about to part the clouds and wag an omnipotent finger at me. I started to say something smart and then just let it go. I felt like I had just dodged a bullet and was feeling pretty good about it. That afternoon, I watched City beat Chelsea 6-2. It was good day to be alive.

Later that evening, I was lying on the pavement with Gary shining a torch under his car.

'She meant it, you know. About the girls, I mean.' His attempts at man-talk were punctuated by prolonged periods of silence when he was forced to concentrate on a particularly tricky period of fiddling. 'If you want to go away. We know it wouldn't be for ever. And we'd be glad to do it.' Like most men, he wasn't great at this kind of thing, any more than he was capable of keeping his car on the road. An elaborate spread of spanners and other tools were arranged on the pavement next to me. Each time he asked for a tool, he would say the name and then have to tell me what it looked like.

'You're bloody useless at this,' he grumbled, 'But at least you can hold a torch steady.'

I didn't know what to tell him. I was still no closer to knowing what I wanted to do. I told him as much.

'The thing is, son, you've got an opportunity to make your life better we never had.' He cursed under his breath as something refused to slide into place and he skinned his knuckle. 'It's not something to throw away lightly.'

'I know that,' I replied, 'But you're happy enough, right?'

'Of course. I've got everything I need.' He grunted and the piece finally did as it was supposed to. He sat up triumphantly and started to gather up the tools. 'But that doesn't mean we don't dream of better. Both of us. There's a great big world out there, you know.' I knew he meant well, even when he stated the obvious. Sometimes the simple truths are the easiest to miss, the hardest to hear. He patted me on the back, a great big bear of a man who didn't know his own strength. 'And as for that girl of yours...' His voice trailed off admiringly. 'I hope you realise that she's the one who thinks she's lucky. You're a great lad, you know, even if you do support a shite football team.'

'You want to be careful,' I cautioned him. He was on enemy turf and he knew it. This was a proper man talk, quickly moving onto football banter before things became too sentimental, but I really appreciated his attempts to offer support and his approval genuinely meant a lot to me. I helped him pack away.

As we put things in their proper place, I took the opportunity to raise something with him that was bothering me. I hated the way he let his brother talk to him sometimes, as if the size of the car you drive somehow equates to the calibre of your person.

He didn't answer for a while, grunting with the effort of lifting his tools back into place.

'It's just always been that way,' he said, finally, 'ever since we were little. He's always been motivated by money, making good by putting other people down.' Everything was in its rightful place and he led me back towards the house. 'It doesn't bother me, if that's what you're asking. If truth be told, I guess I feel sorry for him if he feels that's how he has to be to feel good about himself.'

I could see Maxine shuffling around in the kitchen going through cupboards in search of something we didn't have. He must have sensed my reluctance to go in.

'Go easy on her, eh,' he said. 'She wasn't always like this, you know.'

'That's just it,' I reminded him. 'I don't know. I can't remember her any other way. This is all I know.'

'That's as maybe,' he said. 'I suppose that's how it is with my brother. He's always been a prick but he's the only family I've got left so I just accept it for what it is. I don't know any different.'

That made a strange sort of sense. He put his great arm around me. 'I meant what I said, though. About moving away. We wouldn't have offered if we couldn't manage.' He opened the back door. 'And get some sleep, he said. 'You look knackered, and you're working tomorrow morning.'

'Yeah, yeah, you old nag.' He laughed and closed the door on me.

'What were you two on about like that?' asked Maxine, still rummaging for god knows what.

'Nothing for you to worry about,' I said. 'You just carry on looking for something to drink.' I sidestepped her and headed for the stairs.

'Couldn't you be nice for once?' she asked, her voice slurred as if she had only just woken up.

'If that means, could I find you something to drink, then no.' She was right in that I did find it hard to be nice to her. I felt I owed her nothing, and that's exactly what she got in return.

'You're a cocky little bastard,' she snapped back at me. 'Just like your father.'

I stopped on the stairs, stung by her remark. 'I'm nothing like him,' I retorted, 'because here I am, still stuck here putting all with all your crap.' I was reminded of Tom's jibe about the umbilical cord needing to be severed as she loudly shushed me in case I woke up the girls.

'Fuck you, Maxine,' I said as quietly as I could so that she could still hear. I didn't like her, any more than I liked myself when I was with her, her last nasty little gift to me. For completism, I hated my father, too, never once considering that

117

maybe he had run away because she was so awful. Long after I retired to the relative sanctuary of my room, she continued to stumble around downstairs until I put on my headphones and drowned her out with some Joy Division, something beautiful and self-loathing to see out the night. As I lay there, I thought about the concept of dirty rainbows, and realised that in a way that's what we all were, something dazzling just waiting to be set free.

Ten

O n his breaks at work, Tom had been busy networking with the subcultural underworld of Manchester, making himself known and insinuating The Manifesto anywhere and everywhere that the right sort of people might chance upon it. Comic shops, clothes stalls, certain carefully-selected pubs and cafes, Piccadilly Records. Wherever I went, there it was, spreading the good word. We even got a favourable mention in the Manchester Evening News in the Friday

supplement which featured a what's hot guide to the city's cultural life. I was particularly pleased when I attended a signing session at Odyssey 7, the comic shop in the university precinct. Alan Moore was there, grumpily signing copies of Watchmen, and looking distinctly uncomfortable having to embark on something so degrading as a promotional tour to boost sales. Adrian took a photo of us with a copy of The Manifesto on a shelf in the background. It was a small thing, but it made my day.

Things were starting to happen, just as Tom had predicted.

We had no idea how many copies we had sold, but as fast as he could print them off and sow them into the murky seed-beds of the subterranean scene, they would sell out. Accounting was impossible and we entered into a strange world where everywhere we went people would hand us beer or money as payment for whatever they had been able to collect for them. The idea had really appealed to people that they could charge what they liked or accept whatever people were able to afford, and there was no such thing as being ripped-off because everything that came in was a bonus. We started to realise that there was an alternative economy that sat invisibly on top of the normal world of transactions, where people would give you things in exchange for the cultural capital we were able to provide, even at such a low level. A wise man might have once declared that there was no such thing as a free lunch, but free beer and T-shirts bearing cyrillic slogans we couldn't even translate were a very different matter. I shared the thought with Tom who laughed, but at me rather than with me.

'That's not quite what he meant,' he said. We were in a pub on Platt Lane which we liked for its proximity to the City training ground. Occasionally, some of the players would sneak in there for a cheeky pint or two after training was finished. It had been done up a bit and the new landlord had placed a sign in the window which parodied the nationalistic signs we had grown up with regarding blacks and the Irish:

NO TORIES
NO COCKNEYS
NO REDS

We went over to the bar trying to imagine what the slogan read on the T shirt I was wearing, a square-jawed Soviet muscleman proudly wielding a hammer.

'I'm with stupid?' Tom suggested. 'Gullible Western tourist?'

We were making our way over to an empty table when the landlord shouted over the jukebox to ask if I was Maxine's lad. I didn't quite know what to answer but I knew what was coming.

'Tell her to stay away,' he said menacingly. 'She's in here every other afternoon making a bloody nuisance of herself. She's not welcome in here.'

I didn't like his attitude or the idea that I was somehow responsible for her. The sign had made us laugh and we had hoped for something better, but it turned out that the landlord was every bit as unlikeable as his predecessor. 'Like I have any control over what she does,' I snapped back. I didn't want to think what she might have been up to.

I turned away from him and exchanged a quick look with Tom. We both had full pints so I bit my tongue.

He took my silence as weakness, which was a mistake. 'Just make sure you tell her, eh.'

'I'll tell her, for all the good it will do.'

Behind the bar, he was furiously wiping glasses as if he was expecting a mid-afternoon rush. 'Don't you be taking that tone of voice with me or you'll get a fat lip, sunshine. You think you can just come in here and swagger arrogantly around, like you own the place, eh?'

I'd had enough. 'I'm not her bloody minder,' I snapped. I swallowed half my beer and stood up to him.

'I never said you were. I just asked you to give her a message.'

'Yeah,' I said. 'Whatever.' All I wanted was a quiet drink. I started to drink up but he over-reacted, making his way over to confront me. He was out of condition and his face was heart-attack red but he was the size of a brute as he told me in no uncertain terms to get out. I mostly drained my glass and launched it in his general direction from about fifteen feet, not intending to hit him but close enough to make a point, the dregs sloshing all over the empty space between and around us. The glass disintegrated harmlessly behind the bar but it did the trick.

Tom calmly drained his glass and put it down safely on the table. 'Cheers,' he said, and off we went. The landlord started out after us, cursing, but thought better of it as soon as he reached the exit. We made sure he wasn't following us and sauntered away, never to return.

'Sorry about that,' I said.

'Sorry for what? He was a total prick,' said Tom nonchalantly.

'Sorry for losing my temper, that's all.'

He had spilled some beer down his top and was wiping it away with his hand. 'No apology required,' he replied. 'I like it when you lose your cool. It suits you. Bloody Maxine, though. I don't know how you cope with her. Can't you just throw a bucket of water over her and let her just dissolve into a dark little pool of malevolent slime?'

I wished it was that easy. I liked that he hated on her so much as it saved me the effort while we were together, though I preferred simply to forget she existed. We were near Darren's, so we made the best of things and spent a pleasant afternoon listening to records. There had been enough drama for one day and it felt good to turn things down a notch or two, doing our best to work out why *Pet Sounds* was so highly regarded and drinking endless cups of tea.

Even though we hadn't drunk anything, we sang along to the ones we knew best.

> *Wouldn't it be nice if we were older*
> *Then we wouldn't have to wait so long.*

It didn't take Darren long to run out of words he could remember, but he creased us all up making up stupid or obscene lyrics that seemed to fit. After a while, Tom stopped singing, closed his eyes and just listened.

'Not bad,' he said as *That's Not Me* came to a close and the static hiss and crackle cued up the next track. 'You can actually hold a tune.'

'Thanks,' said Darren.

'Not you, you daft sod. You sound like a kitten being drowned.' Darren pushed him and Tom slopped the dregs of his tea down his top as he evaded further punishment with an acrobatic movement across the room. 'Bloody hell,' he shouted. 'Not again.' But he was laughing harder than all of us.

In the end we decided that its classic status was simply a case of music journalists doing their level best to demonstrate that they just knew more than you did, but we all really liked the record anyway, so it hardly mattered one way or another. All the same, just before he lay back, shut his eyes and allowed the music to dominate the room I could see in Tom's face a determination that one day he would be the one dictating matters of taste to other people, rather than the other way round.

*

It had been a couple of weeks since we had been out properly, which was a lifetime. My only outlet had been football, and that just wasn't the same since Tom had stopped playing. I had been moved into his position in the centre, but I was a pale shadow of him. I worked hard, but I couldn't do what he could, dominating the game and effortlessly running the show. At least City were doing the business for once, making it to a cup final, albeit a dodgy one no one had heard of before. We could just see the Maine Road floodlights from where we were, beacons of hope in an otherwise bleak landscape.

We talked about what came next, thankfully not another discussion about university but with regards to The Manifesto. We were both tentatively working on stuff for the second issue, but it felt important to let the first one have its moment and play out fully before we impetuously rushed on to the next one, but we were too full of energy and ideas and it had to come out somehow or we might burst.

The Pastels were playing that night at the Boardwalk, a relatively new venue that had opened up on Little Lever Street, and we decided to check them out, although they were a little twee for my current tastes. Still, it was better than nothing. Zoe agreed to come along, too, and her redhead friend who I learned was called Gemma. When he got there, Darren and

Colin were in the queue and Jake, too, making more of a night of it. At the bar, I noticed The Manifesto on sale, on plastic display stands which made it look even more professional, somehow. Tom was talking to the manager, a nice supportive guy called Colin we had spoken to before about interviewing bands for the fanzine, before we had decided against it.

'Take my advice,' he had cautioned. 'Don't bother. If you're going to meet your idols, do it as equals, not as star-struck fanboys.'

Tom came back over, looking really pleased with himself. I gave him a quizzical look, but he shook his head as The Pastels shambled onto the stage more like technical crew rather than the star turn.

'I'll tell you later,' he said.

We had hoped the Mary Chain warm-up had been a blip, but The Pastels were terrible, amateurish and largely devoid of charisma, although I liked some of the songs and admired what they were trying to put together back in Glasgow, trying to establish a mutually supportive music scene. I put it down to a bad job by the sound technician, but that was probably generous. Zoe and Gemma seemed to like them, and afterwards Gemma bought a T-shirt from their merchandise stall, which she immediately put on in front of us, though it was a good size too small. She stuffed her other top into her handbag.

Jake was scathing about the performance. The band's, not Gemma's.

'Honestly, I could do better than that,' he declared, and we didn't doubt it.

'You need to put your money where your mouth is, though,' said Darren. 'That's the thing.'

Tom put his arm around Jake's shoulder. 'Bobby's right, you know. You need to get a decent band together.'

I was confused. 'Who the fuck's Bobby?'

Darren smiled proudly. 'That's me,' he said. 'Ever since I pulled that cracker at The Venue. Bobby Dazzler.' He puffed out his chest and struck a pose. 'Most handsome man in Manchester.' His laugh was as infectious as cholera. The Pastels' set had at least been mercifully short, and we stayed afterwards and drank and danced until Gemma's dad came to pick her up and we blagged a lift home along Oxford Road and beyond. As we passed the Toast Rack, I jumped out with Zoe, though Tom stayed put.

'See you around,' he said. I gave him the same look he had given me about the girlfriend thing, and he just grinned back at me. He was more drunk than I realised. I looked at Zoe and she just shrugged. The car drove off and then stopped, reversing back up to where we stood. He wound the window down and shouted out:

'I forgot to tell you. There's a big festival this Summer. Ten years of punk or something. And I've got us free tickets.' He waved pieces of cardboard at me out of the window, then tapped three times on the roof to signal that it was okay to take him to wherever they were going.

*

At home, it was the same old story, Maxine comatose in the darkness. Had there been a fire, I highly doubted she would have stirred, but at least Gary and Deb were vigilant next door. We nimbly made it to the stairs where we silently dissolved into each other's arms. One of the girls stirred slightly when we went into my bedroom but mercifully went straight back to sleep, leaving us to it. I had heard Just Like Honey at The Boardwalk before the band came on, and it was still in my head because that was how I felt with Zoe, something beautiful emerging from swirls of chaos, even though I knew that Jim Reid was singing about smack. If it some kind of warning, it wasn't one I was ready to hear just yet.

On the wall by my bed, I had created a collage of Colin's photos, including one of Miranda taken against a post-industrial vista of an abandoned factory that resembled a post-apocalyptic urban hell, its roof-tiles stolen so that the grim sky could be seen through the crumbling walls.

Zoe was aghast. 'Seriously?' she said. 'You've got a picture of another girl on your fucking wall?' She punched me on the arm, not playfully.

'It's a beautiful image,' I protested.

'Oh, it's beautiful alright. She's stunning.' She was physically pulling away from me. 'So why is there no photo of me up there?'

I shrugged defensively. 'Because I can't afford a camera? Because you haven't given me one?' I sat upright, trying to calm her down before she disturbed the girls.

'Just to be clear,' she said, 'I am mortally offended right now.' She couldn't take her eyes off the photo. 'What is it with you and this girl?'

'There's nothing between Miranda and me,' I said. 'I like her, that's all. She's cool.' I put my arms around Zoe to reassure her, but she was cold to the touch. 'I'm here now, with you. That's what I want.'

'And I want that photo to be taken down right now,' she whispered, squirming to avoid me.

I did as she bid, although the space it left when I peeled it off the wall was as artless to me as the photograph was beautiful, and I resented her for making me remove it. Against the derelict backdrop, Miranda was like the first snowdrops pushing through the hard earth, exquisitely formed, a thing of beauty. Her cheekbones caught the tentative light, as sharp and precise as the metal girders that framed her all around. I felt like I was suddenly playing a game where somebody had neglected to inform me of the rules so that every move I made was destined to place me in a disadvantageous position. I didn't much care for it.

*

Apparently, Zoe had made a prior arrangement with Gemma, and presumably Tom, to pick her up in the morning so I could get on with getting the girls ready for church without having to worry about her. I dropped them off with Deb and Gary.

'You've got a free morning,' said Gary. 'My brother called. He's not well or something. Says he'll still pay you, though, for your trouble.'

'It's no trouble,' I said. 'I'm really grateful for the work and he's a nice kid. He doesn't need to do that.'

'I know,' said Gary, 'but it's fine. He's loaded.'

Typical. It was a good outcome, but now there was no need for Zoe to have gone so early.

I went back inside where Maxine was awake.

'So, who's the girl?' she asked. It was obviously a lucid day. I was tempted to play dumb and act like it was another hallucination, but she had enough problems without me gaslighting her.

'Just a girl.'

'She's lovely,' said Maxine. 'A real class act.'

I looked at her in disbelief. 'Really?' I said. 'You really think you get to have an opinion.' I headed upstairs to tidy up, the only part of the house I could control.

'Don't be like that,' she called after me. 'I was just saying, that's all. She seems lovely. Anyway, shouldn't you be next door?'

'I can manage my own life, thanks all the same, Maxine.' I couldn't believe the cheek of her. 'You should try doing the same.'

I had a ton of work to do, essays and revision. Even on a good day when all I had to endure was her fake niceness rather than the usual demented vitriol, any brief encounter with Maxine was enough to inspire me to put pen to paper if the alternative was staying here much longer. An essay on the Bolshevik coup came easily to me, so I allowed myself the luxury of starting a new piece for The Manifesto. I started to write about graphic novels and the new wave of science fiction championed by JG Ballard, who wrote provocatively apocalyptic novels about urban alienation and the psychological impact of bad urban planning. It was something I could easily identify with, growing up in a city where even the architecture seemed oppressive, claustrophobic, looming buildings shutting out the light. The Hulme flats which housed a multitude of people to the south of the city centre were true monstrosities straight out of one of his novels, and I could hear a lot of his influence in much of the music I listened to. If you were to dramatize his work, Numan or Joy Division would be the perfect soundtrack capturing the icy horror of his psychotic protagonists. My working title was The Concrete Island, named after the one book of his I hadn't read. Even the book exchange on Shudehill had let me down, even though every book I was interested in seemed to wash up on its grubby shores sooner or later. It was easy to identify with his work, growing up hemmed in by brick and concrete so that the horizon was never more than a few feet away. It was a big city but a small world, or at least that's how it felt sometimes.

I made a decent start but ran out steam and even drifted back off to sleep until the girls came rushing in telling me all about Jesus and all the good things he had done. I indulged them, listening to them retelling the parables extolling the virtues of being a good person and helping others less fortunate, working on the basis that there was little harm that could come from feeding them such ideas. Soon enough, reality would disavow them of such fanciful ideas, or else they would follow Deb's footsteps into sainthood. Although they were old friends, I had heard Maxine complain that she was only like that to get a fast-pass to Heaven, and maybe that was true, but either way she was more of a mother to me and the girls than Maxine would ever be, and a better person, too.

I carried on working through the afternoon with a little more focus. Miraculously, Maxine was still relatively lucid and I allowed myself the luxury of allowing myself to focus on college work on the assumption that things were quiet downstairs and so presumably the girls were safe. As I tired, I became distracted, which was never a good thing. I tried to get into The Cult's new album which had seen them take a dramatic turn towards the rock market and presumably greater prospects of mainstream success. I was certainly not averse to the concept of bands evolving their sound, but it sounded over-produced and I couldn't help feeling a little betrayed by the more commercial sound, as if they owed anything to me. Part of me knew it was ridiculous, and I certainly didn't begrudge anyone making a decent living out of their art, but I needed to feel that they were being true to themselves rather than following a trend in order to gain more recognition. It might have been cool to be obscure, but if that was how you made a living, then even I had to concede that cult status was a poor consolation in every sense of the word. The track *Revolution* finally did for me, sounding so retro as to become a parody of itself, as if we were still living through the revolutionary days of '68 rather than the slow chokehold that Thatcher had placed on the country, so I turned off the stereo.

Downstairs, it felt too quiet. Years of anxiety about the girls had heightened my senses. If they were playing next door, I could usually hear them squealing through the walls. In the house, they constantly chattered to each other, a sort of low-level babbled dialect that was somehow soothing. They experienced everything through the prism of their sibling before anyone else was invited in and that manifested itself in their shared secret language.

I went downstairs and found Bella hugging Sindy, whose face was red. Instantly, I could see she was choking. Her eyes bulged with fear. I slapped her on the back a couple of times to no avail and then did my best to imitate something I had seen on TV, placing my arms around her and squeezing, taking care not to apply too much pressure and crack her little ribs. Bella was sobbing.

'Deb!' I ordered. 'Go get her!'

I didn't have much of a clue what I was doing but it was all I had. Rhythmically, I squeezed as hard as I dared. The back door went and I was aware of Deb coming in as Sindy convulsed and spat out some kind of food then collapsed into my arms.

I could hear myself shouting 'It's okay, it's okay!' over and over again, as much to reassure myself as my sister. After a while, Deb eased me aside to take a look at Sindy, whose was still quiet and unusually subdued and red of face, breathing hard.

'Where's Maxine?' asked Deb.

'Not a clue. She was down here with them earlier. It seemed okay. She was having a good day.' Of course I should have known better.

'Mummy went out,' Bella explained. 'She said to be quiet because you were working.'

I exchanged glances with Deb. We both knew what it most likely meant when Maxine went out in the afternoon.

'We need to get her to the hospital,' said Deb. 'Get her checked out, just in case.'

'Can I go?' asked Bella.

'You stay with me,' said Deb, taking her hand. 'Come over to mine. She'll be fine, just you wait and see.'

'I'm sorry,' said Bella. 'We were hungry so I got something to eat.'

I gave her a hug, a bizarre parody of the dramatic embrace I had just given her sister. 'It's fine,' I said. 'You did nothing wrong.' I felt her squeeze me back as hard as she could, pleased to be absolved. 'You're the best sister anyone could hope for.'

Deb pulled her away. 'Come on, love. Let's see what we can find to do.'

Gary was out with the car and I didn't have the money for a taxi so I decided the bus was the quickest option to get her to Casualty, which was only a mile or so away. There had to be some benefit of living on the busiest bus route in Europe. She was a little distressed but it didn't seem like an ambulance was in order. Her face was still blotchy, and she was very quiet as I wrapped a coat around her shoulders and carried her outside, pulling the door to.

They were lovely with her at the hospital and made a real fuss of her, giving her a sticker for being brave and even a lolly reserved for the prettiest patients. Tom's mum was working a shift and she came over to have a word as soon as she saw me. She gave me a hug and checked the charts.

'She's fine,' she said, nodding.

'Thank God for that,' I said.

'Thank you, God,' Sindy echoed in her tiny voice, looking up into white polystyrene ceiling tiles which I guessed could resemble heavenly clouds if you were young enough and oxygen deprived, doubly so with flickering fluorescent lighting.

'Where was your mum?'

'Your guess is as good as mine,' I replied. 'I'll bloody kill her when I find her.'

She gave me a sympathetic look, tinged with a note of caution. 'You need to take care of your sister,' she reminded me. 'She's your priority. She had a close call today.'

The reality of what had happened hit home and it took an effort to keep from breaking down. She patted me on the arm.

131

'Go home, she said. 'Do something nice together. She's fine, honestly, but just keep an eye on her all the same. If you think you need to bring her back in, don't think twice, okay?'

'Better safe than sorry, eh.'

'Exactly.'

On the bus home, I saw Maxine stumbling along the street, the worse for wear. Sindy saw too and waved energetically, but her mother was too far gone to notice. I almost stopped her hand but decided it wasn't my place to shatter the myth just yet that mummy loved her. That wasn't any kind of love that I could recognise, just a lingering emotional connection left behind when the cord was cut. When she came home an hour or so later, she had a Curly Wurly in her pocket for each of us and it was so truly pathetic that I couldn't even be angry. Her mind had been anaesthetised by alcohol so she could neither think nor feel, and even if I had possessed the energy and the words to let her know what had happened, it wouldn't have made the slightest difference. It could wait till morning.

I went to bed with the girls to keep a watch over them as they went to sleep, reading them a chapter of Five Children and It before turning out the light. I didn't think sleep would come, but it overwhelmed me as soon as I shut my eyes, dreaming all night of broken dolls so that when morning finally came, I was shattered.

Eleven

Still, life went on. Later that week, we had arranged to meet up with Colin outside Affleck's Palace so he could show us the latest batch of photos he had taken. If anything, he was getting better. He was even having some success selling some of his work which meant he could afford to buy more film, but we made sure we gave him some of the money we had picked up over the past few weeks, so he felt a full and valued part of the creative team working on The Manifesto. All along, we had wanted it to be a collective project, providing a showcase for the various talents of the friends we had accumulated over the years.

There were a lot of photos of Miranda in there, too, not just the ones he had taken in the café but all around what he fancifully termed the beauty spots of the city. As he had suspected, she was the perfect muse and his technical prowess lent an ethereal gracefulness to her innate good looks. The monochrome aesthetic perfectly captured both the inherent bone structure and confidence as well as the city's soft-focus melancholia. She didn't really look like other girls I knew; there was something exotic about her, an enigmatic quality as if she didn't quite belong to any particular time or place.

'These could be published in Vogue,' Tom remarked, as if that was the pinnacle of success.

'She gives good face,' he said, then blushed when we both started laughing. 'Oh, grow up,' he protested. 'You both know exactly what I mean.' He walked round with us while we dropped off more copies of The Manifesto and discussed ideas for the next issue with him and found him as receptive as ever.

'Is your work not getting suspicious about the amount of paper that's going missing?' he asked.

'He's good at keeping them distracted,' I explained enigmatically, so Tom had to explain what was going on and Colin insisted on walking with him into the printers so he could check her out.

'What about that other girl?' he asked.

'Gemma.'

'Yes, the redhead you were with the other night.' He was so lost in his art that he found it hard to keep track of what the rules were when it came to social interactions. He was fine with us because we generally indulged him by letting him talk about his work. I could happily listen to almost anyone talk about something they were obsessed by and expert at, vicariously feeding off their passion.

'She's just a mate,' said Tom.

'A mate? I thought you were...you know.'

Tom laughed. 'Well, yeah, sure, but she knows how it is. It's just a bit of fun. I'm too busy for anything serious and I'll be going away soon.'

'Does she know it's a just a bit of fun, though?' asked Colin. He could be very serious sometimes. We were standing outside the printers. 'And what about this one?'

'They both know the score,' he said reassuringly. 'I never make any promises. And I can guarantee that they're having a lot of fun.' There was a cheeky glint in his eye. 'You jammy sod.'

Tom started to walk off laughing to himself, but Colin called him back. 'She asked me to give you these,' he explained.

'Miranda. She only went and got the part in that play she was auditioning for.' He handed us a load of tickets for a production of *Medea* at the Contact Theatre. 'And she got me a job taking photos for the programme. I got fifty quid. I went to rehearsals and it's good. A bit weird, and I didn't understand all of it, but it's worth going to.'

I walked with Tom as far as the printers.

'I could get quite used to this,' he said. 'People offering us free tickets for things.' The previous night we had been on the guest list at The Boardwalk to see The Waltones, a fun lightweight pop act whose singer would achieve national attention many years later as the heroic survivor of an unprovoked terror attack at Victoria Station.

'Yeah, I agreed. 'You could even give up this shitty job. We keep losing without you.' Saturday mornings had become depressingly routine.

'It has its benefits, though,' he reminded me.

'For you, maybe. I don't get to shag the girl in the leather skirt.'

'True, but we're effectively getting free printing, so it's still worth it. For now, at least. It won't be forever. Wish me luck,' he said, bouncing up the stairs.

'When did you ever need luck?' I called after him, but he was already gone.

*

As if to prove a point, college provided him with a pair of return rail tickets to London to attend his interview at the LSE as part of a policy to support aspirational students of modest means. The other ticket was intended for his mum but she couldn't change her shift at the hospital, so I went with him. Gary and Deb stepped up and ordered me not to pass up the opportunity to broaden my horizons, so off we went on an adventure.

Typically, he refused to dress up for it.

'They can have me as I am or not at all,' he insisted. We bought a four-pack at the station and spent the journey comparing articles for the second issue which was coming together far quicker than the first although he hadn't started work on the design. As we neared London, we got talking to a

135

guy on the seat opposite who claimed he worked for Smash Hits and suggested we send him some articles if we were looking for work. He was nice enough and full of praise for what we showed him, but when we arrived at Euston I saw Tom throw the guy's contact details in the first bin we passed.

'Bullshitter,' he had decided, and that was that. Either way, the incident reinforced our prejudice that London was unfairly blessed as the place to be if you wanted opportunities to fall in your lap, whereas we had to work hard for everything.

I assumed we would head straight off, but we had got an early train and Tom led us via a hand-drawn map to Tavistock Square to show me something. In a row of imposing houses, he located number 21 and informed that that Lenin had briefly lived there before the revolution had given him better things to do. It was hard to imagine that at another time less than a century earlier, one of our great heroes had inhabited the very spot in which we were standing. I felt like I was standing in a science fiction film, as if his essence still inhabited the same spot years later.

A man tapped me on the shoulder. 'Can I help you?' he inquired.

'We're looking for Lenin,' I explained.

'Well, he's not here,' the man said. He had a brolly with him like something out of an Ealing film.

'We know that,' I said. 'But he was.'

The main pointed with his brolly 'You want number 27,' he said. 'They changed the numbers. They want to put a blue plaque up for that filthy communist, you know. Can you believe it? We lie in our beds worrying about the reds dropping the bomb, and the idiots in control of London want to commemorate him.'

I expected Tom to put him in his place but he let it go and walked across to the right house. We stared up at the windows as if that great domed head would appear and wave. 'I know what you're thinking," he said, 'but there was nothing I could say to influence someone like that other than to tell him to fuck off, and I'm trying to be on my best behaviour.'

Still in no hurry, he led me off towards the British Library so we could check out the Magna Carta on display, the significance of which he had to explain to me. It just looked like any other piece of ancient parchment.

'This is important,' he said, 'because it limited the absolute power of the monarchy.'

I remembered something from a history lesson. 'Absolute power corrupts absolutely.' He nodded. I was good at the broad strokes but not so good at the finer details.

'Except it's not as revolutionary as it sounds. All it did was gave more power to the Norman lords. None of it passed down to the commoners. It was just a power grab by the rich and powerful.'

'So just like now.'

'Exactly,' he said. 'Nothing much ever changes. The rich getting richer at the expense of the poor.'

It was a timely reminder that his interview was looming. It was hard for us not to feel overwhelmed by the sheer size of the capital, though the convoluted transport system tends to distort distances to make it seem bigger than it really is. We walked as much of it as we could, trying not to be impressed by the wealth of history that appeared around each corner, memorialised in blue plaques for rich and powerful ghosts or scraping the sky with huge phallic constructions that sprung from the fertile streets. Occasionally, we stopped to get our bearings and take in the view. It was hard not to be impressed, and we were trying pretty hard, as if we were cheating on the city we loved.

Subconsciously, we were doing the 'Manc swagger' through Bloomsbury, shoulders swinging as we stomped through unknown territory, hoping to breathe in some of the literary air, but not too much. We caught our reflection in a shop window and laughed at the sight of us, but it didn't stop us or even slow us down. The clock was against us but even with our scrawled notes we made our way unerringly to Westminster, past the Courts of Injustice to the appointed location. I wished him luck and located a pub where I tried to make a pint last two hours while I read the New Musical Express, Melody Maker and Sounds in turn before he returned.

'How was that, then?' I asked.

He seemed a little unsure of himself, but nodded affirmatively. 'It was good,' he responded. 'Interesting.' It was a bit of an effort for him to respond as if his mind was elsewhere.

'When will they let you know?' I was interested in the mechanics of university applications on the off chance that I actually found the nerve to apply.

'They already did.' He did not elaborate on his answer, so I feared the worst for him. He took a drink to savour the moment.

'I'm in.' He even allowed himself a little self-satisfied smile.

'That's great,' I said. 'I'm really pleased for you.'

'Yeah, thanks.' He wandered over to the bar to get a drink, pulling a face at the exorbitant price compared to what we were used to. 'It's dependent on grades, of course,' he said. His voice trailed off as it was almost an inevitability that he would achieve the required tariff with room to spare. 'It was a strange old interview. Not at all what I expected. They asked me what statue I would erect if I had a free choice.' He shook his head. ' 'Trying to catch you off guard.'

'I guess do. Or trying to see if you can think on your feet under pressure. I suppose they get sick of hearing the same old crap from every applicant.'

I honestly had no idea what his answer would have been.

'It's a brilliant question, if you think about it. Catching you off guard, your answer is going to reveal a lot more about your personality and the way your mind works.'

'So, what was your answer.'

He laughed. 'I started by saying I didn't agree with the concept of memorialisation. I mean, who gets to choose?'

'And yet you love sitting under that statue of Marx,' I reminded him.

'True, but it doesn't really mean anything, does it? It's just a way of trying to gain vicarious credit for Marxism, when all he really got out of being in Manchester was a sense of the human horror of industrialisation. It's just a photo opportunity for lazy tourists, when for me it's more about remembering my dad taking me there and telling me all about Marx and Engels and the importance of the struggle.'

I couldn't argue with that.

'Anyway,' he went on, 'the interviewer wouldn't go for that argument. I had to pick someone. To buy some time, I talked for a bit about going to Lenin's house but decided erecting a statue of Lenin in Tavistock Square would be as meaningless as a statue of Colonel Sanders. It would be divisive. You could see that in the reaction of that guy who came out to redirect us to the right house. It would mean different things to different people.'

'You could have suggested a war memorial,' I offered. 'They bring people together in a common cause, to remind future generations what others have sacrificed for them.'

'Yeah, tried that one, too,' he said. 'Also rejected. I had to pick a person. A real person, too, not something emblematic like the fallen soldier or an honest square-jawed worker in a hard hat. They were the rules.'

'This is hard.' I conceded. He went and ordered more drinks while I gave it some thought. I could see the importance of statuary as civic art, as a means of honouring good service and sacrifice. The Marx statue in Manchester was, after all, one our favourite haunts to take a break and gather our thoughts, as if some of that great wisdom would elevate us in some nebulous way. Having recently been marched through Trafalgar Square, I could readily understand the visual impact of monumental figures of the great and good, people who embodied universally acknowledged virtues to which we should all aspire. They also endow a greater sense of gravitas to a particular place, so those virtues of courage and sacrifice and leadership or whatever become bound to that place for as long as the statues remain, granting observers some social and historical perspective. To orientate themselves in time and space. The problem, of course, is the question of who gets to decide what those values are and who those influential people are who represent the greatest attributes of any given period.

'Just imagine,' he said upon his return with the drinks. Apparently, he could work out what I was thinking from my pained expression. 'In our lifetime, people will try to erect a statue of Thatcher.'

The thought was shocking, but I could see he was right. It was a matter of perspective. One person's champion was another's person's monster, someone who destroyed communities and stripped honest people of their dignity. In effect, the question at hand perfectly illustrated a significant social problem, that the erection of monuments was a devious means by which the elite reinforced their own status and hegemonic power.

'Rich white men erecting statues of rich white men,' I concluded.

'Exactly,' said Tom. 'Or women, if you can call Thatcher a woman.'

'So, who did you choose?' I knew him well enough to know that he would have come up with something interesting, especially as he had already told me that he had effectively passed the test.

He gave me a mischievous smile. 'I went for Edith Nesbit,' he said. 'You know, the writer. It just popped into my head. I decided the best option was to do to him what he was trying to do to me. He never saw it coming.'

I immediately gave up. 'Explain.'

'For starters, she was one of the founders of the Fabian Society. Remember we studied them last year. I know they're a bit wet, a social revolution over the course of a century and all that, but their hearts were in the right place.'

I remembered. 'The wolves in sheep's clothing.'

He laughed approvingly. 'They couldn't even stick to that because it was too aggressive-sounding, but yes. The point is, they set up the LSE, the first part of the social revolution. A place for radical thinkers to do their thing.'

'And she's a woman. So, she's a good choice from the feminist angle.'

'Now you're getting it. And she was a writer so she fused art with radical politics.'

I wasn't having any of that. 'Come off it. It's not like *The Railway Children* is *Das Kapital* for kids.'

He was unmoved. 'I never said she was the perfect choice. But she did the trick, didn't she. Picking her showed that I had done my homework into what the LSE stood for. And she wrote *The Enchanted Castle*, remember. What's not to like?'

'I love that book. I was terrified when the dinosaurs came to life.' We both loved that book as it turned out.

'And as luck would have it, so did the guy doing the interview,' Tom explained. 'He's a huge fan of the Crystal Palace dinosaurs. He's part of a group trying to get a preservation order for them. The acid rain is dissolving them, apparently.'

'Now that's what I call a great statue.' I did a T Rex impression, flimsy arms and terrible jaws. Someone on the next table gave me a funny look, which I ignored. The realisation started to hit home that he was going to come and live in London and I would be left alone in Manchester. 'I just don't know how you get so lucky.'

He shook his head. 'You know better than that,' he said. 'It isn't luck, not in the way you mean. You have to put yourself in a position where you can take advantage of opportunities that come your way. That's the hard bit.'

We finished our pints and we set off again. We hadn't even noticed it wasn't raining. It wasn't what you would call a pleasant day, but it wasn't wet and it wasn't cold. Deb and Gary had pressurised me not to be home early. The idea was to get a late train back home so we could take in as much of London as possible, walking and using buses so we could take in the sights. Taking the Tube seemed pointless and disorientating as we had no interest in seeing underground London, except in the cultural sense.

We strolled past the Wellington Memorial on the long hike to the Rough Trade record store, Tom delighting in telling me that the statue was made out of captured cannons as a great fuck you to the enemy. He loved that sort of detail. We wondered what his E Nesbit statue would be made out of and decided that it should be constructed of papier mache consisting of pulped novels by bad right-wing writers or pampered members of the elite whose work had seen the light of day only because of vanity publishing. Then we moved on to whether it would stand up to the elements, although Tom convinced me that if substantial sections of the Great Wall of China could be made of hardened rice, there was no reason why not.

At Rough Trade, we agreed for them to stock a dozen or so copies of The Manifesto and both bought an LP just so we could walk around with the iconic bags. I bought *Bad Moon Rising* because Sonic Youth were booked to play The Boardwalk in a few weeks and they were a band I felt I wanted to know better. Tom spent ages choosing and eventually went for *Shoulder to Shoulder* by Test Dept., not because he particularly wanted it but because he felt a sense of loyalty to their support of the Welsh miners.

The thin London light was failing when we eventually left the store. The thought struck me that even if they sold out of The Manifesto I would never get to see any of the money, although the point was just to get the word out there in as many outlets as possible. Then I remembered that this was to become Tom's new home, that this would be his regular record store and that in the next few months everything I thought I knew was going to be taken apart and would never be quite the same again.

On the train home, he was unusually quiet for the first part of the journey, probably thinking much the same.

'You're going to love it there,' I told him, not because I was trying to reassure him but because I knew it was the truth. In his head, he was already moving on.

'In the interview, we talked about The Manifesto. He wasn't really interested in what I was doing in college. I guess that's the same for everyone so what's the point? He wanted to know what I did for fun, how I used my time, so I told him.' 'And?'

He shifted uncomfortably in his seat. 'And I listened politely enough. He let me talk for a couple of minutes and then he said...' His voice trailed off as if he was trying to recall the exact words. 'Basically, he told me not to place too much importance on it,' he said. 'It's just a fanzine. Just a bit of fun to fill the time. He was a bit more interested in the pricing thing,' he went on. 'Asked how much people tended to pay. I started to explain what it was about, why it was important, but he sort of shushed me. He said it was fine, a good thing to have done, but that was it.'

'Bloody cheek.'

'I know, but maybe he had a point.' It was disconcerting to see some doubt creeping in, a little shadow tainting the bright sunlight of his soul. When he looked at me, I could see in his eyes that a little of that youthful lustre had gone. 'When I come back home,' he said, 'I'm going to be a different sort of person.' He stared out of the train window at the world that seemed to be rushing past us, his eyes fixed on the infinite distance.

I didn't have an answer or a word of comfort, if that was what he required of me, so we sat in silence for a while.

'It really wasn't luck, you know,' he said apropos of nothing as we hurtled through Stoke-on-Trent, mercifully spared the views as evening fell with a sudden urgency. 'In the interview. There was a photo of him and another bloke on his desk standing next to a fibreglass Iguanodon. I just put two and two together.'

'Elementary, my dear Barton,' I mocked him. 'There I was thinking you're some kind of genius, and in fact you're just a total chancer.'

'I think you'll find it's much the same thing, old chap,' he replied. 'See your chance and seize the moment.' The mood lightened and we rolled into Piccadilly station right on time, which was a miracle, a little embarrassed by its squalid, functional design after having walked a few hours earlier past the gothic majesty of St Pancras which was like a portal to a magnificent adventure. We caught a ride onto Oxford Street and raced down the steps to the Salisbury Arms just in time for last orders. In some indescribable way, the pollution smelt sweeter somehow, and it felt great to be home again.

We ended up back at Tom's. His mum was still up psyching herself up for the graveyard shift at the hospital but still excited to hear what his day had been like. I loved being round there, the mutual respect and good food and the feeling that it was a real home. Because of the very real life-and-death nature of her job as a nurse, she was very grounded. There was no pressure on him to stay that others at college talked about, no desperate cloying maternal need to infantilise him and keep him at home. She wanted him to grow up and move on, not because she didn't love being around him but because that was what nature

144

demanded, that the next generation are encouraged to be independent and find their own place in the world. I could see all this remotely as they interacted, like a scientist coldly examining something they had never experienced themselves, but it didn't make me feel sad. I was pleased for him, for both of them. They were lovely people, and it made me feel good that they had invited me into their lives.

'How's your sister, by the way?' she asked.

I nodded. 'She's good. No harm done.'

'She's such a sweet pretty girl,' she said. Her voice sort of trailed off and I could feel the regret in her voice, that sad knowledge of what was waiting for her when her innocence faded.

'And what about you?' she asked.

I shrugged. 'What about me? I'm fine.'

'Oh, come on, you know what I mean.' She was used to my little ways. 'Have you made any decision about what you're going to do next year?' She put her arm around me. 'You don't have to stay here forever, you know. People would understand.'

I hugged her, feeling the alcohol soften me. 'Thanks. I do know. It's just so hard. Every choice I make seems so huge. People get hurt whatever I do. The thought of going away to study just feels so self-indulgent.'

'You've always been a lovely boy, Alex,' she said. 'I know you'll make the right decision when the time comes. You've got a big future just waiting for you out there, you know.'

She seemed genuine and I wished I believed it, too, but it wasn't that easy. 'Tom's going to love it in London,' I said, changing the subject. 'I hate to say it, but I had a great day. It's too big and too smelly and too rich, but you're going to love it there. But if you come back a Chelsea fan, I'll beat you senseless.'

He smiled. 'Support the rent boys? No fucking way.'

'Tom, no swearing,' his mum chided, but she was laughing, too. She poured us another drink. 'Have you thought about studying in Manchester?' she asked. 'It's a good uni.' 'And I've heard it's a great city,' said Tom.

I had thought about it. Zoe's mum had mentioned the same thing, but it felt pointless. What I thought I needed was escape, independence, a chance to discover who I would become when unburdened by the responsibilities that been forced upon me. On the table, there was a photograph of a younger prettier version of her with Tom and his dad taken on a beach that must have been Blackpool.

'Getting a degree would still open a lot of doors,' she persisted. I loved her for the care she felt for my wellbeing, but she could see I was unconvinced so she tried a different tack. 'Come on, Tom,' she said. 'What would you do in his shoes?'

He was silent for a long time, as if he was about to say something he knew was contentious. He didn't look at me when he spoke. 'Honestly, I don't think I would go away. I think it would hurt me. If I had fun, I would feel guilty. If I did well, it would feel selfish.'

'Bloody hell,' I joked. 'I wasn't expecting that.' It felt like a slap. He looked at me and I could see that the alcohol had finally got to him, loosened his tongue. 'Don't take this the wrong way,' he said. 'Please. I'm just telling you what I think. I know you. I really know you, how you think, how you feel.' His eyes were red in the electric glow. 'In the end, I just think it would make you sad. You would have a degree, but I think what you came home to would just disable you.'

'So, do what then?' asked his mum. It still seemed incredible to me that she valued his opinion.

He was less sure of himself now. 'Yeah, that's the thing. I sensed he had spent more time thinking about this than he had his own possibilities. 'You've got to believe in yourself more.'

'Easier said than done.'

'This city is going to change,' he said. 'It's been starved for so long, but it's starting to change. Things are happening all over. It's starting to evolve. Everything that happened in the past, it's going to kickstart a regeneration. A renaissance. All those little things that are starting to happen, it's leading somewhere that I think you'll want to be a part of.'

'So, what are you saying?'

He was staring right through me. 'Honestly, learn a trade. You pick things up so quickly when someone gives you a shove. It doesn't matter what. An electrician, a bricklayer, whatever, it doesn't matter what you pick. Just be the best you can be and things will happen for you. I'm sure of that. They're going to take this city and build it right back up again and make it something special. So, what should you do? Stay. Become a part of it. You need to keep doing what we're already doing, breathe it all in.'

'You're pissed,' his mum told him.

'I am,' he said, 'but it's all true, every last word of it. You're going to come and see me in London and I'll feel jealous every time you head back home.'

'Sorry boys, but I need to head off,' his mum announced, checking her watch. It was late, and the relentless morning was waiting so I decided to leave, too. His mum hugged me again as she got ready for work. I needed some air and some headspace to take it all in. Tom hugged me, too, and kissed me on the forehead. As the cold air of the streets hit me, I didn't know if he was right or not, but by the time I was in bed and sleep had overwhelmed me, I had a vison of someone standing on top of a skyscraper staring out over the city and I honestly couldn't tell if it was me.

Twelve

I had a late start at college so I walked the girls to school with Deb. I suspect she sensed that I was still freaked out by the choking incident, and more than a little guilty that I had been upstairs indulging myself while my sister had been close to death a few feet away.

'Sindy's fine, you know,' she reassured me. 'No harm done.'

'And a lesson learned.'

'Well, yes.' We waved them off and headed back.

'Nothing's changed, you know,' she said. 'The offer's still there. We would love to look after them.'

'I know, and I love you both for the offer, but it's not that straightforward, is it?'

'I'm sure we could sort something out,' she insisted. 'Between us, I'm sure we could work out some kind of arrangement that would keep Social Services off our backs.'

I stopped waking and looked at her. 'Deb, I know you and Gary mean well and I completely trust you, but we need to be realistic. We can't even get Maxine to agree to clean out the house.' I felt exhausted, defeated. 'She's totally useless, a waste of breath. Her crap's everywhere. If I bring a girl home, it's just totally humiliating. We live like animals. If I try to tidy up, she just destroys everything again. She just wants to wallow in her own chaos and drag us all down with her.'

'Not chaos,' said Deb. 'Misery. Your mum's not the Wicked Witch of the North West, you know. She's had it hard, too.'

'Yeah, poor Maxine.' I hated to hear myself sound so bitter.

'Don't be like that, love. She's broken, but she still has good days. She pretty functional most evenings, and if she's on a bender at least she lets you or me know so we can look after the girls.'

'Like the other day, you mean?' I snorted derisively. I forgot where I was and mis-stepped, treading in some dogshit. 'For fuck's sake!' I did what I could to scrape the worst of it off on the kerb. 'Let's face it, if the Social get involved any more, we'll be totally screwed.'

'I know,' she said. 'I know, love. We could start by cleaning out the house. Let's not give her a choice, eh? Me and Gary will help. I'll get him to drive it all to the tip and then we can try to start again.'

Inevitably, it stared to drizzle and the sky turned a dirty shade of dark. Looking up, the rain was not at all refreshing, although at least there might be puddles to wash my shoes a little cleaner. Tom called this a Golgotha sky, a desolate vista that made you feel hopeless, trapped. 'Thanks, Deb,' I said. 'That would be great. Really.'

I stopped obsessing about my shoes and we carried on towards home. 'Just so you know, I've been thinking of maybe not going away but learning a trade instead. A skill.'

'And waste that big brain of yours?'

'I dunno. Maybe I could put it to better use. I'm sure uni would be great but I'm really not all that smart. What would I do afterwards? I'd basically be in the same position I am now.'

'Yes, love, but with a degree.'

'True, but if I learned a trade, I would have three years of experience behind me. With money in my pockets.'

She could sense my uncertainty. 'I know you've got a lot to think about. You should talk to Gary about it, too, see what he thinks. All I can say to you is that we are here to support you in any way we can for as long as we can, but don't make a decision you come to regret later.'

As ever, her heart was in the right place, but she missed the point that you can only have regrets when it is much too late to do anything about it.

Sometimes, I felt like a person torn in half. My social life was epic, college was going well and I had a great girlfriend, so by most measures my life was pretty good. But it was self-deluding fantasy world. At home, I found myself increasingly tormented by the burden of responsibility and self-doubt about my future. I was trapped in the past, present and future all at once, like someone in a science fiction film caught in a time-loop paradox.

I had more than enough misery and melodrama in my life and needed some escapism, but we hadn't seen Miranda for a while, so seeing her performing in a Greek tragedy made a strange kind of sense. I didn't really know what to expect apart from a lot of violence and suffering and hysteria, according to Tom, so in that regard we were not disappointed. She was playing the lead role as the eponymous witch following the heroic Jason across the Mediterranean in search of adventure with his argonauts. The actor playing Jason was a muscular actor in his mid-20's who was really hands-on with her on stage and delivered his lines as though he was reading football scores, reciting rather than emoting. I had dragged Zoe along and teased her that she fancied him, largely to distract her from the incredible spectacle of Miranda on stage, doing her thing against a bleak backdrop of Colin's angular monochrome shots of Manchester's industrial heritage. The programme notes indicated that they were used to show how the protagonists were imprisoned in their own private hell of boredom and regret and betrayal, which I couldn't really argue with one way or another. Miranda was fantastic, really living the part of the tormented wife. You couldn't take your eyes off her, and I could see why the play was named after her character rather than her heroic husband who had once stolen the golden fleece. As Zoe yawned next to me, the play slowly drew me in

and at the climax, when he betrays her and she slays their
children in retaliation, I was totally numbed. Whatever I had
expected, it wasn't that. There was no hope, no redemption.
We clapped the actors robotically and stumbled out into the
night.

'Fuck me,' said Tom. 'That was intense. Who knew those
Ancient Greeks were so hardcore? That was brutal.'

'I thought the set was amazing,' Zoe said to Colin, which I
thought was kind of her. 'I thought you said they just used your
photos for the programme.'

He grinned sheepishly. 'It did look great,' he said. 'I'm really
chuffed.'

We sat on a bench outside the theatre, drinking and waiting for
Miranda to appear so we could fuel her ego.

'At the end, did she remind anyone else of Myra Hindley?'
asked Tom. 'With all those images hemming her in, the image
just popped into my head.'

'Jesus, she's a lot better looking than that evil hag,' I responded.
Zoe kicked me in the shin. 'I am still here, you know,' she said.
She was making it as clear as possible she wanted to go home.

'Yes, of course she is,' Tom agreed. 'The simple joy of a
beautiful woman in a toga and all that. But you know what I
mean, though, right? That cold-blooded despatching of little
kids. It was pure Myra.'

'You're sick,' Darren teased him. 'I never knew you had a thing
for Myra.'

Tom punched him playfully on the arm as Miranda emerged
from the bright lights of the theatre into the darkness, still
pulling pins out of her hair. He flashed Darren a look. 'Don't
you dare!' he hissed.

'So, what did you think?' she asked. 'Be honest, be kind.'

'Brutal,' I answered, honestly.

'Me?' She looked hurt.

'No, it. The play. I'm emotionally drained.'

'Great,' she said. She breathed out a melodramatic sigh of relief. 'So, what about me? Was I amazing?'

'You know you were,' said Tom. 'You totally stole the show.'

She bowed. 'Why, thank you kind sir. To be fair, the writing kind of made it easy.'

'And the toga,' said Tom.

'Oh, don't you bloody start,' she said. She had changed into her normal clothes, a pair of jeans and DM's. 'I've only just escaped the sweaty clutches of the octopus.' She mimed pushing off the unwelcome advances of an over-amorous suitor which was highly entertaining. 'Bloody actors,' she said,' always after something extra once the lights go out.'

'I assume you mean the heroic Jason?' I asked. 'Want us to go and sort him out for you?' I mimed a violent punch to the gut and she laughed.

'No, I think he's finally got the message, but thanks for the chivalrous offer.' She accepted a can of lager and took a big swig. 'Got to lubricate the throat,' she explained, helpfully. 'Anyway, I've got to do this every night for a week so I need someone to be up on stage with me.'

'Jason was, erm, something else,' I said. 'Zoe really liked him. I could tell.'

She wasn't blessed with much of a sense of humour, especially if she felt she was the target of the joke. 'Hardly,' she snapped. 'He's like an ape.'

Miranda laughed. 'Yeah, he is. But then he is supposed to be Greek.'

'Are you allowed to say that?' asked Colin.

'I can say what I like,' she said. 'I just meant Mediterranean men tend to be quite hairy. I'm sure that's why they cast him. It certainly wasn't for his acting.'

'You can say that again.'

'He does have a lot of muscles,' said Zoe unhelpfully.

'Ha, I knew you fancied him,' I cried.

'You can have him,' said Miranda, looking gratefully towards Zoe. 'Honestly, I'll be happy to sort it for you.'

Zoe grabbed my arm and pulled me towards her protectively. 'I'm all sorted, thanks. He's all yours.'

We were passing the cans of beer around as fast as we were talking and laughing. In the distance, emerging glumly from the stage door, we saw the much-maligned Jason skulking off to hail a taxi and we all waved at him over-enthusiastically although he couldn't possibly have understood why.

Tom stood up and delivered some of his lines, word perfect, flexing his muscles theatrically as he went. 'I'm sure I could do it,' he said when he had run out of steam. 'What do you say?'

'That was actually pretty good,' said Miranda admiringly. 'How did you do that?'

'I was paying attention,' he said, 'and I 've got a good memory. I just said the lines like I knew what they meant.'

'Wow,' said Miranda, laughing hard. 'That's what they call acting. You're a natural.'

'He's a natural smart-arse,' said Darren. 'And a show-off.'

Some of the other actors came over to join us. 'All actors are show-offs,' one of them remarked.

'And whores, don't forget,' said another. They were heading off for a Reclaim the Night demonstration. Miranda hesitated. 'After the mauling I've just had, I know it's the decent thing to do,' she conceded, 'but I'm knackered.' She looked at Zoe. 'What about you?'

'Me? I've got an early morning,' she politely declined. 'And my parents are coming to pick me up any minute.'

'I'll come,' said Darren hopefully. Some of the actresses were attractive and he was on a winning streak.

'It's you they need protecting from,' I joked. He looked hurt so I apologised. 'He's a lovely boy, really,' I explained.

'To be clear,' Miranda explained, 'it's not protection we need, except legally, in the courts. We just need men to stop being so rapey.'

'Amen to that.'

Suddenly I felt ashamed, though I had no idea why. 'Give 'em hell!' I said for no good reason.

'Thanks for coming all of you,' said one of the actresses, heading off. 'Tell your friends to come, too.'

Zoe's parents turned up and offered to run me home, but I decided to stay. I went to kiss Zoe, but she turned her face and offered me her cheek instead which seemed a bit off. I assumed she was tired or that she had hated the play, but I shrugged it off.

The beers kept coming as one by one people drifted away. Miranda was still drinking with us, too hyper after the show to think of calling it a night.

'Seriously, where did you learn to act like that?' I asked her.

'I was trained from birth,' she explained. 'My dad was an actor and a total hippie so I got dragged all over the world with my parents. Months in India eating lentils and discovering our spiritual selves and all that bullshit.' Her face clouded over.

'Is he famous?'

'Only in his own head.' She brightened again. 'Oh, you will definitely have seen him in stuff but nothing of any importance.'

Neither of us had ever been further than London, so the idea of travelling independently in other countries seemed intoxicatingly exotic. 'India must have been amazing,' I said.

'We lived like peasants,' she said, 'and that's never good.'

'Especially when you had a choice to live that way and they didn't,' Tom felt obliged to say.

She clapped her hands. 'That's exactly what I used to say to them. Why are we playing poor? I mean, it wasn't all bad. I remember seeing some really cool stuff but most of the time I just felt tired and dirty and really hungry. Sometimes, we would dress up and pretend to be wealthy tourists and run up huge bills in luxury hotels. I think that's where I learned how to act. We would make up crazy backstories and then run away before we had to pay up.' She shook her head. 'I guess they never quite got over the culture shock.'

'Was it really that bad over there?' I asked innocently. She gave me a queer look.

'I mean being back here,' she explained. 'Having to work to make ends meet. It destroyed them.'

'What do they do now?'

Again, the look. 'They're hippies,' she said. 'You know what they do.' She theatrically mimed someone smoking a spliff whilst nervously checking over their shoulder.

'Could be worse,' I said.

She seemed unconvinced. 'I'd like to know how.'

'Well, my mum is a non-functioning alcoholic for one thing,' I explained, 'and my dad is a living ghost.'

Her face was animated, eyes wide, taking in all the details I could offer. 'What does that even mean?' I started to see that she was one of those actresses who loved to borrow emotions from real life so I fed her some pain.

'Well, I've no memory of him at all.'

'Is he, you know, dead?'

'He might as well be.' Tom was very quiet, his eyes flicking back and forth between us, but I was aware that this was getting a little close to the bone for him. 'Anyway, fuck him,' I said, switching off. 'His loss.'

She gave me a big empathetic hug which felt genuine. 'Maybe you win,' she said. She yawned. 'Is it just me or is it totally exhausting to bare your soul like this?'

We walked with her over to a taxi rank and waited with her until one arrived.

'Thanks for coming to see me,' she said.

'Our pleasure.'

'And thanks for the beer. Sonic Youth on Saturday?'

'Yeah,' said Tom. 'Of course. Wouldn't miss it for the world. It's gonna be a big night.'

We waved her off then headed off across the road to catch our bus which rattled our weary bones away from the centre.

'She's quite something, isn't she,' said Tom. It wasn't a question but I answered anyway.

'Yup, sure is.' I was still a little bothered by Zoe's coldness and Tom could read me well enough to know exactly what was bothering me.

'Oh, that,' he explained. 'It's a girl thing. Miranda's stunning. Zoe knows it. You know it. I know. I wouldn't worry about it. It will all blow over by the weekend.'

I knew he was probably right, but as we headed off towards home, I couldn't help remembering the last time Zoe had felt insecure

I had caught her draped around some random boy at The Ritz the first chance she got. Maintaining the illusion that everything was going to be okay was getting increasingly hard and sleep was becoming elusive. I tried to fall asleep listening to music to block out the white noise of my anxieties, but even that failed me. It was going to be another long night.

*

The second issue was coming together well. Second time round, we were more efficient and had a template to work to, but it wasn't quite the same. If anything, the content was looking better and we had contributions from other people who had written in to the address we had included in the first, so it was more rounded, too. Someone had sent in an interview with the band james and Norman from The Housemartins had drawn a great comic strip showing a great new dance move how to pogo on a fascist's head. They weren't a band we were particularly fond of, but they were getting a lot of airplay and it was perfect fit as we were conscious of trying to get the right balance between entertainment and more serious pieces.

The aim was to try to get it ready to start selling at The Festival of the Tenth Summer which was the city's big summer event. Organised by Factory Records, it was a bold and visionary attempt to reinforce the city's cultural identity to the outside world to be hosted inside the newly refurbished GMex centre, a council funded arena to host major cultural events. Tom wrote an article which was to be the centrepiece of the second edition as it supported everything he had been saying about the regeneration of the city. It was hard to believe he hadn't known about it when he started telling anyone who would listen that Manchester's future was on the upturn, which was particularly ironic as he about to depart for the blinding lights of the capital. I assumed that one of his father's union friends had filled him in on what was starting to happen around the city.

In his article, he likened it to Blade Runner, describing what he called the retro-utilisation of a delapidated urban centre, repurposing buildings for a different kind of future. The city would effectively become a pimped version of itself, a new megacity crafted around the existing infrastructures so that it looked like a new city superimposed over something that was starting to fall apart. As we sat on The Stoop, drinking and dreaming and fooling around, we could start to see it happening right before our eyes, entrepreneurs starting to buy up empty warehouses in the centre and the surrounding areas at rock bottom prices, just as had happened in Manhattan in the previous decade when the punks and junkies had been forcibly kicked out by venture capitalists whose hunger for greater wealth knew no limits. For the time being, the warehouses were left empty, but over time the process of repurposing them as desirable yuppie flats and bars would commence, boosted by the city's regional and national reputation as a cool city. Boards were hammered in place over windows and doors, security measures installed and in some cases scaffolding erected to encase buildings that would see no workmen for years to come. It was a feeding frenzy of greedy investors pickpocketing the Council who were desperate to raise any kind of funds to see out the recession.

GMex itself was a prime example of what was happening. Occasionally, Tom had taken me over to watch it being refitted for a new purpose. Originally the city's central train station and linked to St Pancras architecturally by its vast wrought iron roof, it had stood as a monument to the city's decline, an abandoned transportation hub that symbolised the disconnect between the city and the capital like a severed artery spurting out money so that Manchester suffered as London grew ever more wealthy. Like the Ballard acolyte I was, I could see some kind of beauty in the rows of cranes that encircled the structure like carrion feeders stripping a carcass. Tom explained that GMex was not quite what it appeared to be. It heralded a new form of elite thievery in the form of a public-private project whereby wealthy investors supported the council in the redevelopment of the city centre in return for a share of the spoils that would hopefully follow, but without the risk that normally accompanies such a venture. Their profits were guaranteed.

'Guaranteed by who?' I asked innocently. 'The council is potless.'

'By us,' he replied. 'That's the beauty of it.'

All the same, it was hard not to be excited by the festival that Factory had planned, all the musical heavyweights of the region's cultural scene, headlined by New Order but with a great supporting cast.

For my part, I was trying to write a piece for The Manifesto to sum up what ten years of punk had meant but it was hard going, partly because I was a little too young to fully appreciate the seismic cultural shift that punk had precipitated. I could recall the thrill of seeing the word 'bollocks' on posters around the city, and the visceral shock of punks with mohawks and safety pins congregated, weirdly, around the entrance to Boots on Market Street.

'Punk was the game changer,' my article began. 'It was the harpoon that speared Mary Whitehouse and that generation of proto-Victorian puritans whose backwards-looking outlook had sought to trap us all in the joyless post-war years where even fun was rationed. It was the grenade that exploded the self-indulgent drum-kits of prog-rockers whose idea of entertainment was the twenty-minute drum solo. It was the bent safety clip that released the shackles of bloated major conglomerates who sought to enslave creative people in prohibitive contracts.

Punk was the war cry of the culturally dispossessed, seizing the means of production and showing that it was possible to write record and distribute music at a grassroots level and take on the majors at their own loaded game. It revealed that talent was not the preserve of the elite. It put words into the mouths of the common people and turned guitars into guns...'

Increasingly, what seemed really important was the democratisation of music, and all forms of culture for that matter, that idea that you no longer needed access to industrial processes to be creative. Effectively, what punk showed that anyone could do anything. The same was true for film and, of course, journalism. But I was stuck. I stood by what I had written, but maybe I wasn't the person to be writing it. I admired almost everything that punk had stood for, and everything I loved in some way owed a huge debt to what punk had fought for, but it didn't quite feel mine. Seeing the Jesus and Mary Chain had been an incendiary moment. This was music that felt like it belonged to me, the zeitgeist, in a way that restaging the moment the Pistols played Manchester couldn't compete with. It seemed significant that Pete Shelley was on the bill at GMex, playing his new solo stuff that had a distinctly modernist electronic element that was a world away from The Buzzcocks, with their perfect three-minute punk anthems. The world had moved on. I could see that it was worthwhile to pay homage to the pioneers, but I was far more excited by Sonic Youth bringing their New York indie vibe to Manchester than anything that Factory had recently put together.

*

Almost everyone we knew had got tickets and were packed tight inside The Boardwalk. Jake and Simon were getting on like old friends which, as it turned out, they were. Miranda had sent a message via Colin that she would be there as soon as the play was over. She had a taxi booked to take the short journey across town and insisted we warn the doormen that she was on her way and to let her in.

'She said she's going to read her lines quicker so she can get in time,' Colin laughed, and we didn't doubt it. Sonic Youth were a new breed of band, very much part of the New York underground scene but with an indie vibe that had brought them a lot of acclaim on this side of the Atlantic, too. It didn't make sense that they were playing such an undersized venue, but we weren't complaining.

We had all been drinking and there was a great buzz about the place at they took the stage. Technically, they were real risk-takers, detuning guitars and pushing the boundaries between music and noise so that the songs had to fight to be heard through waves of distortion and feedback. Thurston Moore was as insouciant as ever, his blonde hair tumbling across his brow as he hunched over his guitar as if he was struggling to contain something dangerous, then grabbing the mic and making his voice heard through the beautiful chaotic mess. You could see him exchanging excited looks with Kim in her pink plastic sunglasses as the songs changed pace, lulling you and then smashing back with a ferocity that took your breath away. The crowd soon got into it and Zoe dragged me into the pit as the band found their groove and roared away at us, songs melting into each other so that there was no such thing as start and end, just a seamless endless whirlwind of poetry and noise.

Halfway through and Miranda came smashing into us, her face alive with a smile as the stormy crowd sucked her in and away again. Briefly, in the tumult I caught a glimpse of Darren trying to do a stage-dive, but he didn't quite get it right and rather than ecstatically surfing the mosh-pit, he plunged heavily into the crowd and caught someone straight in the mouth with a flailing foot.

And when it all stopped and they had gone away, we were a horrible sweaty mess, deafened and happy to be alive. Wordlessly, Jake had wandered over to the stage as roadies began dismantling the equipment, desperate to learn more about how they had created that sound. You could see in his eyes that they had ignited something in him, that for all his technical skill he had been taught a lesson about the difference between proficiency and art. The best musician is not necessarily the finest songwriter.

Tom went over to the merch stall and was persuaded by the American girl running it to trade his *Unknown Pleasures* T-shirt for her phone number and a *Youth Against Fascism* shirt that would become his second skin.

Outside, in the fresh Manchester night, we hung around and traded superlatives until Jake reappeared and started to try to explain to us in technical terms what we had just experienced.

'Don't ruin it, you muso twat!' Darren shouted at him. They didn't know each other that well, but he had a way of abusing people so that they always took it as a joke. 'It just was what it was, a thing of mad beauty. You can't use words to describe something like that.'

'Point taken,' said Jake. 'I was just blown away.'

'Exactly,' said Darren, 'Just let yourself be blown away. Feel it, don't think it.'

'Glad you could make it,' I said to Miranda.

Zoe was clinging onto me, being a bit weird, and I couldn't tell if it was the drink or something else. 'She always makes it,' she said.

'By the skin of my teeth,' said Miranda.

'Of course you were,' someone said, but I couldn't tell who. I was distracted by a girl talking to Colin. There were a lot of people there we didn't know from out and about and she was really in his face, bothering him. He wasn't good in these kinds of situations.

'You need to watch yourself,' she was saying.

He had his hands up in the air defensively. 'I swear I didn't do anything,' he said, as much to us as to her.

'There's something about you,' she said. 'I don't like it.'

It was too dark to see if she was high, but she was freaking him out. She put her hands on both side of his face and kissed him on the forehead. 'You need to take care of yourself tonight.'

When she had walked off with her friends, he was still at a loss. 'What was that all about?' Tom asked.

'Damned if I know,' he said, clearly shaken up by the interaction. 'Never seen her before in my life.'

We made our way up Little Lever Street towards The Hacienda, although the music on a Saturday night was getting a bit dancey for our tastes. A queue snaked round the block, on in one out. We moved on towards The Venue, which was less fashionable and consequently less busy. In the first half hour we were there, every track was by a Manchester band, and we couldn't even tell if it was a conscious thing or simply a reflection of the strength of the music scene. The Smiths. The Bodines. New Order. James. Big Flame. The Stone Roses. The Chameleons. The sweat hadn't even dried on our young bodies and we all up again, taking over the dancefloor like we were spinning in the centre of the universe, and it was all ours, the music, the city, the future, all of it.

When I sat down, Tom and Miranda were making out.

'You must be gutted,' said Zoe.

'What are you on about?'

'Tom getting in on it before you,' she shouted in my ear. 'I know you like her.' I couldn't really make out what she was trying to say. She pushed in closer and shouter harder. 'I know you really like her.'

'I do,' I said. 'She's great.'

'You don't get it,' she said. There was an edge to her voice. 'I know you *like* her.' She stressed the word like with a kind of animalistic snarl.

'Yeah, she's cool,' I admitted. 'I do like her.'

'Well, good for you,' shouted Zoe. 'I don't.' She was glaring at Miranda's back. I followed her gaze.

'I don't like her like that,' I said, getting annoyed. 'I'm here with you, aren't I. I thought we were good.' I didn't like the look she gave. 'If they want to stick their tongues down each other's throats, so be it. I'm glad for them.' It just then occurred to me that Zoe's friend, the redhead, had gone home at some point. 'If this is to do with...' I was suddenly too pissed to remember her name. She shouted it but I still couldn't make it out. I had no idea where all this emotion had come from and it overwhelmed me. I pushed my way past them all and headed outside for some fresh air. Some guy was crouched against a wall by the snooker club sobbing for some girl who didn't want him, bleeding from a cut on his mouth.

Zoe was by my side and pushed me. She started shouting that I didn't want her and the guy looked up at me resentfully that I could be with a girl so pretty and not let her know it.

I probably should have kissed her, but I just didn't feel it.

'Why are you being like this?' I protested. 'I haven't done anything.'

'It's all about her,' said Zoe. Her voice was slurred. 'Everywhere we go, she's there all of a sudden. And you, you're just drooling all over her.'

'What the hell? You don't even know her. She's smart, and funny. That's all.' The moon had slipped behind clouds and it was suddenly very dark. Her eyes were just glints of furious colour where they caught the streetlights. 'It's you I came out with and you I'm going home with.'

'You wish.'

'What do you want from me?' I tried to keep my voice calm, steady.

'I want you to want to be with me,' she hissed. 'Not some other girl. I don't care how fucking perfect she is.' She was struggling to stand up and stumbled against me.

'I want to be with you,' I said. 'She's downstairs. With Tom. And that's absolutely fine. I fact, it's fucking brilliant. I hope they have beautiful children together.'

'What's wrong with you?' she screamed at me. 'Why aren't I enough?' Her eyes glistened with tears. 'She even said it herself the other night. She's a whore. Don't you get it?'

'She was joking,' I said. 'And you're just jealous.'

That lit the fuse. 'You know the problem with you?' she spat. I was hardly going to answer that one, but I had to wait for her scrambled thoughts to gather themselves. Even standing upright was becoming a challenge for her, let alone rationalising her thoughts. 'Your problem is that you think all women are virgins or whores, and you can't even tell which is which.'

'Is that supposed to be clever?' I asked. I think it was.

'Which is witch,' she slurred. 'You hate your mum and I get it, but when you think about what happened, she's got every reason to be fucked up.' Her hands were pushing hard against my chest. 'And you, you don't cut her an inch of slack, do you?

164

You've no pity in you, no understanding for what she went through. You're a total woman hater.'

She smiled at me through her drunken fury. 'What the hell do you know about it?' I shouted back at her.

'More than you, apparently. Have you ever bothered to look at those newspapers piled up everywhere?' I was totally taken aback from the randomness of her comment, so she took her chance and pushed me away. The crying guy struggled to his feet and said something threatening to me and I told him to back off. He lunged at me, and I would have hit him but I summoned some pity for him instead. There was no more fun to be had tonight. Enough was enough. The noise in my ears was like a shell from a storm-hit beach, not the glorious aftershocks of Sonic Youth but my own anger boiling up.

She had totally lost control and started hitting me with her tiny fists, beating against my face and chest. I pulled her away towards the bus stop before she really got herself in trouble. Then just past the Ritz, someone reached out and grabbed Zoe's arm.

'Is this kid bothering you?' he asked. He didn't even bother to look at me as if I was nothing. He had mates with him, stepping out of shadows.

Her eyes were full of tears. I grabbed her arm back and she shouted at me. 'That hurt, you dick.'

The guy pushed me hard in the chest. 'You want some?' His voice whistled menacingly through a broken tooth.

Normally I would have looked for a way out but this was not that sort of a night. I was in no kind of mood for backing down from anything. 'Why don't you just piss off and mind your own business,' I said.

His smile was sinister. 'The girl's upset. Let her speak for herself.' He tried to push me again, but I managed to knock his arm away. 'Is this kid bothering you,' he asked her. 'You want to be with a real man tonight?'

He tried to grab her again and she struck out violently with all her pitiful weight behind it. One of the bouncers came over and told us to clear off while he stood in the way of us and them to give us a chance to get away. One of them punched me on the ear and I stumbled while Zoe ran towards Oxford Road, stumbling onto a bus before anyone could follow. I ran hard but it had pulled away before I could reach the stop and then stood there, cursing hard. I waited a couple of minutes and another bus rolled up so I decided to jump on. If I was lucky and it picked up passengers by the university, it might even catch up and I could make sure she was okay.

But it never worked out like that. We got close and I thought I saw her get out in Rusholme by Platt Fields Park so I jumped out and ran after her, right by the spot where Morrissey had sung about a kid stabbed at a funfair. Everywhere in the city had a mythology. The park was empty except for me and whatever ghosts hung around just out of sight. A strange fear took hold of me, fuelled by hormones and alcohol, a cocktail that had destroyed far better people. For no good reason, I was convinced that something terrible had happened.

Then the clouds cleared, and stars lit my way and I headed to the lake in case she had plunged herself into the murky depths like some melodramatic heroine from a Kate Bush song or those classic novels she loved. Constellations danced and wavered in the water like mischievous nymphs and I almost waded in but the cold began to sober me and I gave up. Exhausted, defeated, I headed home.

One of the girls was crying in her sleep when I got home but it was just a bad dream and I quickly calmed her by holding her tiny hand. I couldn't even tell which of them it was, but her cries gently subsided to a whimper and then she was quiet. After everything that had happened, I had no real hope of sleep, but when I shut my eyes I instantly surrendered to the darkness.

Thirteen

The morning sun mocked me when I woke up. It was fiercely hot through the flimsy curtains and I was badly dehydrated so that my brain felt like it was bouncing off my skull as I moved. I poured myself a glass of water and woke the girls, so I poured out two bowls of cornflakes and was amazed to see that Maxine had remembered to put the milk back in the fridge for once so it was actually cold and raised hopes that she might be having a functional spell. The inside of my head was a horror-show and I stuck my head under the tap by the sink to try to take some of the ache away. It was a Sunday morning, so the girls were excited about the prospect of church. I could relate as I, too, was suffering like a nailed-up Nazarene and I had to face up to the prospect of trying to be keep things together for what would be two very long hours of tutoring.

The girls were quiet and self-contained but still disturbed Maxine, so I took the opportunity to slip out of the house and give Zoe a call just to check she had made it home safely. The nearest phone box had been vandalised and the next stank of stale piss so I cursed when I anxiously fumbled the coins and had to stoop to reclaim them.

Zoe's mum was not best pleased.

'Yes, she made it home,' she said, 'but no thanks to you. She was in a sorry state.' There was a long pause but there was nothing I could say but for whining excuses, so I kept my mouth shut. 'Anything could have happened to her.'

'I'm just glad she's okay. We got into some trouble and she ran off.'

'Yes,' she said. So I gather.' Again, there was a pause. 'She's still very upset. She doesn't want to talk to you right now.' She must have been feeling a lot worse than I was, so I very much doubted that she was anywhere close to conscious, but I decided not to challenge her.

'Okay,' I said numbly. 'Please just tell her I called.'

'I will.' Her voice changed. 'She was worried sick about you, you know,' she said. 'Are you okay?'

I wasn't really in a fit state to process the question. 'I will be,' I said. 'I'm sorry for any trouble.' The pips went and the line went dead. I still didn't feel I had done anything wrong, but the situation had spiralled way out of my control and could have ended far worse, and I was certainly sorry for that much.

By the time I had stumbled back home, Tom was there, his eyes red-ringed. He looked terrible. Maxine was making him a cup of tea and she poured one out for me, too, when I walked in. I could see immediately that something was wrong. There was blood on his Sonic Youth t shirt although I couldn't see a mark on him.

'Colin's mum called up,' he said. 'He never made it home.'

'Maybe he got lucky,' I suggested but when I saw Tom's face, I instantly wished I could take it back. Colin was one of those poor unfortunates who never seemed to catch a lucky break. 'What do we do?'

Tom stood up with an effort. 'We go and look for him, I suppose.'

Gary was none too impressed when I knocked on his door and told him I couldn't do the tutoring, but Deb silenced his protests with a look once Tom explained why the urgency. The unseasonal sunshine seemed wildly inappropriate as Tom paid my bus fare into town. On the way, he unravelled a sorry tale of the night before once me and Zoe had stormed off in our own selfindulgent melodrama. After I left, the others had stayed until the end and then made their way towards the bus station and home. 'It was one of those great nights,' Tom said. 'And then all of a sudden it really wasn't.'

'Yeah, I noticed you had your hands full.'

Somehow, he mustered a sheepish smile. 'Miranda? It just happened. Anyway, what happened to you? One minute you were there and then...' His voice trailed off as the bus crawled through the curry mile, the sun glinting off a thousand shiny bangles in the saree shops and we choked on diesel fumes.

'Zoe had a total meltdown,' I explained. 'Out of nowhere. All to do with you and Miranda. She went crazy, accusing me of being jealous.'

'That's called displacement,' he said out loud.

I ignored him. 'Anyway, she was pissed and angry and jealous and starting hitting me. She was a complete psycho. Then some dickhead tried to grab her by The Ritz and she ran off and I couldn't find her. It was a nightmare.'

'By The Ritz? Probably the same idiots we got into it with.'

His picture of the night before was imperfect, what Darren called Sunday vision, half-remembered hazy memories of things that may or may not have taken place, seen through the distorting prism of way too much booze.

Someone had punched Simon in the back of the head and knocked him clean out. Tom had headbutted someone and a fight had broken out, hence the blood on his shirt. He remembered Miranda booting someone on the pavement. There was a chase and they had become separated. Tom and Miranda had run into a burger place and leapt over the counter, escaping through the back while the staff grappled with their attackers. Darren had called him up in the middle of the night to say he was with Simon and Jake at the hospital getting checked out, but they were okay. No-one had heard from Colin but assumed he had got away.

Now we weren't so sure.

My head was killing me, and a devastating feeling of guilt started creeping into my thoughts, that me and Zoe were somehow responsible because we had run away so they had picked on an easier target. It must have been written all over my face.

'No more of that,' he said. 'It wasn't your fault. You were just protecting yourself. How could you have possibly known what would happen?' We jumped out by the ballet school across the road from the BBC and walked up towards Whitworth Street through litter which danced on the light breeze. We had no idea if the two assaults were even connected, but in our heads it seemed the likely assumption. As usual, we had nothing else to go on but our wits. In the distance, we could hear church bells, a sound as rare as songbird and as pretty, although it potentially signified unpleasant truths to be uncovered.

There were signs of homeless people all around, cardboard carefully laid out in doorways under arches, not the customary Dickensian tramps of old, but a new breed of wretched underclass who, like the Biblical bad seed, had fallen through cracks in the system. Apparently, this was the acceptable price of Thatcherism, when community ties were severed, and the state turned a blind eye to the losers in the deregulated shake-up.

Outside The Ritz, everything seemed fairly innocuous, the brightness of the day bleaching away any sense of lingering peril. By the adjacent snooker club, Tom found a brownish stain that was unmistakeably stale blood and rubbed his head to indicate that this was where the confrontation had taken place.

'I can't remember much,' he said hesitantly, walking up and down. He closed his eyes and willed himself to recall any helpful detail. 'Over there...' He pointed back towards The Ritz. 'Someone stepped out and smacked Simon in the head. He went down hard and Daz jumped in and started grappling with someone.' He opened his eyes and looked hard at the ground. 'Someone hit Colin and he screamed.' There was a smaller pool of brown staining the pavement and then a trail of smaller pools leading off towards Oxford Road. Tom showed me where the drips had little tails to show directionality and we dutifully followed.

'I can't be certain,' he said, 'but I think this is him. It was chaos. People shouting, punches being thrown. Daz had some twat on the ground and Miranda booted him right in the face. I remember that. Jake was with Simon, that I'm absolutely sure of.' He was still looking all around him, trying to piece the shattered image of it all back together again. 'I think someone came over to help, one of the bouncers maybe.'

We were still following the trail of blood, one drop at a time, spaced further apart.

'Looks like the bleeding was stopping,' I suggested.

'Or he was running. Being chased.' It made sense. We followed the drops across the road towards Great Marlborough Street, under the train tracks and deep into shadows where nothing good ever happened. A taxi sped by and honked its horn at us, but we disregarded the warning.

It must have been some chase. He turned left at some point and crossed Oxford Road again and headed down the old canal paths near the gay hang-outs, constantly zagging towards bright lights and anywhere more people might be about at that time of night. We didn't speak. Our fears were intensifying the further we went, sensing his fear and desperation as god knows how many people had been chasing him down as he ran for his life. He had lost a lot of blood by the time the trail came to a stop in Sackville gardens by the Rochdale Canal. You could see the disturbance of gravel where he had finally given up, skidding to a halt to suck in some desperate lungfuls of sweet air and ready to make some sort of last stand. Years later, they would erect a statue of Alan Turing here, the gay martyr. On a nearby bench, there was more frothy blood and what looked like a couple of broken teeth.

'Shit.'

I don't know which one of us even said it. It could have been anybody's blood, of course. Homophobic attacks were a regular occurrence before the gay village became a tourist spot and adrenaline was making our imaginations run wild. We both thought the same thing. The canal was a few feet away and we shared a morbid fear that he had been beaten and thrown in. Wordlessly, incapable of articulating what we both suspected, we walked over to the water's edge and peered through the gloom. We could see nothing. We threw stones into the water to break the surface to see if it cleared, but it was no good, a fruitless act at the end of a futile search. I would have cried if I could, but I was too dehydrated.

We wandered back towards the centre and found a functional phone box where Tom checked in with Colin's mum. He mostly listened. Outside, I heard him say 'nothing, there's no sign of him.' I wasn't so sure that was accurate, but it was certainly kinder. The pertinent point was that he hadn't wandered in mid-morning, hung-over and covered in blood, but alive. He had become another living ghost, neither alive nor dead.

I waited while he made a series of calls, to his mum, to Adrian, Jake, anyone he could think of. Nobody had any better news to impart, no words of hope or comfort as we baked under the formidable sun. All we knew was that Simon was okay, a bit concussed but nothing too serious.

Tom's face was a grim mask. It didn't matter that we had no idea who they were and no way to track them down other than to hang outside The Ritz like a pair of vengeful vampires all dressed in black and with nothing but bad intentions. It might as well have been a bomb for all the damage it inflicted, a single act of violence with multiple casualties.

We went to the Lass o'Gowrie to collect our thoughts. I still had no money but Tom was flush and bought a round. We sat in silence and drank like automata, mechanically tipping the glasses to our lips.

'You alright, lads?' Someone I swear I had never seen came and sat with us, a middle-aged guy named Keith who knew Tom. He drank with us, and Tom explained to him what we were looking for as the shock wore off.

'There's some right nasty bastards out there all right,' he said. 'I got jumped one night and beaten black and blue. Your dad came and sat with me in the infirmary all night. He was a great man like that, your dad was. It was when all the trouble was kicking off, when the strikes were being planned. You know, just before...' His voice trailed off and he went and bought another round. 'I'll ask around, he said. 'Sometimes people hear things. I'll let you know if anything useful turns up.'

'Cheers, big man, that would be great.' Tom shook his hand like men do.

My head was spinning as we stumbled outside into the unseasonal sunshine, and we decided to walk home to sober up and clear our heads. There was nothing more to be said and we set off like soldiers after a losing battle, while the merciless sun tracked us all the way. Emotional exhaustion loosened Tom's tongue as we walked through Rusholme, our senses awakened by the lingering smells of exotic spices and sweet shops. The end of Empire had its advantages. I liked the idea of a cultural melting pot, quite literally adding vibrant colour to the monochrome city we had inherited. Again, there was that sense of the past and the future coming together at the same time, the imperial past giving way to a new multiculturalism that was refreshing the city. Already, a sizeable immigrant community was moving into the run-down parts of the city, while the native population moved out of the city one prosperous village at a time, just as Thatcher had predicted.

The walk had done us some good, as if the further we moved away from the canals, the harder it was to fear the worst. Tom started talking about his dad, about the strikes he had helped arrange when a business developer had started cutting corners and his men's safety had been compromised. I knew there was a mystery about his death, various people had alluded to it over the years, talk of a conspiracy and a cover-up. None of it helped a bereft boy comes to terms with the loss, a father memorialised to near-mythic proportions by a thousand sympathetic drinkers he had helped over the years. He had to share him with so many others. His dread anxieties about Colin were stirring deeper agonies he had suppressed for so long but I let him talk. Better out than in. There wasn't much to say other than to give voice to his fears and lingering frustration that he would never have closure about what had happened, a psychic scar that would never heal. He had been struck by a speeding car in broad daylight on Deansgate and died instantly in front of horrified shoppers. Nobody had got so much as a license plate and the case had been closed as a tragic accident that nobody could really accept.

'It's so hard,' he was saying. We had stopped to get something to drink. 'There's literally nothing I can do to make it better.'

'Think how well you're doing. The LSE and all that. You've got some future to look forward to. You must make him proud,' I said, though my words sounded hollow even to me. 'Once you're done with London, you can finish all the things he started.'

He walked on in silence, past the technicolour saree shops to the very edge of the curry mile, where it started or stopped. 'I'm not so sure anymore,' he said. 'My dad would always talk about revolution, what would happen when the workers rose up, but it just seems like a melancholy dream.' We moved on past Platt Lane where City trained during the week, past rows of repossessed houses. 'As bad as things are, where's the anger?'

he wondered out loud. 'If this isn't enough to people to want to fight for change, how much worse does it need to get?'

At college, people wore badges and talked about how to make things better, but it was all empty rhetoric. The reality was that working people were starting to buy into Thatcher's anti-ideology, believing in nothing more than their own selfish ambitions. To own a house, buy a car, wear designer clothes. Move away from areas where the immigrants were moving in. She had managed to make people ashamed of who they were.

'I love it here,' he said, 'but it's shit. Isn't it?'

I didn't have a good answer. I hated hearing him sound so nihilistic, though he had lost none of his passion.

'We should be fighting to make things better, that's what I believe in, but all we're actually doing is fighting each other. And for what? Because you support the other team? Wear your hair differently? Is this what we've been reduced to?' There was despair in his voice. 'Look, I can't let this go with Colin.' His voice was cold, mechanical like a trigger. 'I need to find out who did this.

Make the bastards pay.'

'Of course,' I agreed. 'I'm with you all the way.'

He hugged me and I could his body shudder with emotion he was struggling to contain. Someone drove past and called us faggots through an open window. You weren't permitted a minute of weakness in this city. Tom threw his can at the car and it smacked against the rear windscreen. The car skidded to a halt and reversed up Yew Tree Road so Tom invited the driver to step outside with a taunting smile. The car was full but none of them fancied it and they quickly drove off.

'Unbelievable.'

To distract him, I changed the subject to The Manifesto and he took the bait. We allowed ourselves to get lost in the minutiae of articles and images and deadlines. The plan was to get it ready to sell at the Festival of the Tenth Summer where we should have access to a huge market of like-minded people. We would get there early, sell whatever we could and then spend the profits on as much alcohol as we could feasibly consume.

Just before we parted, he stopped. 'You know, there's a lot more to life than music.'

'Of course,' I agreed.

'It's not enough to define yourself by the music you choose to listen to, the clothes you wear. I'm not saying it isn't important, but it's not the be-all and end-all. We all have to decide what we're going to do with our lives.' I wasn't quite sure what had brought this on, but it was clearly something he needed to articulate. Presumably, he was reminding me that I had big decisions to make, or thinking about Colin, picturing him the way we always would, with a camera in his hand, framing life into tiny slices of art. 'Music,' he went on, it's just the soundtrack, you know what I mean.'

I shrugged. 'I guess it is, in the end.' I didn't really know what else to say.

'Thanks for coming with me,' he said.

'I wouldn't be anywhere else.' He shook my hand, which was an oddly formal thing to do. 'You know I love you, right?'

'Of course. You, too.'

*

When I got home, Gary had hired a skip which sat right outside our front door where our family car would have stood if we were a normal family and had any money. Shockingly, I saw Maxine with armfuls of junk walking outside as I approached and dumping inside the skip.

'Look what the cat's dragged in,' she said.

'Don't start,' I snapped.

Maxine actually looked hurt. 'It was a joke,' she said. 'Come on, there's a houseful of this crap.'
'Tell me about it.'
Sindy took my hand to show me what she had been doing. 'We're making the house nice,' she told me proudly. I told her what she wanted to hear, that she was a good girl.
Deb had them well organised. The girls were throwing things into bags, Maxine and Gary were lugging things outside, while Deb was on her hands and knees orchestrating things and scrubbing wherever a bit of floor or wall emerged from the chaos. It didn't seem possible to accumulate so much clutter and junk into one modest house, even if it was stacked floor to ceiling. The skip was soon getting quite full, so we lifted the girls inside and they danced and stomped on the rubbish to flatten it, then the graft recommenced. It was just what I needed, mindless backbreaking work to dissipate all the latent energy I needed to release. I didn't need or want to talk so I put my headphones in and listened to Echo and the Bunnymen as my body went through the motions. I smiled at the sight of felt tip marks on an inner doorway charting the height progress of the girls over the years. Whether we liked it or not, time simply rolled on. Twice, I collected piles of old 2000AD comics from my bookcase and started to carry them to the skip but then put them back, weighing up the need for space as part of the collective household effort with the fact that I still read and enjoyed them. In the end, I saved my favourite issues and let the rest go.
'It's just stuff,' I told myself.
To her credit, Maxine pulled her weight and kept going, never once fighting to salvage some piece of rubbish onto which she had placed undue sentimental value. It all had to go.
By late afternoon, the skip was full, and Gary called a halt to proceedings for the day. Maxine took the girls back to hers to prepare some food while Maxine carried on sorting things out

inside so Gary could assess what size skip he needed for the next day, or if the rest could just be driven to the tip, or burned. The day had cooled, and I sat outside on the pavement, my back against the house as the sweat evaporated in the gentle breeze. The house was transformed. There was actually space to move around, although the décor was revealed in all its hideous squalor. Miserably, I wondered what kind of children could thrive in such a place. Still, it was a start. Gary and Maxine even talked about what they do to improve it, while I phased out, turning up the volume as *Go Out and Get 'Em Boy* started so I couldn't hear them inside through the angry jangle of guitars and David Gedge's poetic sensibilities.

Deb stepped outside and smiled at me, lost in my small little world on the pavement. I don't really know why but I started to tell her about the argument I had with Zoe, how it was all my fault. She nodded and smiled sadly, then reached into the skip and eased a newspaper from a bundle wrapped in string. She tossed it onto the pavement next to me.

Things all started to make a little bit more sense. It was an old edition of the *Evening News*, with a story about a car crash and a kid who had been killed in the collision. The pretty woman in the photo looked strangely familiar to me and I realised with horror that it was an earlier incarnation of Maxine. A drunk driver had smashed into her on Hyde Road and her three year-old son, Matthew, had died instantly. Another child survived and as I scanned the article, I realised I was reading about myself. There was an implication that the children had not been safely secured inside the car which seemed unnecessarily harsh as the other driver had evidently been in the wrong and she had suffered such unimaginable loss. I wiped away tears that been all day coming. Deb was still there standing next to me, arms crossed.

'It really wasn't her fault,' she said, 'but your so-called father couldn't cope, couldn't forgive her. The guilt, all she had lost, it just destroyed her.' She placed her hand on my head. 'She bought every copy of the Evening News she could find so no one could read about it as if that would somehow bring him back or make it all go away. God only knows why you weren't hurt, but then you've always been a little miracle.' She ruffled my hair. 'You okay?'

I shook my head. 'Not really. It's all too much. I don't want to have to deal with any of this.' I pulled my knees up to chest, trying to make myself as small as possible.

'No luck finding your friend?' I shook my head. 'I assume you tried ringing round the hospitals.'

'Tom's mum did it straight away. She said we wouldn't believe how many people have to be patched up on a Saturday night.'

'You know you can always talk to me,' she offered, 'or Gary, if you think that's any use at all.'

'What should I do?' I asked, holding up the newspaper.

She smiled at me sadly. 'I can't tell you that,' she said. 'You need to decide what's best for yourself. I would definitely take some time to process it. Talk to her if you feel it will help. You know, in all these years, she's never once talked to me about it. She just started drinking one day, and she never really stopped. It's so sad. She was my best friend.'

I stood up and hugged her hard, my surrogate mother. 'You're still her best friend,' I told her. 'We wouldn't have made it this far without you.' I felt her shudder in my arms. 'Why did you never tell me?'

She indicated the bundles of newspapers filling the skip. 'It was always there hidden in plain sight. We assumed on some level you always knew,' she said. 'We thought you'd deal with it when you were good and ready.'

I tore the front page from the copy in my hand and folded it in my back pocket, tossing the rest into the skip.

'Let's go and eat something,' she said. 'You look like you're going to faint.' I watched the last of the sun dip behind the terraces opposite and felt the burn of it in my eyes as it disappeared with a final glare, feeling like what I was, a young man with a heavy heart clinging onto the remnants of childhood.

I rejoined my family and ate mechanically without pleasure, then got my sisters ready for bed. When they had finally shut their eyes, I went to bed myself, pulled the covers over me and tried to surrender to the darkness. Finally, I gave up and killed time any way I could, absent-mindedly helping the girls with some homework. Anything to switch my brain off, my emotions. I even did a bit of revision while I listened to Stuart Hall on the radio to see how City were getting on in the meaningless Full Members Cup Final but my heart wasn't really in it. Bizarrely, they had played United the day before and got a creditable come-back draw much to Gary's annoyance but must have been knackered and, predictably, they were 5-1 down by the time I switched on. Even scoring three very late goals didn't make me feel any better. It was that kind of day.

*

I couldn't face the idea of college so I stayed away, even though we had mock exams coming up. I kept myself busy on my hands and knees scrubbing anything that didn't run away with bleach like a modern-day Cinderella with two beautiful sisters and a fairy godmother living right next door. To her credit, Maxine kept at it, too, but I was in no way ready to talk to her. There were years of pain and rage and frustration to work through before there could be any kind of reconciliation or forgiveness, but I sensed a stealthy softening in my animosity that suggested a ceasefire might be on the cards. Whatever tragedies had befallen her, I had been forced to bear the brunt of her weakness and self-indulgent guilt for far too long and that was not something I could easily let go of.

On the Wednesday, Tom came round to check up on me and bring me some college work I had missed. Maxine even said hi to him as he hovered in the doorway. There was still no word from Colin, and I agreed to walk over to his house to see his parents that evening, glad for any excuse to get out of the house for a while.

'By the way, I love what you've done with the place,' he mocked gently.

In truth, it was still looked fairly awful, but given the poverty of what we had to work with it was a decent start. Gary had found some old tins of paint and had helped me slap a couple of coats on even though it was supposed to be his day off. Like real men, we worked hard and avoided talking about anything meaningful, and I appreciated him for it, although at one point one point he gave it a go. He was so clumsy, I could tell that Deb had pushed him into it. To give us time and space, Maxine had walked with her and the kids to school, which was unheard of.

'Your mum seems to be doing a lot better.' I stopped slopping paint on the wall and looked at him. Your mum? He looked so uncomfortable I decided to let it go. We carried on in silence but I started to wonder if maybe he was right.

'Should I have done this years ago?' I asked. I painted a question mark on the wall to emphasise my uncertainty.

'You were just a kid,' he said, pretending to focus on a stubborn bit of wall. 'It wasn't your place or your responsibility to do anything. She just needed time to work her work through it.' He finished the bit he was working on and put his brush down carefully. 'But I think she's had enough. And you're not a child anymore.' He came over to inspect my work. 'You've done a decent job,' he said. 'You should be proud of that.' I couldn't tell if he was talking just about the paintjob or all of it, but I reddened with pride all the same. He wasn't one to hand out praise lightly, so it had real value.

I showed Tom my raw hands and he grimaced sympathetically. 'No gain without pain, right? At least you look more manly. And it looks a hell of a lot better from where I'm standing.'

I ignored him and grabbed my jacket.

'You spoken to Zoe?' he asked.

'Not so much.' Not at all, if truth be told. This was the first time I had set foot outside the four walls since the weekend so I had no access to a phone.

'Everything okay with you two?'

'I've no way of knowing,' I remarked, trying to sound casual about it. 'Is anything okay with anyone right now?'

'Fair point. I've seen her a bit around college, but she's been fairly low-key. Asked about Colin, but not much more than that.'

'Asked about me?' What is it they say about not asking a question if you don't care to know the answer?

He let it stand for a moment. 'Not so much,' he admitted.

I didn't really have the headspace to process it at that moment. 'More pertinently, what about you and Miranda?' I was in a mood to hurt myself.

'It was a one-off thing,' he shrugged. 'She even said as much to me. I'm a witch, remember. You can't expect anything from me.' He did a poor impression of her voice. So much for his acting career. 'Anyway, she's got some big audition coming up,' he announced. 'A speaking part in a Werner Herzog film. I meant to tell you, but, you know, with everything that's going on.' I was ready for any good news. 'That's literally incredible. Was that why she kept speaking German the other night?'

'Who knows with her,' he said. 'But yeah, I guess so.'

I was glad for her. A small glimmer of optimism was suddenly magnified and the oppressive gloom lifted a little. Every little bit helped. We rounded the corner into the outskirts of Withington, on Burton Road near the cinema. Colin's parents' house wasn't much but it was bigger than we were used to.

His mum answered the door, pleased to see us and all that, but her eyes were glassy like a waxwork whereas normally she was full of life, so we knew the doctor must have prescribed something. 'Heard anything?' she asked mechanically, but she already knew the answer.

'Nothing to report,' said Tom.

'I'm so sorry,' I added.

His dad was sitting in an armchair, trying to man his way through it so he looked terrible, gaunt and severe and tiny in an armchair he used to fill. His eyes met ours.

'Thanks for coming over, lads.'

'The least we can do. We'll head out after this,' Tom explained. 'Have a wander round, talk to some people, see if anyone saw anything.'

His mum made a round of tea and brought biscuits on a willow pattern plate that no one touched.

'The police have been round,' his mum was telling us. 'They were good. Really good. They've been trying to find some CCTV footage to see if they can find anything.' 'That's good,' I said.

On top of a pile of red bills and unopened mail, they had left a blown-up image of a face presumably taken by a security camera. It showed a face that was like one of those scream paintings by Munsch depicting existential horror. It may or not have been him, a blurred ubiquitous face of anonymised terror. Behind the face was another, much smaller, pursuing him like a ghoul, white, close-cropped hair, a visage of malevolent rage.

'Yes. At least they're acknowledging that something might have happened. At least it's like he mattered.'

I hadn't even noticed, but I saw Tom wince at her use of the past tense to describe him.

'He matters all right,' said Tom. 'We'll keep looking.' His voice and his eyes dropped. 'We won't give up on him, Mrs

Wilkinson.' In that moment, I could see him throwing up his whole future, a wilfully self-destructive act rooted in survivor's guilt. It was the same look I had seen in Maxine, medicated to the point of oblivion, floating in some parallel dimension, in the pathetic look of gratitude she would give me when I picked her up off some pavement, too drunk to stand or even recognise who it was who was dragging her pissy carcass home.

'Of course,' I said. 'We'll do whatever we can.'

She hugged us both, surrogates for her beloved son.

'You're good boys,' she said. 'Thanks. Call as soon as you hear anything.'

'Cheers, lads.' His dad couldn't even look up, fiddling with an ill-fitting piece of anaglypta wallpaper where he sat. 'Thanks for checking in.'

As we turned to go, she called us back. She handed us a bag containing loads of his photos, dozens of them. 'I wanted you to have these,' she said.

Tom refused to take them. 'I can't,' he said.

'He'll want them when he comes back,' I cut in. 'Won't he? He'll wonder where they've got to.'

She smiled and patted my cheek tenderly. 'Of course,' she said. 'But take them all the same. He'd want you to have them for that magazine of yours. And believe me, boys, there's tons more where these came from.'

I lacked Tom's fortitude and accepted them in spite of myself.

We can't have been there for more than half an hour, but on the street we both had to catch our breaths. The accumulated emotions were as suffocating as the clouds of cigarette smoke. We caught a bus and rode into the city centre in silence, both trying to erase the same terrible image from our minds.

Starting on Whitworth Street, the trail of blood had almost gone, lost in the mingled filth of the city and the oblivious footfall of pedestrians, but we followed it all the same, all the way to the gardens. We sat for a while and sorted through the

184

photos which had assumed a greater poignancy. Like the metaphorical natives who feared that photographs would steal their souls, Colin had left a little piece of himself in every image he captured on film. It was a way of seeing the world though his eyes, that gift he had for seeing the poetry in bricks and mortar, of making the mundane seem mythic. I would never be able to see the city the same way again. We followed the path of the canal for miles, looking for any trace of him, but there was nothing.

The sun slipped away, dipping behind buildings that once had purpose.

The hours of decorating had taken its toll on me. 'I need to eat.'

He looked at his watch. 'I'm meeting Miranda in a few minutes on Oldham Street. They sell decent enough food where we're going. She's off to London tomorrow for the big audition so I thought we could wish her well. You coming?'

'Sure,' I agreed. 'Why not. I could do with something to brighten the day.' I fumbled in my pockets to see how much cash I had. 'Is there anywhere that still owes us? Turns out I'm skint again.'

We took a meandering route through various stores and bars to see how well The Manifesto had done. Pretty well, as it turned out. There was something strangely gratifying about all that hard work putting food in our bellies. In any event, we turned up late, but then so did Miranda, who came in looking a bit flustered.

'What's up?' asked Tom.

'Nothing,' she replied. 'You know, the usual. Some idiots who think they can try to touch you up if they feel like it.'

I watched his hands instantly pull into fists. He was on a short fuse, all right. She noticed, too.

'It's all in hand,' she said. 'I took care of it, but I resent having to, you know. Why does it take a knee to the balls to make some moron realise he doesn't have the right to assault me?' I couldn't tell if she was joking but right on cue a furious looking bloke appeared in the doorway. He had friends with him. Tom was up at once, but she expertly stood up and eased him down with a hand on his shoulder.

'Don't,' she said. 'It's done. I don't need protecting.' Tom glared towards the door where a member of staff had intervened and he slowly let it go and relaxed into his chair. She sat in between us. They were not overly physical with each other, and I was grateful for that, though I didn't really understand why that mattered.

'Well,' she said. 'You boys sure look like sandblasted shit.'

'Thanks,' I said. 'It's been a long day.' She leaned towards me and pulled some paint from my hair.

'No news?'

'No good news,' I confirmed. 'Unlike you, I hear.'

'I know, right.' She positively glowed with excitement although I could tell she was really trying not to be inappropriately upbeat given the circumstances. Tom got a round in while she filled me in on the details which he had already heard.

'Herzog, though. That's crazy. He's a total genius.'

'That's what people keep telling me. I just keep telling myself it's not a done deal. And he's probably just some old perv. All he's seen of me is a photo. What does that tell you?'

'That you've got a good agent?' I suggested.

'Most likely.'

Tom came back and she swigged back half a pint in a single gulp.

'Look,' she beamed. 'My glass is literally half full.' She indicated the pint glass with her bewitching eyes. 'Colin will turn up safe and sound with some Swedish nymphomaniac he ran into. I'm going to get this role. Hollywood beckons. Tom is going to set London ablaze with his brilliance and run the country. And you...' She came to a sudden halt.

'What about me?'

'That's the thing,' she said. 'I don't really know. My crystal ball is a bit murky when it comes to you.'

My face must have fallen. 'No,' she said quickly. 'It's all good.' She put her hand on my knee. 'I just can't quite see what it is.'

'You and me both.' We ordered some food and told her all we could about the Herzog film Adrian had made us watch to broaden our cultural horizons, as he put it. Some of them we had really liked. Heart of Glass. Fitzcaraldo.

'He's batshit crazy,' I said. 'You've got a lot in common.'

The conversation was better than the food. Eventually, I had drunk enough to bring up the revelation about Miranda. And the brother I knew nothing about.

'Did you know any of this?' I asked.

Tom was evasive. 'A little,' he admitted. 'More than you, apparently. My mum remembered it happening. It was all over the papers.'

I still had the front page folded up in my back pocket which I showed them.

'I didn't know how much you knew,' Tom was saying as Miranda read it. 'I saw the papers the first time I went round yours. It was all right in front of you so I just assumed you must have been in denial, or something. I'm hardly an expert.' He took a hard swig of beer. 'I could just never get past how awful Maxine was, what she put you though.'

'It can't have been easy for her either,' said Miranda.

'But she was the adult,' Tom disagreed. 'That's what it is to be a mother. You have to stand up, be strong. Not keep breeding with any dickhead who'll have her and leave it to everyone else to raise them.'

'Not everyone is as strong as you, though,' Miranda insisted. 'Your mum seems amazing, but not everyone is as lucky as you. Nothing is that simple.'

'I never even knew I had a brother,' I said. 'I mean, what the hell.'

Miranda shook her head. 'I think you must have known, on some level. Look at how you follow Tom round like a beautiful little puppy.'

I laughed so hard I spat out a mouthful of beer. She had a clever way of cutting close to the bone without causing harm, defusing situations. 'Just for the record,' I said, 'he's the one who follows me round like a puppy. He asks me to join him at college, asks to borrow my music. He turns up at my football team asking to play. Honestly, I could go on and on.'

'Yeah,' she said. 'Whatever you say.'

'On the subject of football, good news. I've packed my job in,' said Tom. 'I'm playing on Saturday.'

We were on a depressing losing streak, so it was good news, but I was surprised all the same. 'What about the printing?'

'All taken care of,' he explained. He looked unusually sheepish. 'I may possibly have been caught in the act, but someone in the office has kindly agreed to carry on the good work for us.'

'So, now you have a new disciple?' Miranda teased him.

He laughed, but wisely declined to elaborate. 'Something like that.'

'What about the money?'

'We won't have to pay for anything. It's gratis. Anyway, I thought we could raise the cover price.' He raised an eyebrow to indicate that he may be joking.

'What does that mean? Pay twice as much as you think it's worth?'

'Yeah,' he said. 'Why not?'

I finished my drink and left them to it, emotionally drained and in desperate need of sleep. Tom had threatened to drag me into college if I spent any more time away but I needed more time. Even though I was on that familiar sluggish bus route taking me one node at a time from the centre to the outskirts, it felt like everything was changing at an extraordinary rate, the world whooshing past as I stook stock still, a colourless blur seen though a rain-streaked glass panel.

Fourteen

I held out all week, using decorating as a pretext and as a useful means to physically exhaust myself so I could sleep. I had heard nothing from Zoe who had no means of contacting me, and I felt fine about that in my little amniotic bubble. I wondered absently if I subconsciously held her accountable for what may have happened to Colin. If she hadn't freaked out about Miranda, if she hadn't been so pissed, if she hadn't wandered recklessly into trouble and set off a violent chain of
events...

Most days, though, my mind was a glorious blank. I blasted out tunes and lost myself in the hard graft. Other days were harder, my mind playing out endless scenarios where things turned out differently. I could have taken the beating outside The Ritz that was eventually doled out to Colin. None of it helped bring him back or make me feel any better about any of it. At least the house started to look much improved. When they came back from school, the girls got stuck in, too, and even Maxine got her hands dirty with us. We didn't have the money to replace any of the worn-out furniture but Deb had sourced a sofa that her workplace was throwing out and Gary drove the old one to the tip for me, which made a huge difference.

'It almost looks like a home,' said Maxine admiringly.

'It takes more than a coat or two of paint to make a home,' Deb reminded her, 'but yes, it does look much better.' On the Friday evening, with Deb's help, she even cooked a meal. We sat and ate together on the sofa and it wasn't awful. I even managed to bite my tongue whenever Maxine said something that grated rather than taking the bait. I had rarely seen the girls look so happy.

On the Saturday, Tom came to get me and we made our way to Hough End together to play against a cynical team from Urmston who had the audacity to play in red. He was unusually taciturn and I assumed he was just psyching himself up for what would be a hard game or concerned about the exams coming up the following week.

'You're done hibernating,' he told me tersely as we warmed up. 'I'm coming round to pick you up on Monday morning, whether you like it or not.'

A couple of times in the first half, he got caught with late tackles that normally he would have danced away from with ease. I even wondered if the break had caught up with him, that he had slowed a little. Still, he was in complete control, commanding the game from the middle of the pitch, and we went in with a slender advantage. A man approached as we huddled at the interval and pulled him aside. A City scout was watching, and he was advised to put on a show in the second half to impress. 'It's not me you should be watching,' said Tom. As I attended to a gash on my knee, I could see he was completely unfazed by the attention. 'Jason's your man.'

In the second half, he took complete control, setting up two early chances that Jason smashed home. He got caught again with an elbow to the face and went down, but was instantly back on his feet. He squared up to the one who had caught him, his teeth stained with blood, grinning, not backing down an inch. He was loving it, and I realised he had allowed himself to be caught like that, to show he couldn't and wouldn't be intimidated.

The ref spoke to both players and the game went on. The ball broke in the middle of the pitch and Tom went in hard and late on his opponent, snapping his shinbone which forced itself through his sock. His white sock quickly blossomed as he lay there, screaming and clutching his leg. Both teams squared up as someone ran off to call for help and it all kicked off. The ref hadn't even brandished a red card, but I could see Tom already walking away, head held high, totally indifferent to the brawl he had instigated. I had my hands full dealing with one of their players who was trying to smack me around. Eventually things settled down. The ref abandoned the game, and I ran off after Tom to check he was okay.

'I'm fine,' he said. As we walked off, he checked his teeth with his tongue and spat out a mouthful of coagulated blood. 'That was just what I needed.'

'Tom, you crippled the guy,' I said.

He took to look at me, his eyes bright and defiant. 'You saw him,' he said. 'He had it coming.'

I couldn't argue with him. 'What about the scout?'

'What about him? I'm out of here soon, aren't I,' he reminded me. 'Off to the big city. It's a distraction I didn't need.' A year or two earlier, and it would have been the most exciting thing ever to happen to him. 'Anyway, he got what he was looking for. Jason was on fire today. All the scout needed was a name.'

I looked back over my shoulder and, sure enough, the scout was deep in conversation with Jason, just like Tom had intended. He had a rare gift for making things happen like that. I tried to detect in his voice a faint trace of regret, a sense of an opportunity wasted, but there was none. As I had suspected for some time, he was moving on.

'You up for a film night with Adrian?' he asked. 'He called me last night. Invited us over. Daz, too.'

It was undoubtedly the best offer I was going to get.

'Of course. Sounds great.' I asked if he wanted to come over to mine so we could travel in together but he said he would rather meet me there.

We were supposed to meet up later in the afternoon to watch City's dreadful losing streak continue in front of a bigger crowd than they deserved, but he said he couldn't make it. Even though tickets were priced for the common man, the money men in the game had squeezed too hard and fans were turning their backs on the game. The plan of blending talented youth with experienced journeymen had not really worked out. It was that thing again, the past and the future colliding, but not always to good effect. Still, we had done enough earlier in the season to be safe and to console ourselves with the naïve optimism that things would get better.

*

Darren turned up in the early evening to pick me up as his older brother was driving him into town. I watched him from an upstairs window as he knocked on the door and enjoyed hearing his confusion as Maxine opened the door.

'Um, sorry, wrong house.' I watched him step back onto the pavement and check the numbers, looking left and right to see if he had the right place. He was literally scratching his head, trying to make sense of it. 'I don't get it.'

'Darren, right?' said Maxine. I had no idea she knew his name. 'You can come in, you know. He's upstairs.'

I met him on the stairs. 'What the fuck?' He saw the girls and started apologising. 'Sorry, ladies,' he said. 'I thought I was in the wrong place.'

'Yeah,' I laughed. 'I've been busy.'

'Hey,' said the girls as one.

'He means we've been busy,' said Maxine. I hadn't even noticed but she had brushed her hair, made some effort.

'Well, it looks like a bloody palace,' he said. He threw his arms wide in admiration.

The girls chuckled and gave each other a high-five, an Americanism they had picked up from TV that I didn't really approve of, but they outnumbered me. They kissed me goodnight and out we went. I stuck my head back through the door as Darren's brother honked the horn impatiently.

'You sure you're gonna be okay?' I asked Maxine. Gary and Deb had gone out, too, but not far away and had promised me they were not going to be late.

'I'm good,' she said. Subverting the parent/ child dynamic, I watched as she held out a hand and kept it steady. 'Honestly. You go. Have fun.'

He waited until we got to Adrian's before he commented on Maxine's appearance. 'She looked...' He searched for the appropriate word. 'I dunno. Decent. She looked decent.' He blushed. 'I didn't mean it like that,' he blurted out. 'I just meant, she looked nice, you know. I don't know what you've done but the place looks great, really.'

'I know what you meant, you daft sod.'

Adrian had laid on a fine assortment of drinks and we indulged ourselves with rum and cokes, or Cuba Libres as we correctly called them in honour of Fidel and his boys.

'Where's Tom?'

Adrian shrugged as he struggled for some ice in his freezer. 'I assumed he was with you?'

'He told me he was meeting us here.'

'Well, he'd better get a move on or there'll be nothing to drink.'

Adrian lived in one of the Hulme flats, brutalist monstrosities crafted from cheap materials that suffered in the mancunian climate amidst serious misuse from the local residents. It took us until ten to realise that something was up.

'I've got an idea where he might be,' said Darren. 'One of you needs to come with me 'cos I'm not walking round here at night on my own. We won't be long.'

'You're not afraid, are you?' I teased.

'I've not got a death-wish, that's for sure. Just shut up and get your coat on.'

It made sense for Adrian to stay in case he showed up late, so I pulled on my leather jacket and followed Darren out through the door.

As we reached the ground floor, he stuck his head over the balcony and shouted at us to bring more drink and some ice if such a thing was possible. This was Manchester on a Saturday night in the early Summer. Anything was possible. Except modern housing fit for human habitation. Hulme was a giant cage, and we made sure we kept our wits about us as we made our way towards the city centre. I could see Darren was ill at ease, so I entertained him with an impression of Tom snapping the guy's leg earlier in the day. It wasn't funny, but I did an impression of his screams that made him rock with laughter.

'That's what I'm afraid of,' he said as we hurried along. 'He's been something fierce all bloody week. I knew something was going to give.'

As we made our way through the concrete labyrinth of the Mancunian Way, through underpasses and walkways laced with protective barriers to prevent debris being dropping onto vehicles passing below, the ambient whoosh of traffic made conversation tricky. Needles and condoms and fast food detritus littered the way which was illuminated by the sodium glow of outdated streetlights that gave everything a nightmarish quality like an arthouse horror film from the European *avant garde*.

'How can people live here like this?' asked Darren.

'You're assuming they have a choice.'

I could see he was on edge, and we quickened our pace through the strange man-made terrain from an era where functionalism eclipsed aesthetics as if designed to make us feel disconnected from our environment, strangers in a strange land. It was almost impossible to imagine that this could have once been fields, that anything good could possibly have grown here. We passed a church that seemed absurdly dislocated, like a temporal shift had transported it from a bygone era when people clung to their faith that things would only get better, or that there something better to look forward to when you passed on. Now it was encircled by motorways as if the saviour himself had been reincarnated in a world imagined by Ballard.

Unerringly, Darren us led along Lower Mosley Street and down Great Bridgewater Street, nimbly circling GMEX where the Festival of the Tenth Summer was to be held.

'It's going to be amazing,' said Darren, pleased to be able to hear his own voice.

Tom was right where Darren had predicted, in the shadows across the road from The Ritz, watching, waiting, dressed all in black like a preternatural apex predator from folklore. His face was a grim mask, psyching himself up for retribution however he could take it. He was so focused, it took him a moment to recognise us.

'This isn't the way,' Darren told him. He positioned himself between Tom and The Ritz so he couldn't look away. 'I get it, I really do, but this isn't what he would have wanted.'

The streets were getting busier and he was still straining to see past us as people walked past.

'Tom,' I said. 'You know he's right.' I put a hand on his shoulder, forcing him to make eye contact. 'Not like this.'

He shook my hand off. 'I can't just let it go,' he said. He was so tightly wound that I could hear his teeth grind.

'Of course you can, you daft sod.' Darren had a knack of making him laugh. He threw his arms around him and they grappled until he felt Tom relax. Across the road, the doormen at The Ritz kept watch without being amused. 'You're too damn pretty to be a brawler,' he said. We had stopped at a shop and he produced a can of beer. 'Here. This will help.'

With a final effort, Tom shrugged him over his shoulder and Darren crumpled to the pavement. He opened the beer and drank in triumph. A little light had returned to his eyes.

'Seriously, this isn't you,' said Darren, sheepishly hauling himself up from the dirt. 'You can't throw away your future like this, skulking in shadows, hurting people, hurting yourself. You're the brilliant one. You're the one reaching escape velocity, getting out. You can't give all that up. Not for this.'

'But what if I've got everything I need right here, Daz?'

'We're not going anywhere. We'll always be here for you to come back to, whenever you need to.'

Darren took a beer himself and gave one to me. Subtly, he made a move towards a taxi rank nearby and Tom followed without even thinking about it. I followed close behind, laughing at the ice already melting, each slow drip metaphorically washing away the trail that Colin had left for us to follow.

'You know he's right,' I said. 'This isn't who you are.'

Tom turned and looked at me. 'Stay gold, Ponyboy, right?'

I laughed with a mouthful of beer, half choking. We loved that book, that film.

Darren insisted on getting a taxi back to Adrian's using the melting ice as cover and we were happy to go along. Adrian knew better than to ask what Tom had been up to, I suspect intuitively guessing where he had been.

'Just so you know,' he informed us cautiously, trying to judge the mood, 'I've been asking around on the scene to see if anyone saw or heard anything last week. Nothing much so far. I met one guy who thought he had maybe seen something, but he was vague on details.'

'What was his name?' asked Tom. 'Could we talk to him?'

'God, I didn't ask him his name.' He almost blushed. 'He just said he vaguely remembered a bit of a scuffle. Assumed it was queer-bashers, you know. Made himself scarce.' He sensed our disappointment. 'I'll keep asking around, though. You never know.'

He had lined up a couple of promising films, and the cuba libres flowed, although Darren misheard and insisted on calling them cobra libres instead, a term which stuck for ever after. Adrian had sourced a decent bootleg of *The Texas Chainsaw Massacre 2* complete with a manic Dennis Hopper, but it was played for laughs a little too much and lacked the gritty visceral gut-punch of the original. By the end, we were barely watching. Someone had put on a Velvet Underground album, and I closed my eyes and lost myself. The conversation came round to The Manifesto and when the next edition would be ready.

'Well, basically, all we're waiting on is your film reviews,' said Tom, 'so I guess that's up to you.'

We told him the aim was to get it ready for the big festival and how we were going to drink ourselves unconscious with whatever we could get for them.

'I'll do what I can,' said Adrian. 'I won't let you down.'

'Cobra libres all night long,' I suggested, but Darren was too far gone to even notice. He started dancing around the flat, a lurid impression of a Latin dance move. He performed it for us all round the room.

'What the fuck are you doing?'

'Shaking my maracas.'

'Shaking your mad ass?'

'Same thing.'

'You know what I think. We should form a band, get Daz in as the dancer. It's the logical next step, don't you think?'

'That's a great idea.' Darren was always over-enthusiastic when alcohol was involved. 'But why can't I be the singer?'

'Because you're totally talentless,' said Tom.

Darren looked a little hurt, but I knew he was just acting. 'Okay, I'll be the dancer,' he agreed. 'You know, for the ladies in the audience.' He thrust his crotch at us rhythmically, but it was far from erotic.

'We still need a good name,' I pointed out. It was a conversation that every group of young men must have had at some point or other. We went round the room with suggestions, each more ridiculous than the last.

'Jailbait,' Adrian suggested.

'That must have already been used,' I said. 'It's too good.'

Tom always opted for something a little confrontational. 'Front Towards Enemy.' Then he looked at us and recalled our earlier conversation. 'Or how about The Outsiders?'

Darren was stumped. 'What about A Molotov Cocktail? As in, Good evening, Stockholm. We are A Molotov Cocktail.' He had a potential career ahead of him as a public announcer.

My turn. For once, I was devoid of inspiration. They waited expectantly, but my mind was empty. I was tempted to suggest The Dick-Swing Children again, but it had become an old joke. I liked the idea that Pop Will Eat Itself had named themselves after an article they had read about the postmodern cliff that popular culture was teetering on the brink of, self-referential and repetitive to the point of parody. Alcohol had dulled my brain. For some reason, I thought of the infamous Falklands headline in The Sun.

'Gotcha!'

Tom shook his head. 'Nah. People will assume we're bloody Thatcherites.'

'You make a fine point.' I thought of the last novel I had read. Suddenly, it came to me, even down to a logo, a cool squared-off font rising up vertically with tapered leading lines reaching up aspirationally.

'High-Rise.'

'You know what,' said Tom thoughtfully, 'that's actually decent.' He was unrecognisable from the grim-faced avenger in the shadows a few hours earlier.

It was far too late for my own good, so I announced I needed to go and Adrian insisted on calling a cab for me. He earned a decent wage and I was in no fit state to argue so I just let it happen. From a distinctly unpromising beginning, the evening had been highly entertaining, and I felt better than I had in a while, more clear-headed even though the drink had dulled my senses. In the morning, all that would pass, and I felt like I could start to move on.

All the same, that night I dreamed that Colin was standing on the edge of a canal, peering in, with seductive nymphs poking through the deceptive stillness of the surface, though it was hard to imagine what kind of creature might thrive in the polluted primordial waterways of Manchester. Enraptured, Colin leaned in further and further, and when the inevitable splash came, I woke up every time.

Fifteen

As promised, Tom came round on the Monday morning and dragged me into college where I did the exams on autopilot. A weak northern sun tried to force its way into the cavernous hall through ill-fitted curtains bleached over the years to a sickly shade of pink. The sound of birdsong was an irritating distraction as my pen scratched hieroglyphs onto exam booklets that I knew would be sufficient, but my mind constantly wandered to our missing friend and I learned the extent to which it is true that what kills you is the hope. Every day I yearned for someone to rush over and tell me he had been found, and I was crushed every time it didn't happen, like a telephone that never rings.

When Zoe told me on the Wednesday afternoon that she had met someone else, it felt totally normal. Mechanically, I watched her pretty little mouth form the words but I just shrugged it off.

'Okay,' I said.

She looked up at me in a way I suspected she thought was appealing, but suddenly all I could see were her flaws. She was vain and needy, and she had soulless eyes. 'You're not upset?' she asked.

'Of course,' I said. 'But not about this.'

She was a little taken aback. 'I don't believe you,' she said. 'It's okay to be upset. And I want you to know it wasn't you. I just met someone else. It happens, you know. And he's got a car.'

'Wow,' I said. 'That must be exciting.' I didn't mean to sound sarcastic. I felt relieved, freed from any burden for her emotional neediness. I was annoyed that she had inadvertently referenced a Primal Scream song I loved, so that every time I heard it, I would now picture her silly little face trying to make me feel trivial.

'You don't have to be like that.' She folded her arms defensively.

It was hard to think of a more prosaic reason to be dumped, but I couldn't have cared any less. 'Seriously, I'm very pleased for you.' She hadn't moved and I wanted to be anywhere else. 'Look, I've no idea what you want me to say or do,' I informed her.

'You could try caring,' she said. 'What the hell is wrong with you? Did you get what you wanted from me and now you're not interested? Is that it?'

It was hard to believe she had to ask, as if she was the centre of the universe and everything else revolved around her own high self-regard. I was in a weird space inside my head and I found her anger somewhat entertaining.

'Zoe, it's fine. You don't want me anymore.' My voice was strangely calm which I think freaked her out. 'That's fine. I get it. Maybe I'll see you out with some other guy and I'll burn with envy. Who knows, eh. But that's what it means to dump someone. I'm not yours anymore. You don't get to dictate the way I react. You have to get over it.'

I started to walk off and she pulled at my arm. 'Am I not good enough for you?' she asked. There were tears in her eyes and I didn't want the melodrama. She had asked me that before and I had no desire to become her Heathcliff.

'I loved being with you,' I said. 'But that was then. The world isn't the same anymore. Everything I thought I knew is just an illusion. Go and be happy.'

She quite literally couldn't let go. 'Is this about her?'

For a while, I didn't even know who she was talking about. 'Who? Maxine?' I laughed out loud so that people turned and stared.

'It's never been about her.'

Her face was streaked now with mascara. 'You know who I mean,' she hissed. 'Her. Fucking Miranda.' Her eyes were downturned and she reached out to take my hand in hers.

Reluctantly, I realised I would have to give her something. 'Okay,' I said, trying not to sound flippant. 'Sure. Why not. It's Miranda. I am madly in love with her. From the moment we met.'

Finally, she pulled away. It felt like an emotional exorcism, a burden suddenly let go. 'You know what?' she said, trying to hide her hurt, as if she was the one being wronged. 'You pretend to be nice but you're a bastard.' Bizarrely, she looked really beautiful as she said it.

'Thanks,' I said. 'I've been told.'

Finally, she stormed off and I waited for a couple of her friends to go after her to make sure she was okay. I felt gloriously disconnected from the pain and melodrama of it all, like something had flicked a switch in my head or shoved a needle in my arm, and the stray thought struck me that this was Maxine, that I was becoming her, one and the same, anything to stop the hurting.

I hung around as far from other people as possible until Tom and Jake finished their exam.

'Don't even ask,' said Jake before I could even ask him how it went. 'All I could see all the way through the exam was Tom sat in front of me just writing and writing and writing.' He glared playfully. 'It was so off-putting. Let's just say I won't be going away anytime soon.'

'I'll sit at the back next time,' Tom suggested. There was no need to ask him how the exam had gone; there was only ever one answer. Fine. He was staring at me. 'You look...weird,' he remarked.

'Thanks.'

'No, I mean it. What's happened? Have you heard something?' There was rising hope in his voice, especially as we had agreed to visit Colin's parents again. They said it helped to have young people around and it was the very least we could do. 'Not that,' I said. 'I just got dumped. For someone with a car.'

'A nice car, I hope,' said Jake.

Tom was little more concerned. 'You okay?'

'Relieved, if truth be told.' He slapped me on the back. 'Maybe it will hit me later.'

'Or maybe not.'

'That's rich girls for you,' said Jake. 'Everything has relative value. She thinks she's traded up, but she'll soon see she was wrong. It's her loss.'

His parents lived quite near the college so it didn't take long although we went a meandering route so we could talk and prepare ourselves. In the house, it was like time had stood still, not in terms of the outdated décor, but in every conceivable way. Mail was piled up by the door and nothing had been touched, as if the house was slowly transforming itself into a shrine. Automatically, his mum disappeared into the kitchen.

'The police have been round again,' said his dad. 'Not that they had much to say for themselves.'

A tray of tea appeared, with biscuits. 'At least they're trying,' said his mum. 'They're doing everything they can.'

It seemed a poor metric to judge someone's usefulness. What we needed from them was some helpful information so we could get some positive news, or some closure.

'Have they at least tried talking to people at that bloody nightclub?' It was the most animated we had seen Mr Wilkinson. 'Somebody there must know something.' If only it was as easy as that.

Colin's mum went and stood by him, put a hand on his shoulder where he sat. 'Don't get excited, dear. It doesn't help.' She was a blanket of calm thrown over the household, fussing over refreshments and keeping things ticking over as if it would help everything soon blow over. 'Everyone's doing the best they can.' She almost made you believe that any time now Colin would come bounding through the door, camera slung over his shoulder, wondering what all the fuss was about.

When I got back home, I expected a return to the usual chaos, but the house was tidy, though there was no sign of Maxine and I assumed she had started to go back to her old ways, though she had taken her medication. I went next door to make sure Deb had the girls but they weren't there, either. Immediately, I feared the worst.

By the time I had got back home to get my jacket, she was back with the girls who were both carrying a bag of shopping. It was mostly processed crap, but it was better than nothing. The girls had sweets, too, which was something new.

'How did the exam go?' asked Maxine. For a moment I couldn't answer, and she looked concerned.

'It was fine,' I said. I had no idea she even knew.

'Come on,' said Sindy. 'Help us put the shopping away.' Just for a second, it was almost like we were a real family. I helped them cook fishfingers and chips and we watched Top of The Pops together. Most of it was awful, but The Primitives were on, and the girls said they wanted to look like Tracie which gave me hope that one day they would grow out of the Disney princess phase and join the real world with the rest of us, and then felt bad for wanting them to grow up before they were ready. When I started to get them ready for bed, Maxine came and joined us and even read them a story, though she wasn't very good.

Later, I pretended to do some revision and listed to the radio absent-mindedly, though Peel played some Public Enemy. Chuck D ranted like a politicised prophet and I liked what I heard. It made me realise that maybe, just maybe, music didn't necessarily have to be guitar, bass and drums. It was a revolutionary idea.

Every day for a fortnight followed the same pattern, stuck on repeat. It was merciful release to go and see Big Flame at The Boardwalk the night before our last exam. To demonstrate their cultural worth, John Peel loved them and they had shone on the NME's *C86* cassette that had helped define an emerging scene of disparate bands united by that same desperate yearning for a creative outlet that we felt as we toiled to get the next edition of The Manifesto ready for printing.

They were great, a stunning live spectacle, but you could already see on stage that the thrill of it was starting to dissipate for them. That rush of adrenaline that came from performing in front of an audience was becoming a pressure to maintain it and move on, where commercial responsibilities started to matter more than the sheer delight of making music. When they played an encore, you could tell that they really meant it when they said they were calling it a day and we applauded until our hands hurt not just for the show but for being true to their word when they had promised to release a few singles, burn brightly, and then make way for the next generation of bands to come along.

As we sat back on the steps and finished our drinks, I didn't ask him outright, but I suspected that Tom was starting to feel the same way about The Manifesto, that he had achieved what he had set out to do, proved he could make it even better and was ready to move on to the next challenge. London was calling.

*

'So, what do you think?'

Gary had arranged with a builder mate of his to offer me a month's work over the summer.

'It will be hard graft,' he said. 'He's got a big job over in Bramhall and he needs to take someone on. No guarantees, but if you get on alright, he says he may look at something more permanent. If not, if you decide to go away, then you've still helped him out of a hole.'

It wasn't what I had planned for the summer. I felt hollow and exhausted and intended to do as little as possible, but it was hard to turn down the money, or the opportunity to maybe learn a thing or two of a more practical nature. I'm not sure if Gary saw my reticence, if Deb had encouraged him to put me off. I knew that deep down she wanted me to go to Leeds, especially as Maxine continued to keep her shit together.

'It's long days,' he said. 'He works you hard. But it will make a real man out of you.'

'What?' I joked. 'Like you?'

He had hit middle age hard of late, but he proudly flexed a manly muscle and smiled. 'Exactly.'

I prevaricated, but we all knew the answer would be yes. I just needed time to get my head round it. 'When do I need to let you know by?'

'End of the week should do it. It starts on Monday.'

I walked round to Tom's, slowly coming to terms with the inevitability of my decision. The Manifesto was almost complete. We were just putting in the final flourishes and then it was off to the printers, so there was no good reason to say no. I had nothing to lose but my freedom.

When I got to Tom's, he had virtually finished all the work, so we mostly just listened to music while we laid all the pages out and debated the running order of articles while his mum cooked us eggs and bacon.

'It's looking good, boys,' she said. I noticed there was still no price on the cover.

'Really? Again?' Sometimes, he could be exasperating, like he had forgotten how frustrating it had been trying to negotiate a price. 'We only just got away with it last time.'

He was clearly amused by my reaction. 'It's our USP,' he insisted. 'It's what makes us different.'

'Tom, we just forgot last time. It was a mistake, remember.'

He was still enjoying my frustration, and it was good to see that his dark mood of late was starting to lift. 'It was a beautiful mistake,' he corrected me.

'Just because it impressed them at the LSE doesn't make it a good idea, but I don't care strongly enough to fight you.' He wore an enigmatic smile, as if to say, isn't that always the way with us?

'Did Tom tell you he's been offered an internship?'

'Nope.'

'I only just heard,' he said, a little defensively. 'It's a month or so with the union my dad worked for, or what it became after loads of them amalgamated. They're paying me, too.'

'It was too good a chance to pass up,' said his mum.

'Of course. That's great,' I said. 'It will be great experience for you, getting ready to take on the world.'

His mum had a lovely laugh, warm and honest. 'Oh, he's been doing that for years,' she said. 'Like father like son, eh.'

'So I've heard.'

I took the opportunity to tell them about my job offer.

'So, you do listen to me sometimes,' said Tom. 'It will be good for you. A month of hard work and you'll be begging to go away to uni.'

'Or you'll love it,' said his mum. She started cleaning away the plates and commanded Tom to wash up. 'Either way, at least you'll know, one way or the other.'

We sensed that this would probably be the last edition, but we were proud of the flat-plan laid out in front of us. I think we both suspected that we had taken it as far as we could, that our futures would take us down very different paths. It was hard to see that we would have as much time again to work on it.

In contrast to the sombre aesthetic created by Colin's stunning use of light and shadow, the tone was lighter and the tenor less formal. It was less preachy and more fun, still with a strong political undercurrent but more a celebration of our outsider status, an affirmation of youth and the potency of creative energy. Anything is possible. I nodded towards the table where all 32 pages were carefully laid out. 'It's ready,' I said.

'Agreed. I'll get to work.' Whatever that meant. I dreaded to think.

His house was small, but homely. Everything had a place and they worked as a team, keeping on top of it, a far cry from my own. We sat and ate at the kitchen table, the three of us, a warm communal experience that inspired me to use any money I earned over the summer to get a proper kitchen table. I wanted the girls to have it better than me and I liked the way this made me feel.

His mum came and sat with me. 'I hear your mum's doing better, bless her.' That must have come from Tom, and I was a little surprised that he had anything positive to say about Maxine. He was harder on her than I was, and that was saying something. 'I guess so. She's not drinking as much. She even cooked the other day.'

'Give her time love, if you can. I know it's hard for you.'

'Yeah, I'm trying,' I said. 'Old habits die hard.'

'You and her both.'

While I was there, Darren called around to see if anyone had heard anything about Colin, more in hope than expectation. Tom's mum hugged him affectionately when she saw his face, how hard it was to take, the not-knowing.

'Don't you give up hope, she told him. She ruffled his hair and he pulled away to fix it again in the mirror.

I took it as a cue to leave, not that I wasn't always welcome, but I felt I needed to let Gary know that the answer was yes.

I thought I was alone, but Maxine was with the girls in the back yard. There was a lot of noise. Experience had taught me to have low expectations, so I felt the need to check up on them, leaning to see over the detritus on the kitchen windowsill. Carelessly covered in primary colours, they were painting plant-pots and pushing a solitary sunflower seed into the compost. The girls saw me staring and waved, so I stepped outside, feeling like I was intruding on something important. I raised a hand in greeting but didn't want to speak in case I broke the spell. She led them over to the far side of the yard where the sun just about reached beyond the shadow case by the façade of Gary and Deb's house. Once they had settled on the perfect spot and watered the pots, she sent them inside to clean up. She actually looked like she knew what she was doing.

Maxine didn't look up at me as she cleaned up the worst of the mess but she knew I was there.

'What do you think?' she said. She seemed pathetically keen to win my approval, to let me know she was making an effort.

'They seemed to enjoy themselves,' I said. 'You did alright.'

'Thanks. You could have joined us, you know.'

'Nah, you were having far too much fun.' She even laughed. 'Besides, I've had my fill of manual labour for one day.'

I stepped aside so she could get to the kitchen sink.

'Thanks.' She ran a sink full of scalding water and started the clean-up. 'I'm never going to be your mum, am I?' she said. It wasn't really a question.

'No,' I agreed. 'Probably not.' I was so used to being antagonistic with her that I didn't even know how to converse. I wondered if I was being too harsh when she was starting to make real progress. 'But it's not too late for the girls. You're doing alright, for what it's worth.

I sensed her turning round to look at me, finally seeing me for what I was, what I did to keep the place ticking over. 'Thank you,' she said. It was a tone of voice I didn't recognise. Honest, perhaps. No guardedness or self-pity. 'I don't know what I ever did to deserve them,' she mused, her back to me. 'I know I probably should never have had them, but they're growing up to be such sweet little things.'

'Yeah,' I said. 'They're not too bad. For kids.'

She was obviously having a better day, her thoughts quite lucid and self-reflective. 'I think I thought they would fill the hole,' she said. 'You know?'

I did, and I didn't. It wasn't a conversation I could have with her. Not then, probably not ever. She turned over her shoulder to look at me and I instinctively looked away. I had nothing good to say about it. I didn't want to know any more about my father, my brother, any of it. All of it felt like chains I lacked the strength or inclination to carry around. I may have been mistaken, but I felt I was better off not knowing, for what good could possibly come of it? My silence spoke volumes.

'Oh, okay then,' she said. 'I get it.' There was no bitterness in her voice. For once, she was taking her medication properly and drinking in moderation, and it had taken her to a place where she could start to function, more or less, just strong enough to take the edge off. 'One day at a time, eh.' That was as good as it ever got, and it was definitely better than nothing.

Sixteen

The summer turned my soft hands into leather and my shoulders broadened an inch or two. I toughened up in other ways, too. I saw less than I would have liked of Tom and Darren and Adrian but we still went to gigs and watched films, and for once I was able to pull my weight when it came to buying the beers. At least twice a week, some or all of us would meet up and walk the waterways together, tracing a route for Colin to bring him home, but each time it got a little easier emotionally and my expectations of a happy ending slowly subsided into a fatalistic sense that in our own way we were saying goodbye.

A letter arrived one morning, in a florid hand-written hand. There was no note inside, just a solitary photograph that fluttered to the carpet like a feather, landing face down. It was a photo of Zoe, a portrait. She looked good, more natural than how she usually presented herself to the world. I understood that it was to fill the space on the wall where she had removed Colin's image of Miranda. I was bemused by the gesture but I couldn't think of a good reason not to use it to fill the ugly void left by her little fit of pique.

'That's Zoe,' said Bella.

'Yes, it is.'

'We liked her. Why doesn't she come here anymore?' she asked innocently.

I thought about it for a while. 'Because she decided she doesn't really like me,' I said.

'I think she does,' said Sindy, knowingly. 'Why else would she send you a photo?'

I was at a loss to answer. 'What do you two know about it?' I laughed. I didn't feel sad about not being with Zoe anymore. Things had ended with her in The Venue, that night, maybe even before that, just one of those things that was nice but doesn't last. I tried to explain that to the girls.

'You mean, like a rainbow?' I laughed again. I loved their simplistic view of the world. It was so much better than my own.

'I guess so.'

'Don't worry,' said Sindy, sympathetically. 'The next time you get a girlfriend, we'll help you.'

What else could I say? 'Thanks. That would be great. I think I need all the help I can get.'

*

Miranda got a call-back, which necessitated a trip to Germany to meet with the producer. Nothing was guaranteed, of course, but it made us feel like anything was possible. She talked us through the process as we made our way along the Rochdale Canal, trying to distract ourselves as we walked, so we subconsciously took routes we hadn't already taken. The whole thing was quite surreal, joking around on our grim quest looking for any trace of Colin, seeking knowledge that we dreaded finding. There was no such thing as good news, apart from ample evidence of the astonishing durability of wildlife as we saw signs of water voles and other creatures managing to somehow survive in those toxic waterways.

'It will never happen,' Miranda was telling us, but you could detect in her upbeat voice that she believed that she stood a decent chance. 'They took about a million photos of me,' she explained, 'and I had to do a screen test where I had to walk through a doorway and deliver a line of dialogue.' She performed it for us in perfect German.

'What does it even mean?' I asked.

She shrugged. 'I don't really know,' she admitted. 'I think it means I don't love you anymore, but it's possibly a bit more nuanced than that.'

'It's more like *My love for you is over*,' said Tom.

'Same difference.'

'I guess so. Either way, they seemed to like it.' Something broke the surface of the water briefly and then disappeared again. We watched for a while, wondering what kind of monster could survive in such an inhospitable environment. 'The weird thing is, I don't actually like to be filmed. It makes me really self-conscious.'

'Sure,' said Tom.

'It's true. It's the same with photography. I've done modelling before to pay the bills, but it's hard for me.'

'I can't even tell if you're being serious,' I said.'

'Deadly serious. I like acting, but I don't really like being looked at.' She must have been aware of how ridiculous she sounded, standing there like some kind of displaced goddess in those bleak wastelands. 'You can laugh all you like, but when I look in the mirror I'm sure I don't see what you see.'

'My heart bleeds for you,' I remarked.

'It's easy for your pretty little girlfriend,' she said. 'She just has to flash a smile with those perfect little teeth and everyone's happy.

I'm not pretty, as you can see.' She articulated the word *pretty* as if was a profanity.

'Sadly, she's not my pretty little girlfriend anymore.'

'Oh, I'm sorry.' She looked genuinely remorseful. 'I've put my big boot in it in again, haven't I? Are you sad?'

'Not especially.' I answered. 'There are lots of pretty girls. And you might not be pretty, but you're something so much more. You're spectacular.'

Her face lit up. 'I think that's the nicest thing anyone's ever said about me.'

'Really?' said Tom. 'Don't believe a word he says. He's just being nice because he's single and lonely.'

I threw my hands in the air like I had been caught out doing something bad. 'Guilty as charged. Have you talked money?' I asked. 'At least make all that pain worthwhile.'

She shook her head. 'One step at a time,' she explained. 'To be honest, I'd do it for nothing.'

'Christ, don't tell them that,' I said.

'He's right,' said Tom. 'You have to know your worth.'

She stopped and pulled a movie star pose, her hair blowing out behind her in the acrid breeze. 'No problems there.' We had reached a heavily built area where the canal stretched out underneath a flyover and our laughter echoed around the perpendicular slabs of concrete.

'The only time it was okay was when I did that photoshoot with Colin.'

'That's because he's a genius and made you look like a movie star,' I suggested.

She blushed, almost. 'Maybe. But it was like he wasn't there, just me and a camera clicking away. It's hard to describe.' She didn't need to. We had seen him at work, lost in his art, framing the world, seeing beauty to which others were blind.

The call-back fell on the day before the big Festival at GMex, but she had bought a ticket and promised to do everything she could to get back in time.

'I'll just pull my usual trick and read my lines quicker.'

'You're such an idiot.' I motioned to push her in, and she grabbed onto my arm with a perfectly executed look of horror on her face. 'Pretty poor taste, don't you think?' We almost felt guilty laughing so much.

'I was thinking of getting my hair cut into a bob,' she said. 'Going for the whole Louise Brooks thing.' She pulled her hair back with both hands and let strands fall through her fingers to frame her face in the desired manner. 'What do you think?'

It looked great, emphasising the perfect geometry of her face, but I wasn't convinced. 'They obviously like you as you are,' I suggested. 'If they want you to change your look, let them decide for you.'

I watched her with Tom, looking for signs that they had rekindled their romantic feelings for each other, but there was little hint of anything more than an easy friendship.

'Anyway, enough about me. How's the internship going?' she asked.

'It's fine,' said Tom, but he was unconvincing.

'What does that mean?'

He played dumb. 'Fine? It means everything's okay.'

'You know what I mean.'

We had walked all the way back towards the city centre, leaving the wilderness behind as civilisation beckoned. 'It's all good,' he said, 'but it's like I'm living someone else's life rather than my own.'

'Your dad's?'

'Exactly. It's like everyone knows who I am and looks at me like I'm going to be the next big thing. I'm literally walking in his footsteps.'

Miranda hugged him, almost tripping him up. 'But you are the next big thing!'

'Yeah, but I think I need to do it on my terms, rather than because of whose son I am.' He kicked a stone into the canal. 'Is that bratty of me? They're all great and it's really useful experience, but it's not what I really need right now.'

'Then it's lucky you're getting out of here,' I said, stating the obvious. 'At least it's only a few weeks.'

The conversation came back round to the festival, trying to come up with a plan to meet up with her in case she got there late, and she made us swear to her that one of us would make our way back to the main entrance every hour to check if she had arrived okay.

She beamed. 'It's great to have friends you can rely on,' she said. There was no doubting in her mind that we would stick to our word. Talk about knowing your worth.

When we got back to Tom's, his mum had left a note for us. He was to call Colin's parents as soon as he got in.

A body had been found.

We must have missed the police by mere moments, but we saw a patrol car drive off up Burton Road with his parents in the back seat. There was nothing for it but to wait.

We had a couple of pints in The Cavendish, trying to judge how long it might take before we got news. Conversation came harder than it ever had before, each starter leading us down a blind alley as we sat and feared the worst. Eventually, the waiting became unbearable and we headed back. They had been home long enough to have made a cup of tea which had grown cool. His dad looked terrible, greying stubble adding years to him, while his mum could barely stand. We waited for one of them to find their voice.

'Sorry, lads,' said his dad. The experience had visibly shaken him. 'We don't know what to say.' He put his head in his hands, as if shielding himself from the horror of it all. 'It was bloody horrible. They pulled something from the water, but we couldn't say if it was him. They need to use dental records to be sure.'

I had no idea what I was feeling, I was so disconnected from my own emotions.

His mum's voice trembled. 'That thing,' she said. 'That wasn't my son.'

'Of course not, love.' He turned to us. 'We'll know for sure in the morning,' he said. He turned to the TV and switched it on, looking without seeing, hearing without listening. His mum shuffled off to the kitchen where she fussed through cupboards and after a decent amount of time we quietly let ourselves out to slink home through the failing light.

Seventeen

We started drinking early, all of us together, on the cobbles by The Salisbury under the train station on Oxford Road, with the half-decent jukebox to get us in the mood. Almost all of us. We left a seat empty for Colin, as a mark of respect, and only half-dared to believe he might turn up as he so often did, fashionably late and more than a bit dishevelled after crawling round in the city dirt trying to capture the perfect shot and that look on his face that seemed to ask, what have I missed?

Under the table sat six cardboard boxes containing The Manifesto, hot off the press. A girl had turned up shortly after we got there and led us outside where her car was parked and we helped ourselves.

'I've got to go,' she said.

'Thanks for this,' said Tom. 'You're a star.' He kissed her and she drove off while we shook our heads and laughed.

'Was that...?'

'Yup.'

'I won't ask what you had to do to get them.'

'Best not.' He was totally unfazed as we lugged the boxes inside, each containing a hundred copies.

The news about the body had been inconclusive. It was badly decomposed and had suffered further facial trauma in the canals, and the police had concluded that it was most likely not him. There was no shortage of people who went missing under suspicious circumstances. We took it as a good omen and drank a toast to his good health. Darren was eager to get there as early as possible as the line-up was great but was outvoted.

'Let's drink up before we get there,' Simon suggested. 'God knows much we'll have to pay once they've got us trapped inside.'

'If I miss OMD, someone's gonna pay,' Darren warned us.

'These things never run on schedule,' Simon said soothingly. 'We've plenty of time. Remember who's running it.'

It was fair to say that Factory had great flair and an incredible ear for a band, but organisation was not their strong point. FAC 151 could go either way, and we all knew it, but one way or another it would be a glorious mess and it was all ours.

Tom had torn open a box. 'Don't you worry your ugly little mug, Dazzleships,' he said. 'We'll be inside long before anyone gets anywhere near a stage.' He handed round handfuls of the fanzine to everyone. 'Best get selling, people,' he said. 'Remember, you keep what you sell.'

'What do we do if we can't sell them?' asked Jake.

'Are you kidding?' asked Darren. 'Just look at it.' Colin's stunning portrait of Miranda adorned the front cover, a fitting tribute, we felt, for our absent friend and collaborator. 'Who wouldn't want to buy one of these?'

'Just remind me, how much do we sell them for?' asked Simon. Darren rolled his eyes. 'Just look at their trainers,' he suggested. 'If they look expensive, charge them loads. And if they're scousers, double it.' We all laughed. Darren was already up on his feet, barging round the crowded pub, keen to get things moving, trying to shift his copies as quickly as possible before we flooded the market.

We needn't have worried. As we stepped outside, the sun was burning a hole in the sky and the shimmering streets were heaving with people heading towards GMex. The idea that indie music was some kind of small-time cult thing was completely disavowed by the size of the crowds. This felt like the start of something, a cultural tipping point where alternative culture started to become indistinguishable from the mainstream. It had already started to happen with major record labels buying up successful indies as a way to scoop up emerging talent, but also to blur the financial distinction for added credibility. The notion of cool was up for sale, and judging by the numbers of people heading towards GMex, nobody seemed to care.

We spilt up and competitively started selling our stash of The Manifesto so that we were freed up of the burden of lugging them around and in a position to pay the exorbitant prices for beer inside the arena. I still hated the process of trying to convince people to pay for something I had worked so hard on, but getting rid of them was time-sensitive so I was highly motivated to sell. As I took up a position outside on the steps leading up to the entrance, I could hear the sound of bands setting up and it became clear that things were going to start sooner than we imagined. I had expected a lot of haggling over the price, but people were here to have a good time and happy to pay whatever figure popped into my head. My pockets soon filled up with change and the challenge became how to price each issue so I could get as many pound notes as possible and rid myself of jangling coins that soon started weighing me down. It didn't matter too much that some people were buying a copy, flicking through it as they queued up to have their tickets validated and then disposing of them in a bin. There were more where they came from. Right now, I could hear Pete Shelley's adenoidal voice singing Homosapien and every fibre of my being suddenly started calling me inside.

A festival of this size was new territory and it was incredibly hard work getting through the ticket-checking area. A group of lads in front of us had come down from Scotland and were trying to work some scam to get inside without tickets, and the crowd swelled to force them though. The atmosphere was great, though, people from all over the place congregating in the home of music to celebrate. The clash of different accents was amazing, like nothing we had ever heard, like the tower of Babel had toppled on its side, everyone getting on and sharing the same small joys of great music and worshipping the same anti-heroes as they walked on stage and poured their souls out.

Suddenly, someone hand their hand on my shoulder and it was Darren, with Tom and Simon, all of us together in a great sweaty mass of youths all trying to get in at once, until the bouncers gave up and opened the doors and we all came flooding through, fighting to stay on our feet and make our way to the post-Buzzcocks thrill of Pete Shelley trying to reinvent punk-pop perfection. There's Millions of People (But No-one Like You), he sang, and that's just how it seemed right then, a mass gathering of individuals all coming together to share the night. He came and went before we knew it and then we went off in search of alcohol. The nearest bar was heaving, desperately understaffed and so slow that Tom led us off in search of other bars in more remote parts of the impressively appointed structure, though it was far too cavernous to be suitable for music. The space was just too big. The obvious solution was to turn up the volume, but the distortion was awful.

'When the big boys come on, we need to get near the front,' Jake explained. He knew about this kind of thing, and we knew to just go along with whatever he suggested.

Tom's idea had been sound and we soon stumbled across an emptyish bar. For convenience, we bought two beers each as a clear statement of intent and sauntered back towards the main area. Almost immediately, a girl walked up to Darren, smiled and helped herself to one of his pints. He didn't resist so she helped herself to the other then kissed him on the cheek and walked off. He was always the soft touch.

'Bloody hell,' he grinned. 'It's like that, is it? See you in a minute, lads.' He headed off back to the bar in search of more.

We assumed he would be back in a minute or two but we waited and waited and he never showed.

'He's probably been mugged by another girl,' said Simon. It was a fair guess, to be fair. By this time, OMD had come on and beguiled the crowd, although Darren was nowhere to be seen.

They finished with Enola Gay, that bold arthouse masterpiece, arguably the greatest non-love song ever committed to vinyl. Despite their Liverpudlian origins, they had released their brilliant first single on Factory Records so they were the ideal choice for the festival, hinting at a tentative cooling of the cultural animosity between the two rival cities united by their hatred of Thatcher's toxic brand of politics.

I couldn't get that line out of my head: *That kiss you gave is never going to fade away.* It made me think of Miranda for some reason, made me remember to check up on her, to see if she had actually made it.

'He's going to be so pissed if he's missed this,' I said out loud. 'He's probably with that girl.'

'Let's hope so, or we'll never bloody hear the last of it.'

We kept on drinking hard, and things started to become a bit hazy. At one point I was aware of Darren returning, spitting venom. His face looked even crazier than normal. Somehow, he was clutching four pints of beer in soft plastic containers, so I helped myself to one of them, just to make things a little easier for him. His eyes were bleary with booze.

'I can't believe I fucking missed them.'

Tom was with him. 'Don't worry, Dazzleships. There'll be other nights to see them,' he said consolingly.

They were both unsteady on their feet. There was a brief lull, and we took the opportunity to find somewhere to sit, to compose ourselves and then drink some more.

'Colin would have loved this,' said Tom. 'He would have been in his element.' The evening was dominated by his absence.

We could picture him, walking around with his camera, trying to capture the moment while we were busy trying to live it. He didn't experience the world the same way as others; maybe that was why he was so good at documenting the world around him. The alcohol didn't help – or maybe it did – but everywhere was a blur of movement and colour.

It suddenly felt important to change the mood. 'It's heaving in here,' I commented. 'What happened? When did everything get so, um, popular?'

I couldn't quite find the right word. Popularity wasn't necessarily a bad thing, but one of things that had always appealed about the music we loved was its exclusivity. Suddenly, everyone wanted a part of it, people you had never seen before.

'Remember when you could go and see a great band and you could just walk in, buy a ticket on the night?' said Darren.

'Of course, the other way of looking at it is that bands can now actually start to make a decent living out of what they do,' said Tom. We had been shocked to find out that James had done medical trials to fund some of their early releases.

'It's hard to argue against that.'

'I guess it's just not ours anymore.'

'It is still ours, all of it,' Tom insisted. 'We're just going to have to learn how to share.'

We all started laughing at how absurd it all was, how we could care so much about something, even if it was just a way of not having to care so much about all the things that hurt. Like our obsession with football. I remembered being annoyed when Zoe suddenly started dyeing her hair and coming into college wearing cool band T-shirts as if she had always been part of the scene. Despite his personal reservations about her, Tom had bollocked me for being elitist, a cultural snob.

'What difference does it make when she realised that there was life outside the Top 40?' he said. 'Surely the importance thing is that she gets it now.'

Without that, I might never have gone over and started speaking to her. We sat there, drinking away the proceeds of months of hard labour, watching things change right in front of our eyes, hundreds of people suddenly drawn together by a shared love of the same bands, having the time of their little lives. Though it was far less incendiary than punk, this was a vital part of the cultural revolution. As we talked, we hauled ourselves to our feet and started wandering over to the meeting point to see if Miranda had turned up yet. The night was drawing in and there was no sign of her.

'Punk was the Bolsheviks storming the Winter Palace,' said Tom. 'A handful of people who took the future and exploded it in the present, changing everything. This is the next stage, the November Revolution, not just storming the seat of power but taking control of it, forging a bold new direction.'

'Fuck the major labels!' shouted Darren melodramatically.

Somewhere in that huge place, The Smiths were on stage, but it seemed less essential to be there, a part of it all.

'So, in effect, what you're saying is that Morrissey is the new Stalin,' I said, heading towards the music. He gave me a very funny look like his eyes were struggling to focus.

'I think that's exactly what I'm saying.'

'He has got some very odd ideas,' I said, thinking it through. The Smiths frontman was a pinprick in the distance, whirling on stage under polychromatic lighting, delighting the crowd with homespun tales of child murder and repressed homosexual angst whilst Johnny Marr pulled it all together into something that made sense, so that all those individuals felt a sense of belonging to something far bigger than they could ever have dreamed. The rest was a blur.

The details were sketchy by then. At some point I wandered off and made my way alone to the meeting point later in the evening and Miranda was there. She threw her arms around me and kissed me hard. She was as drunk as me and far more beautiful. She said something about Germany, but I had no idea what it was. The soundtrack to that kiss was New Order, quite sublime in that monumental setting. Ian McCulloch of the Bunnymen came on stage and all those wary scousers in the crowd went crazy, the two cities finally coming together. She took my hand and we ran for the main arena in time for the encore, but she was soon pulled away and it was just me again.

The next thing I knew I was with Tom and we were somewhere near the back. He was shouting in my ear but I couldn't really hear what he was saying. Everything was okay. I knew that much. Over his shoulder, I felt someone watching us, a face I knew but I couldn't quite place it. His eyes met mine and I could tell he was thinking the same thing. He walked over. His eyes were dilated and he was sweating profusely. He held out his hand as he approached.

'You want one of these, lads?' he said. A handful of pills. 'Take one. They're fucking magic.'

We had started to notice people popping pills at The Hacienda as the music had taken an unpleasant move towards House music from across the Atlantic, which we despised. The hand was still outstretched.

'Not for me, thanks,' said Tom. I declined, too, with a shake of the head.

'Fair enough. Have a great night, lads.' He turned and started to walk off. There was something about the way he said it, air whistling through a chipped tooth. I turned to Tom. 'It's him,' I said. My voice was tiny against the music that blared all around. 'What are you saying?'

I nodded towards the departing figure. 'That guy. I think it's him.'

He knew instantly what I was talking about. His hands were suddenly fists down by his sides. 'How sure are you?' Coloured lights caught his slanted cheekbones as he turned to look at me. 'Pretty sure.'

'Sure enough?' His face was a mask. I did my best to think straight. 'I think so.'

We both knew what was coming. We started to follow him as we walked around the edge of the crowd. Someone banged into him hard and knocked him sideways. He grabbed onto the other person to stop from falling. They put their faces together and laughed at how messed up they were. He was in a very different place to us. He noticed us following him and stopped. We led him away from the stage, into shadows where no one could see.

'Changed your minds, lads?' he asked. He held out his hand again. 'It's fine. No problem.' He was as close to me then as he had been when we started grappling outside The Venue several weeks previously. I could feel his breath on my face. 'You won't regret it.'

I felt Tom move first, a sudden decisive lunge. He threw his arms around the guy and pulled him close. I feared the worst. I couldn't be sure but his lips were at the man's ear and he might have whispered something though I couldn't even guess what it might have been. Maybe nothing. Over the man's shoulder, his eyes met mine, wet in the skittering light.

'It's all good,' he said to me. After a while, he let go and the guy just wandered off. I looked at Tom, not sure what had happened. He had a strange calm look on his face, gentler now like he had been holding onto to something too tightly and had finally let go. 'It's not what he would have wanted,' he explained. He suddenly seemed stone cold sober, though he couldn't possibly have been. 'Colin. He was a believer, you know. He never talked about it, but he was, in his own quiet way.'

We wandered outside and sat in the cool evening air.

'Miranda's here,' I told him.

'I know. I saw her. She was looking for you.'

'So, what do we do now?' I asked. He clearly wasn't quite sure what I meant. He leaned back on the steps and turned his head to look at me.

'We do what we always do,' he said. 'Whatever we like. We need to just let it all go, move on, all of it. The thing is, there are some things we'll just never know for sure,' he said. 'We can't understand all of it. I guess I'll never really find out the truth of what happened to my old man but ultimately it doesn't make any difference. What matters is what he stood for. Same with Colin.' He didn't sound sad, just older and wiser. 'Maybe he'll turn up one day, maybe not. It doesn't detract from who he was, the things he did, what he meant to us. Nothing can take any of that away.'

New Order had finished and people started streaming out, flowing all around us as we sat there. There were copies of The Manifesto all around, discarded litter, plastic glasses, all that effort and love and dedication just tossed away and we both saw it and laughed. After a while, people started joining us one at a time, Jake and Simon and Miranda and Darren, who was still annoyed about OMD.

'Let it go,' I said. 'It doesn't matter, does it.' I looked at Tom and smiled. We were all hot and bothered and the worse for wear, but we decided to walk home. It was a night we didn't want to end.

As always, the summer was too short and nothing was going to be the same after this. We would all be going our separate ways soon enough. Tom took us on one of his meandering journeys, probably because he was still too drunk to really know where he was. We took a supposed shortcut by the university and ended up on Sackville Street.

'You know what this is?' he asked.

'No,' said Darren, 'but no doubt you're about to give us one of your little lessons.'

'I am', he admitted, 'but I promise it's the last one.' He stopped and made us look, though we didn't know what we were supposed to be looking at. 'This is where it happened,' he explained. 'This is the last time Manchester was the centre of the universe.'

'I thought that happened tonight,' said Jake.

'That was just a big gig,' said Tom. 'I'm talking about splitting the atom. Right here is where Rutherford got the dream team together. Geiger. Bohr. All the superstars of science. And they did the impossible. They literally changed the world. In a thousand years, no one will know who fucking Stephen Patrick Morrissey is, but right here, they opened Pandora's box. Incredible, when you think about what they did. We thought that everything, all that energy, was just permanently fixed in place, and they just ripped it all apart.'

'What are you trying to say?' I asked. 'I don't get it.' Science was not my strong point.

'Neither did they. They thought that they had discovered a way to create free power for everyone, something that would shake up the world for ever. The workers would finally be freed up to enjoy their leisure time. And all that happened was that they ended up being forced to make bombs.'

'Wow,' said Darren. 'That's depressing.'

'That's men for you,' said Miranda. 'Always looking for new ways to blow things up.'

'To be fair, they were aiming for something more noble,' said Tom, defensively. We were starting to get cold and carried on walking. 'It just didn't turn out the way they hoped.'

'When does it ever? I wondered. Colin's absence still weighed heavily on my mind.

He was more drunk than I think he realised. 'So, what am I saying? Good question.' Our footsteps echoed on the

229

pavement as we picked up the pace. Subconsciously, we were now in search of food, looking for an Abduls to get something hot inside of us. 'The thing is, Thatcher's doing the same thing,' he said. 'Society is becoming atomised. All those things that bind people together, that traditionally keep things in place, they're all being exploded.' He helpfully counted them off for us. 'Religion. Family. Trade unions. All those things are disappearing. And there's nothing we can do about it.'

'So what?' said Darren.

'I'm not sure. We're already seeing the start of it but I've no idea where we're heading. Rather than belonging to anything, we 're just a huge floating mass of disconnected individuals, like particles bouncing around randomly. You could see it tonight, all those people. You can start to see it in the clubs, all those sweaty pill-poppers hugging each other when they used to smack each other in the face.'

Miranda joined in. 'Gentle collisions rather than violent ones.'

'Surely that's a good thing, right?' I said. I was thinking of earlier, inside GMex.

'I'm not saying it's either good or bad. It is what it is. There's very little we can do about it, either way.' As he walked and talked, you could hear his thoughts coming together. It might have been the alcohol, or the fallout from Colin's loss, but some of the firebrand idealism was starting to disappear from his voice, like someone who moves to a new city and starts to lose the rough edges of his accent. There was a new hardness to the way he spoke about the future, as if he was forcing himself to toughen up.

'When I go to London, I've decided I'm going to hook up with the richest girl I can find. I'm going to charm them, work my way inside, become part of the family. I'm going to become the virus that corrupts the system from the inside out.'

There had always been an element of pragmatism to the way he conducted himself, like the way he could switch on and off with girls. At least he was honest about it. Whatever had happened between him and Miranda was clearly a one-off, a mutually convenient hook-up, and afterwards they were totally relaxed and friendly with each other. What he was now proposing was the next logical step in his evolution and I found I was unable to summon any pity for the poor unfortunate girl he chose for his project. The odds were stacked against him, and she would undoubtedly get more from him than she was likely to from anyone else she was likely to meet.

Finally, we found a fast-food place that was still open and feasted on heavily salted chips with enough vinegar to turn your lips blue. Darren tried a kebab with all the trimmings.

'Time to try new things,' he announced, although most of it went down his top and then in the bin.

'It's like we've come full circle, said Miranda.

'What do you mean?'

She looked hurt that I wouldn't remember. 'This is how we met,' she said. 'You two were sitting together after a gig and I came and stole one of your chips.'

'The Smiths,' Tom reminded me.

'Of course. How could I forget?' I went all dreamy-eyed. 'They were great that night.'

She gave me a filthy look and I laughed at her displeasure. 'Of course I remember meeting you for the first time,' I reassured her. 'It was the chips I forgot.'

We wandered away from the others. 'I'd love to come back to yours tonight,' she said, 'but I'm not going to.' She placed two fingers on my lips and I remembered that line again: *that kiss you gave is never going to fade away.*

'I'm going away,' she said. 'To Germany, and then God knows where after that. But I'll be back one day, and when I do, I'm going to come and find you.' Her eyes were fixed on mine and it was impossible to look away. 'You need to go and find yourself first,' she said. 'Go and be brilliant. Do you understand?'

I nodded obediently. 'I think I do.'

Tom walked over. 'What are you two whispering about?' he asked.

'I think she just proposed to me,' I said.

She physically recoiled. 'I'm pretty sure I did not.'

Tom ignored her. 'And what did you say?'

I had to think about it for a moment. 'I think I said, I do.'

He slapped us both on the back, harder than I think he intended. 'Well, hearty congratulations to you both. I'm sure you'll make each other very happy. It's about time we had some good news.'

'You, too,' Miranda reminded him. 'You've already married yourself off to some gorgeous socialite.'

'I never said she was going to be gorgeous,' he corrected her. 'Or that I was going to marry her, for that matter. All I said was that I was going to use her to get ahead. And just for the record, I'm aiming for a cabinet minister's daughter.'

'Anyone in mind?' I asked.

He shook his head. 'I'm not too fussy.'

'Thanks,' said Miranda.

We had made our way back to All Saints by the Biko Building and Miranda hailed a taxi. We kissed briefly and she jumped in, pulling down the window as it drove off.

'See you in the future!' she shouted.

'Looking forward to it,' I called back.

We stood and watched as she disappeared from view.

'Well, that's that, then.' A night bus appeared round the corner and we made a run for it. So much had happened that I felt totally overwhelmed to the point that my brain had just shut down. I did everything automatically, paying my fare, going upstairs, taking my seat. When I reached my stop, I totally forgot to move and Tom had to push me off the bus the next time it came to a stop, half a mile or so further up the road. I was suddenly freezing and hurried home. All those months and years when every day had been the same, and suddenly everything came together at once, like waves colliding, and nothing was going to be the same again.

Silently, I let myself in and went to bed without undressing. One of the girls was a little disturbed in her sleep so I rested my palm on her forehead until she settled. It was so dark I couldn't even tell which it was, not that it mattered.

A little feeling had returned to my lips and I put my fingers to them like Miranda had. I had no way of knowing if she was just messing with my head, but I already knew I was prepared to wait as long as it took. There was no way I was going to sleep, so I fumbled around for my headphones and put on my C86 cassette. I made it all the way through to the Age of Chance track at the end, where the sonic rumble finally did the trick and lulled me into submission.

Eighteen

Contrary to popular opinion, Tom was not well-known for being enigmatic with his friends. He tended to be very straightforward in the way he did things, but when he asked us to meet him at The Boardwalk on the Sunday morning, we had no idea what was going on inside his head. I had taken a few spare copies of The Manifesto with me to replenish the display stand behind the bar. Outside, some guy had asked for one to look at while he waited for someone to show up.

'Are we in it?' he asked.

'I dunno. Who are you?'

He stood out a hand. 'Noel,' he said. 'I'm the guitar roadie for the Inspirals.'

'Nice to meet you. Next issue, maybe?'

'Yeah, that would be great. I could set something up.'

He was really friendly and I told him he could keep it. Jake appeared just then, none the wiser about what was going on. He had his guitar with him. There was another guy with him, also with guitar case in hand.

'Any idea what's going on?' I asked.

'Not really. He was a bit vague, to be honest.'

Tom's head appeared from inside the venue. 'Finally,' he said. 'I've been setting up.' He led us inside, to the basement. I had no idea there were rehearsal studios inside beneath the main stage.

Adrian was already there with his drum kit already set up. Tom smiled at me, enjoying my confusion.

Jake and his friend set up, too while Tom located a microphone and stand which he located centrally. It figured he would want to be the main man. They turned on the amps and

Jake ran through a few chords and then the three of them starting jamming, trying to find a groove, lock into it. It took a while, but it started to sound really good. I stood to one side with Tom and we watched admiringly. It made total sense, the three of them, and it was good to watch them, meeting each other's eyes and smiling as it started to come together. I waited for Tom to take the microphone. I had never heard him sing, but he was good at everything. The longer the played, the better it sounded and in my head I started to improvise lyrics that fitted with the hard abrasive music they were creating. It was angry, defiant, like riotous youths throwing bricks or bombs. They grew in confidence, trying more ambitious things, and still Tom didn't make a move. I looked at him. He smiled and shook his head, motioned me forward.

'Not me,' he said. 'This is your time.'

If I had time to think, I would never have done it. Hesitantly, I stepped forward, trying to get a feel for what they were playing, searching for a way in. At first, I didn't even recognise my own amplified voice, but it sounded good. There were encouraging smiles all around as they started to repeat musical phrases to provide a platform for me to join in. Tentatively, I opened with a few repeated phrases and then expanded my vocabulary and slowly started to find my voice. I wasn't really sure where the words came from, just some secret place deep within me.

> *An innocent experience had me on the floor*
> *Did you think I'd beg for more?*
> *You should have known from the start*
> *You were never going to break my heart*

Instinctively, the band responded to what I was doing. I wasn't quite sure what I was saying but I knew in time it would all come together, just like the boys in the band were already starting to add structure to what they were playing, pushing each other to find the right musical form. My eyes were shut so I could lose myself in the music, trying not to over-think it, but just to go with what felt right. The raw power of what we were creating felt immense, like I had become irradiated and was developing new powers, testing the limits of what I could do. I had never felt anything quite like it.

We played around for what must have been ages, although I had no sense of time passing. Literally lost in music. The door opened and someone stuck his head in to tell us our time was up and the spell was broken. When I opened my eyes again, Tom was slowly, silently clapping.

'I knew it,' he said. 'You're a natural.' The rest of the band were similarly excited by what we had managed to do.

'That sounded amazing,' said Jake. 'You swear that's the first time you've sung? That's crazy.'

I had read countless times of bands describing the chemistry between the various members and now I had experienced it myself first-hand, my first real taste of being part of a collective rather than a solitary individual. I was proud of The Manifesto, but already this felt like something else entirely. We were buzzing as we packed up, although that might have been because we had the volume turned up so high that my eyes were suffering, not that I could have cared less.

'Just so you know, I've booked you in for ten weeks,' said Tom, addressing all of us. 'I should be back by then, so you'd better have something to show for it.'

Jake gestured towards the rehearsal studio where the next band was already moving their stuff in and setting up. 'How the hell have you paid for that?'

'Let's just say I got a good deal,' he said. 'And I've reinvested some of what we made from The Manifesto. I've booked you a gig here as well, by the way.'

'What? You are totally evil,' I said.

'I will have been in London for months by then, so I'll be desperate to see a decent band. I've already booked my return ticket so you can't let me down.'

'What are we even called?' asked Darren. The age-old question.

'The Dick-Swing Children,' said Tom mischievously.

'Fuck off.'

He put his hands up defensively. 'Just kidding. I've listed you as High Rise for now. There's plenty of time to come up with the perfect name.'

'We've been trying for ten years,' Darren reminded him.

'Well, now you've got ten weeks. I've got faith in you.' The other band was all set and ready to play so we made our way outside. Noel was with them, holding a guitar case. His copy of The Manifesto was folded in his back pocket and he smiled warmly at us as we left.

'Seriously, boys, that sounded top,' he said.

'Cheers.'

Darren threw the drum kit in the back of a van and offered to run Jake and his mate home. I badly needed a drink and there was a decent pub round the corner.

'I can't believe you did that to me,' I said.

He still wore that self-satisfied smile, proving once again to himself and the rest of us that he knew best.

'Did you enjoy it?' 'It was totally fucking amazing, but that's not the point.'

The pub was fairly quiet and I got the first round in. At that time of day, no one could have had a good reason for being there.

Tom stowed his bag under the table. 'Ask yourself this: would you have done it if I hadn't made you?'

I thought about it for longer than I needed to. 'Probably not.'

'Definitely not. I wanted to make a point. You're way more talented than you ever give yourself credit for. And you need to take more risks.'

I knew he was right so I stopped pretending to argue. I turned the conversation on its head.

'What about you?' I asked. 'Were you serious the other night? I always assumed you'd end up being some union hotshot.'

He took a drink and put his glass down on the table with meticulous care. 'It's been an eye-opener over the summer. They're good people and it's been great experience, but it's over. The days of the unions flexing their muscles with the government, it's not going to be like that anymore. There's no stomach for a fight, not from what I can see. Not the unions, but their membership. They're past caring for anything except themselves. Thatcherism has made everyone selfish, ashamed of having so little and wanting more, even at the expense of other people.' He sounded like he had learned an unpleasant truth. 'So yeah, I think I'm going to try it the other way round, infiltrate the system and fight them from the inside out.'

'And what if you fail?'

'Then I'll be living in a castle somewhere in the countryside smoking cigars rolled on the thighs of Cuban virgins and drinking fine wines.' The way he said it made it sound like a slow death, but we laughed anyway. 'I don't know what's going happen, any more than anyone else does, but I'll just have to give it my best shot and see how it goes. If nothing else, it should be interesting to see how it all turns out.' It hadn't occurred to me that he could be anything other than completely self-assured and I was a little shocked to hear him talk this though, though I tried not to let it show. Besides, my confidence in him was unshakable and I think he knew that without me having to articulate it.

I got another round in. 'When do you leave?' It was a question I had avoided asking.

'This afternoon,' he said. 'I'm catching the train down to London and then my mum's driving up with my stuff the next time she gets a free weekend, whenever that is. She says you can get a lift if you like. She's not used to driving long distances and she'd like the company.' That explained why he had a sailors' sack with him branded with the Identity Clothing logo, all his best gear folded carefully inside.

I nodded. 'Of course, that would be great.'

We made the drinks last and then we slowly made our way up the gradient towards Piccadilly Station. We chatted as if tomorrow was going to be just the same, but of course it wasn't.

I followed him onto the concourse. His train was already in.

'So, this is it,' I said, trying not to sound pathetic. 'Go and change the world.'

He climbed aboard, then turned and waved. 'Only the bits that need changing.' His smile seemed a little melancholy, but I instinctively knew he would be fine.

I waited until the train departed and made my way down the ramp towards the city centre. A pigeon with a crippled leg stood in my way eating a discarded Greggs pastie. Typical Manchester. The sun was shining but still a thin drizzle broke out and, like a hopeful child, I scanned the sky for signs of a rainbow.

Printed in Great Britain
by Amazon

77689148R00139